THEN THERE WAS YOU

HOPE CREEK BOOK 3

LAURA FARR

Copyright © 2022 by Laura Farr

All rights reserved.

No part of this book may be reproduced in any form or by any electronic or mechanical means, including information storage and retrieval systems, without written permission from the author, except for the use of brief quotations in a book review.

Website: laurafarrauthor.com

Edited by Karen Sanders at Karen Sanders Editing

Proofread by Judy Zweifel at Judy's Proofreading

Cover by Shower of Schmidt Designs

LAURA FARR

Then There Was You

PROLOGUE

Seb

$\mathcal{I}$ hang back as my family crowd around Cade and Sophie. They've just exchanged their wedding vows, and everyone wants to offer their congratulations. I do too, but I need a minute. I knew this moment was coming, but even so, it hurts more than I'd like to admit.

Wyatt catches my eye and walks over. "You okay? You're quiet," he says, bumping my shoulder.

I take a deep breath before looking across at him. I've managed to keep my feelings for Sophie under wraps these past few months. No one suspects anything, and I want to keep it that way. Wyatt's my twin brother, though, and the one person who knows me better than I know myself. Playing for the Arizona Cardinals, he's not in Hope Creek all that much. I have no doubt if he had been around, he'd have called me out by now.

"I'm good," I lie, hoping he can't see straight through me.

"It's been a long time coming, right?" He flicks his head to where Sophie and Cade are still surrounded by everyone. "They deserve this."

I give him a small smile. "Yeah, they really do."

He frowns. "Are you sure you're okay? You're being weird."

"I'm not being weird," I tell him, brushing off his comment. "I'm just tired. The bar is full on."

"You work too hard. Let's grab a beer."

I breathe a sigh of relief that he isn't pushing the conversation. I hate lying to him, but he can't know the truth. No one can.

"Aren't we going for dinner?"

He shakes his head. "Not yet. Cade and Sophie are having some photos taken first. We've got time for a drink."

"Okay. I should speak to them first, though."

I force my feet to take me to Cade and Sophie. I smile as Paisley steps out of Sophie's embrace. They're both crying, but they are undoubtedly happy tears.

"Seb!" Sophie exclaims as she dabs her tears away, careful not to ruin her eye makeup. My breath catches in my throat when she smiles at me. She looks so beautiful, and I can't take my eyes off her.

"Congratulations," I whisper as she throws her arms around my neck. I hesitate for a second before circling my arms around her waist and tugging her gently against me. I shouldn't be holding her, especially not today, but I can't *not*. It'll be the last time. It's what I always tell myself, but this time, it has to be. It's too hard otherwise.

"Thank you for coming."

I reluctantly step out of her embrace. "I wouldn't have missed it for the world, Sophie." I drag my eyes off her and turn to Cade. "Congratulations, man." I pull him into a hug and hold him tightly. I might be jealous as fuck, but I love my brother and I know how much he loves Sophie.

"Thanks, Seb." The photographer calls Cade's name and he reaches for Sophie's hand. "I think we're wanted. We'll see you in the restaurant?"

"Sure. Go. We'll see you later."

I plaster a smile on my face and watch as he leads Sophie to the balcony with the Bellagio fountains in the background. When the photographer begins to shoot some photos, Wyatt places his hand on my shoulder.

"We should get that drink."

I sigh and follow him off the terrace. My mind is full of Sophie, and we're both silent as we ride the elevator to the lobby.

"Grab a table. I'll get the drinks," Wyatt says as we walk into the bar.

I nod absentmindedly and opt for a high table in the middle of the room. When Wyatt's been served, he comes over and slides a bottle of Bud across the table before sitting down.

"So, how long have you had feelings for Sophie?" he asks, taking a pull of his beer.

My eyes widen and I freeze, the bottle inches from my lips. I should have known I couldn't hide anything from him. I take a mouthful of beer, giving me a few extra seconds to think about what I'm going to say. It's clear I can't bullshit him.

I place my bottle on the table and drag my hand through my hair. "How did you know?"

"Because I know *you*, Seb."

Fear creeps up my spine. "Do you think Cade knows?"

He shakes his head. "No. I think you're safe. So, how long?"

I blow out a breath. "A while, I guess. We got close. I knew she was still in love with Cade. I couldn't stop myself falling for her, though."

"Did anything ever—"

"No," I say, cutting him off. "Never!"

"Why didn't you say anything?"

I let out a sad laugh. "What would I say, Wyatt? I'm in love with my brother's girlfriend? No one wants to hear that."

"In love with her?" he asks, his tone not hiding his surprise. He clearly didn't think my feelings were that intense.

I sigh. "Yes, but it doesn't matter. She's happy. That's all I care about." It's a half-truth. I love her and I want her to be happy. I just wish more than anything that it was me making her happy.

"What about you?"

I frown. "What about me?"

"We're a close family, Seb. You're going to have to see them together all the time. You're okay with that?"

It's going to kill me to see them together. He doesn't need to know that, though.

"What choice do I have? Cade's my brother and I love him. I'm happy he's happy. I'll be fine."

"That's bullshit!"

"It is not! I *am* happy for him."

"Maybe, but you're not fine. You need to get laid, bro."

I roll my eyes. "Yes, because that will solve everything."

"Seriously. You need to put yourself out there. Move on. When was the last time you went on a date?"

I blow out a breath. "I can't even remember."

"You should come to Phoenix. I can hook you up. There are always women following the team around."

"Thanks, but no, thanks. Even if I wanted to, I can't leave the bar."

"You're allowed a life, Seb."

"I have a life."

He lets out a sarcastic laugh. "A life where you're in love with your brother's wife."

"What?" a voice gasps from behind us. My stomach rolls and sweat breaks out on the back of my neck as I recognize the voice.

I take a deep breath before turning around in my seat. I groan internally when I see both Nash *and* Paisley. I look between them, their expressions a mixture of horror and pity.

"Is there any chance you didn't hear that?" I ask, rubbing my fingers into my temple to ward off the headache I know is coming.

"Fuck, Seb! How long have you felt like that? Does Cade know?" Nash asks, sitting down next to me and pulling Paisley onto his lap.

"No, and he can't ever know. Sophie either. You can't say anything to *anyone*." My tone must give away my desperation, and Paisley reaches over, taking my hand.

"We won't say anything. I'm sorry, Seb," she says quietly, squeezing my hand.

I raise a shoulder in the slightest of shrugs. "Thanks. I think I need some air." I stand from the table, Paisley's hand falling from mine.

"Wait," Nash says. "Shouldn't we talk about it?"

I frown. "There's nothing to talk about."

"But—"

"Leave it, babe," Paisley says gently, cutting Nash off.

Wyatt stands. "Do you want some company?"

"No. I'm good. Finish your drink."

I walk away, sighing when I hear Nash quizzing Wyatt on what he knows. I drop my head and quicken my step. I feel like such an idiot, even more so now that half my family knows. I'm not the kind of guy to wear my heart on my sleeve, and I just want everything to go back to how it was. I have no idea how that can happen now. I know my family. They're going to be asking me if I'm okay every five minutes and trying to set me up on dates so I can move on. Maybe I don't want to move on, and the agonizing pain I feel in my chest is a reminder of something real. A reminder that love hurts and, no matter what, I'm never going to let myself be that vulnerable again.

CHAPTER ONE

Seb
Two months later

A knock sounds on my office door, the noise from the bar spilling into the room as Ryder walks in.

"Sorry to bother you, boss, but it's crazy out there. Can you serve while I bring up some more beer?"

"Sure. I'll be right out."

"Thanks."

He leaves the room, the loud music drowned out as he closes the door behind him. I power off the laptop and shut the lid. The accounts can wait. I should be helping behind the bar. I've been holed up in this office for weeks, hiding away behind invoices and orders. Ryder's been holding down the fort, but it's time I got my head out of my ass.

It's been a couple of months since Cade and Sophie's wedding, and I've avoided seeing my family as much as I can during that time. I haven't been to my parents' house for Thursday roast in weeks. Nash has called me out numerous times, and I know Wyatt would have too if he'd been in Hope Creek and not away playing football. It seemed easier to stay away than to put on a front whenever I saw anyone.

I can't hide forever, though, and tomorrow is Thanksgiving dinner at my parents' place. My mom always outdoes herself at Thanksgiving, and this year both Cade and Nash have the day off and Wyatt doesn't have a game. It's rare we're all together, and I know how excited she is that we can all be together this year. I've decided to close the bar, something I've never done before. I want to give my staff a break, and if I'm honest, I need one too. I've worked pretty much nonstop since I opened Eden five years ago. The bar's doing well, and while there's money to be made if I stay open, family time is important, despite me avoiding mine recently.

I head out of my office and into the crowded bar. Ryder wasn't exaggerating when he said it was crazy. Wednesday nights aren't usually busy, but because it's a holiday tomorrow, more people than normal are out. All the tables are full, and it's standing room only. My eyes flick to the bar, and I smile when I see Paisley loading up a tray with drinks. She doesn't normally work on Wednesday nights, but we're short-staffed right now and she's picking up a few extra shifts.

"Hey, Paisley," I shout in her ear as I come up behind her. "Busy night?"

She turns and smiles before going up on her tiptoes and brushing a kiss on my cheek. "It's wild tonight!" She takes a step back. "It's good to see you, Seb."

"It's good to see you too. Thanks for coming in tonight."

"Of course." She picks up the tray full of drinks. "You're still coming tomorrow, right?"

"Yeah, I'm coming."

"Good." She bites her bottom lip. "You know, it's been noticed that you haven't been around much lately."

Guilt washes over me. "It has?"

She puts the tray down and reaches for my hand. "Everyone misses you, Seb."

"I've been busy," I lie, lowering my eyes.

She squeezes my hand. "You don't have to pretend with me."

"I'm good, Paisley."

She waits until I look up and smiles sadly. "Okay. I guess I should take this order over." She releases my hand and reaches for the tray again. "If you want to talk—"

"You'll be the first to know," I tell her, cutting her off. I appreciate her concern and I know she means well, but there's nothing to talk about. Talking isn't going to change anything.

I watch her walk away before moving behind the bar. I catch Ryder's eye and he nods in acknowledgment before disappearing out the back to bring up another case of beer. There are two other members of staff behind the bar, but even with the three of us, there's a constant stream of people wanting drinks. Not that I'm complaining. Business is good.

A couple of hours later, I lock the door. It's been a long-ass night and I'm more than ready for my bed. When the last of the glasses have been washed and put away, I turn to Paisley.

"Do you need a ride?"

"I'm good. Nash is waiting outside for me."

"I'll see you tomorrow, then?"

"You will."

I follow her to the door, unlocking it and letting her out. I raise my hand in a wave to Nash, who's parked outside.

"Night, Seb."

"Night, Paisley."

A few minutes later, I walk out with Ryder. His car and my bike are parked out back. Up until recently, Ryder rented the apartment above the bar, but he's just bought a house in Hope Creek.

"It's nights like this I wish I still lived upstairs," he jokes, unlocking his car.

I glance at him, only noticing now how exhausted he is. A wave of guilt crashes over me. I know I've been taking advantage of him. He's worked so many hours these past few weeks, often covering the bar when my family's been in and I've wanted to avoid everyone. It's no wonder he's exhausted.

"Take the weekend off, Ryder. You need a break."

He swings his head around to look at me. "The whole weekend?"

"Yes. I haven't been pulling my weight over the past few weeks. You're going to burn out if you carry on putting in the hours you have been."

He drags his hand through his hair. "Are you sure?"

"I'm sure."

He slides his eyes to mine. "Is everything okay, Seb? I've noticed you've been a little distant lately…" He trails off.

I sigh. There's no point lying and telling him everything is okay. Still, I don't need anyone else knowing the reasons I've been distant, so I don't go into details.

"I have some stuff going on, but I'm working through it."

"If you need to talk, I'd like to think we're friends as well as work colleagues."

I smile. "We are friends, Ryder, and thanks. I appreciate that. Get yourself home and I'll see you Monday. Happy Thanksgiving."

"Happy Thanksgiving. See you on Monday."

I watch as he drives away before powering up my bike and leaving Eden behind me. As I ride through Hope Creek, my mind swirls with what a total asshole I've been. I'm so caught up in my own head, I failed to notice that my bar manager is almost on his knees. He was right. I have been distant, and it seems he's not been the only one to notice. I need to do better.

I ride into my underground parking garage and kill the engine. I sit on the bike for a few minutes before I force myself to climb off and head up in the elevator to my empty apartment. While I might hide away in my office at work, I'd rather be there than alone in my apartment. At least there's music and voices and laughter at work. Here, there's nothing but silence, and more often than not, it's the silence that's deafening.

~

I wake the next morning after a restless night. Despite the late finish, I'd struggled to find sleep, only dropping off when it started to get light. Stretching my arms above my head with a yawn, I sit up and reach for my phone on the nightstand. I press the home button and frown when the time comes into view.

"Shit! I'm going to be late," I mutter to myself.

I've overslept. I'm not surprised. My body clock is all over the place, and I can't remember the last time I had a decent night's sleep. My mind just won't switch off. Maybe Wyatt was right at the wedding when he said I needed to get laid. Something's got to give because burying my head in the sand and ignoring everyone isn't pulling me out of the hole I'm in. I'm not big on one-night stands, but I've had a few. The bar is an easy place to pick up women. There are always new faces passing through. Maybe I just need to lose myself in someone for a while and try to feel something for someone else.

I drag my tired body out of bed and into the bathroom. Everyone's meeting at my parents' place at one, and it's already past twelve thirty. I'm going to be late. I shower in record time and throw on some jeans and a shirt, rolling the sleeves up. I push my feet into my boots and my stomach grumbles, reminding me I need food. I'll have to wait until lunch now. I'll be even later if I stop to grab breakfast.

I push down the nerves that bubble up as I ride the elevator to the parking garage. It's ridiculous to feel apprehensive about spending time with my family, and I hate that I feel this way. I want more than anything to go back to a time when I didn't have feelings for Sophie. I know I'm going to see her and Cade today. I *have* to get over this. I *have* to get over her.

CHAPTER TWO

Taylor

"Are you sure it's okay? Thanksgiving is for families. I feel like I'm intruding."

Paisley rolls her eyes. "Nash, will you tell her?"

He chuckles and leans down to fix Max's leash. "It's more than okay, Taylor. My mom made me promise to bring you, so if you don't come, I'm going to be in trouble."

My eyes widen in surprise. "She did? But we've only met once."

"You must have made a lasting impression. As soon as she found out you'd moved from Pittsburgh and were staying with us, she told me I had to bring you over for Thanksgiving."

"See? I told you! Now get dressed," Paisley says, gently pushing me toward the stairs.

When I reach the bottom step, I turn and pull her into a hug. "Thank you," I whisper, holding her tight. "You too, Nash," I say over Paisley's shoulder. "I know me staying here isn't ideal. I still can't believe my rental fell through. I promise I'll find somewhere else as soon as I can."

"You can stay here as long as you need to, Taylor. I'm just sorry you're on the sofa," Nash says.

I smile. "Thank you. The sofa's actually pretty comfy. I just worry I'm invading your space."

"You're not."

"I'm so happy you're in Hope Creek," Paisley says, hugging me back.

I step out of her embrace. "I'm happy I'm here too."

After my mom died, there was nothing left for me in Pittsburgh, and when I saw how happy Paisley was, I thought maybe I could make a new life for myself here too. Although Paisley isn't family, she's the closest I've got, and it made sense to relocate here. A change is exactly what I need.

"You're going to love it in Hope Creek, Tay."

"I hope so," I whisper, smiling before I turn and climb the stairs.

I'm not exactly living the dream right now. Instead, I'm living out of a suitcase in Nash and Paisley's bathroom and sleeping on their sofa. I had a rental set up before I left Pittsburgh, but the owner fell ill the week before I was due to relocate and pulled out. As hard as I tried, I couldn't find anywhere else that I could afford. I'd already given notice on my apartment in Pittsburgh, and Nash and Paisley insisted I still come, offering me their sofa until I could find somewhere else. What little stuff I brought with me is currently cluttering up Nash's garage, and I know I need to find somewhere quickly so I can get out of their way. As much as they insist it's fine I stay here, I know they don't have the space.

Twenty minutes later, Nash parks in his parents' driveway. As I climb out of his truck, I look up at the impressive house in front of me. Nerves bubble to the surface as I wait for Paisley and Nash.

Despite Nash insisting I'm welcome, I still feel like I shouldn't be here.

"Looks like everyone's here except Seb," Paisley says as she passes me, chasing an excited Max into the house. Nash chuckles as he follows her.

"You coming?" he asks over his shoulder.

I take a deep breath and nod before climbing the porch steps and following him into the house. I can hear voices and laughter, and the smell of something incredible invades my senses as we head to the kitchen.

"Paisley, Nash," Mrs. Brookes says as we walk in. She hugs both of them before leaning down to fuss Max. Her eyes go past Nash to me, and she smiles. "Taylor, it's so good to see you again."

"You too, Mrs. Brookes. Happy Thanksgiving, and thank you for inviting me today."

"You're always welcome here, sweetheart, and please, call me Tessa."

I'm surprised when she pulls me in for a hug, and I quickly hug her back.

"Everything smells great, Tessa. Do you need any help?" Paisley asks.

She steps out of our embrace and shakes her head. "No, no. Everything's under control. I was just checking on the turkey. Come on. Everyone is in the living room."

She smiles at me before walking out of the kitchen, beckoning us to follow her. The voices and laughter get louder as we make our way through the house. When she pushes open the door to the living room, Ashlyn jumps up from where she's sitting.

"Taylor! It's so good to see you again."

She rushes toward me and pulls me into a hug. "It's good to see you too, Ashlyn."

"Paisley said you'd finally made the move to Hope Creek. Now that you're back, we'll have to arrange a night out."

"I'd love that."

"We'll get a date sorted this afternoon."

"A date sorted for what?" Paisley asks, stepping out of a hug with Henry, Nash's dad.

"Girls' night. You'll come, won't you?"

"Of course. We could ask Bree and Sophie too."

"Ask me what?" a voice says from across the living room. I turn to see Sophie walking toward us. My eyes fall to her rounded stomach, and I smile.

"Hi, Sophie. You look great," I tell her.

"Thank you. I think I'm finally at the glowing stage. It just took me a while to get there." She laughs, and I smile.

"Congratulations on getting married. Paisley showed me some photos. It looked amazing."

"It was." She looks across to where Cade is talking to his dad. "It still feels a little surreal, if I'm honest." Her hand strokes her swollen stomach.

"I'm so happy for you."

Paisley told me a little about Sophie and Cade's relationship and what they'd endured to finally be together. I'm glad they managed to get their happy ever after, and with a baby on the way, there's still so much to come for them.

"It's good to have you back in Hope Creek. I know how much Paisley missed you," Sophie says.

"I think she'll be sick of me soon if I spend much longer on her sofa."

She frowns. "What happened to the house you were renting?"

"It fell through. I'd already given notice on my apartment in Pittsburgh, and Nash and Paisley insisted I stay with them. I flew in a couple of days ago. I'm hoping I can find somewhere soon. I don't want to overstay my welcome."

"Like that would ever happen," Paisley says from behind me.

"So, girls' night," Ashlyn exclaims. "Should I count you in,

Soph? We can decide later whether it's a night at my place watching movies or a night of dancing at Eden."

"Sure. I'm up for either," Sophie says. "Talking of Eden. Is Seb coming today? I haven't seen him in ages."

"He said he was. Maybe he's just running late," Paisley suggests.

After a round of hellos, we sit down. There's not enough room for us all to sit on the sofas, so I opt for the floor, watching as Nash sits down on the loveseat and pulls Paisley onto his lap. He tugs her gently against his chest and whispers something in her ear, her cheeks flushing pink at his words. I might have only spent a relatively short time with the two of them, but it's easy to see how much Nash adores Paisley, and I know she feels the same about him. After everything she went through back in Pittsburgh with her ex-husband, seeing her so happy with Nash warms my heart. She deserves every second.

I sit quietly while they all talk, feeling a little melancholy. The last couple of Thanksgivings I'd spent at the nursing home with my mom. While the staff looking after her had been incredible, it was lonely, especially last year when she had no idea who I was and kept asking me to leave. I'm grateful Nash and Paisley invited me today. Spending the day alone would have sucked.

"Taylor," Paisley says, pulling me back to the present. "Come with me. I want to show you something." She climbs off Nash's lap and holds out her hand.

"Okay."

I place my hand in hers and she pulls me to stand.

"We'll be back," she says to everyone as she gently pulls me out of the living room and into the entryway. She releases my hand, and I follow her out through the front door and around the side of the house.

"What did you want to show me?" I ask, looking around the beautiful backyard.

"Nothing. I wanted to check if you're okay. You were quiet in the house."

She links her arm with mine and we walk to where a wooden swing hangs from a large oak tree. "Are you okay?" she asks again when I haven't answered her. "It's okay not to be, especially after everything."

"I'm okay, Pais."

"You sure?"

"I miss my mom, and today is probably harder than most. She loved Thanksgiving, but…" I trail off and shake my head.

"But what?"

"You'll think I'm a horrible person," I whisper.

She gently squeezes my arm. "I promise I won't. Talk to me, Tay."

I sigh and look at the ground. "I was relieved when she died. I can't believe I'm saying those words, but it was so hard to watch her go through that. She had no idea who I was and hadn't for a while. She was so confused and would lash out whenever I tried to help her. In the end, it wasn't my mom lying in that bed. The dementia had taken her. I lost her a long time ago."

"I'm so sorry, Taylor. I can't even imagine what that must have been like. You're not a horrible person. It was no life for either of you."

"She's in a better place now, and hopefully, I am too. Thank you for inviting me today. I don't think I realized how hard it would be, the first holiday without her, but being here with you all makes it a little easier."

She smiles sadly. "Like I would ever leave you on your own on Thanksgiving, and you can talk to me whenever you need to. After everything you did for me with Connor, I owe you, Taylor."

I shake my head. "You don't owe me anything. It's what friends do."

"I'm so glad you decided to make the move here. I've missed you."

"I missed you too."

She pulls me into a hug, and I hold her tightly. She's like a sister to me, and I really have missed her these past few months.

"Should we head back inside?"

I nod and we walk arm in arm back around the side of the house. As we get around the corner, there's a motorcycle parking on the driveway.

"Looks like Seb's made it," Paisley says.

I watch with wide eyes as he climbs off the bike and removes his helmet. "God, he's even hotter than I remember, especially riding that bike," I mutter as I take in all six foot three of him. He's wearing black jeans and a black leather jacket. Most of his tattoos are covered by his jacket, but I can see a couple on his hands. I've never been attracted to a guy with ink before, but on him, it's the sexiest thing I've ever seen.

She looks at me in surprise. "You think Seb's hot?"

I look at her like she's crazy. "You don't?"

"Well, sure, but you've never mentioned that you thought he was hot."

I shrug. "He's practically your brother-in-law. It's not like he's going to be interested in me anyway. I'll just admire him from afar."

Her forehead furrows in confusion. "Why the hell wouldn't he be interested in you? You're beautiful, Taylor."

"Not Seb Brookes beautiful."

"What does that mean?"

"I've met him, remember? At the barbecue. He wasn't interested. He barely spoke to me."

She sighs. "Look, he had some stuff going on then. He was probably distracted. Come on. I'll reintroduce you."

She propels me forward, calling out to Seb before I can stop her.

"Hey, Seb. You made it." She lets go of my arm and steps toward him, pulling him into a hug. "You remember my friend, Taylor, from Pittsburgh? She was at the barbecue a couple of months ago." She steps back and gestures to me. I give him a small smile, willing my cheeks not to flush pink.

"Sure I do. Hi, Taylor. Good to see you again." He leans down and presses a kiss on my cheek.

"You too, Seb."

He's even more gorgeous up close, and I try not to stare. His hair is messy in the sexiest of ways, and a dark layer of stubble covers his jaw. My skin tingles from where it brushed against my cheek when he kissed me, and my efforts not to stare fail. I lower my eyes before he realizes. I've only been in Hope Creek for a few days. I know how much the Brookes family means to Paisley. The last thing I want to do is come across as some idiot, crushing on her future brother-in-law.

CHAPTER THREE

Seb

I'm grateful to see Paisley and Taylor on the driveway. It gives me time to get my nerves at spending a full day with the family I've been avoiding for weeks under control. I vaguely remember meeting Taylor a couple of months ago when Nash arranged for her to visit from Pittsburgh as a surprise for Paisley. I'm embarrassed to say I didn't make much of an effort to talk to her then, too caught up in my own head to notice anything that was going on around me.

"Ready to go inside?" Paisley asks, raising her eyebrows in question.

"Yep. Something smells good, even from out here," I say, the smell of roast turkey permeating the air.

Taylor goes ahead of us into the house with Paisley and me following. Paisley reaches for my hand, tangling her fingers with mine.

"You okay?" she mouths when I look across at her.

I smile and nod, squeezing her hand. "I'm good," I mouth back.

She holds my gaze before nodding and releasing my hand. I'm not sure she believes me. I'm not sure I believe myself, but I can't avoid everyone forever. It's like ripping off a Band-Aid. I just need to get it over with quickly and with as little pain as possible.

The smell of Thanksgiving dinner is stronger as I get into the entryway, and my stomach rumbles loudly. Taylor laughs from in front of me.

"Someone's hungry," she says, turning to smile at me.

I chuckle and pat my stomach. "I overslept and missed breakfast. I'm starving."

"Seb," my mom exclaims, appearing in the entryway. "It feels like forever since I saw you. Come here." She pulls me into a hug, and I wrap my arms around her, feeling guilty that I haven't made the effort to come and visit.

"I'm sorry I haven't been around. Things have been crazy at the bar." I don't look at Paisley. Things *have* been crazy, but she knows that isn't why I've been avoiding everyone.

"You work too hard," she says, stepping out of the embrace and cupping my cheek. "You look tired."

I smile. "I'm okay, Mom."

She shakes her head. "Everyone's in the living room. You should go and say hi. Dinner won't be long."

I head to the living room with Paisley and Taylor, taking a deep breath as I push open the door and walk in. Paisley slips past me and goes to Nash, who's sitting on the loveseat.

"Hey, guys," I say, raising my hand in a wave as I take a seat between Ashlyn and Wyatt on one of the sofas.

"Hey, Seb," Ashlyn says. "You're late. Everything okay?"

"Yeah. I just overslept. It was after three when I got home last night."

"The bar's closed today, isn't it?" Cade asks from across the room.

I nod, looking over at him sitting with Sophie on the other sofa. I'd avoided looking until now, and she smiles when we make eye contact. My stomach flips as I give her a small smile back. "I wouldn't normally close, but I figured we could all do with a break." My attention is pulled from Cade and Sophie when Taylor sits on the floor across from me. I stand and gesture to the sofa. "Take my seat, Taylor. Don't sit on the floor."

She waves off my comment. "I'm okay. I'm in good company," she says, pulling Max onto her lap and fussing him.

I sit back on the sofa, feeling bad she's a guest and sitting on the floor.

"Where have you been looking for a rental, Taylor?" Ashlyn asks. "Are you looking for one bed or two?"

"Right now, I'll take anything I can afford."

"You're looking to rent somewhere?" I ask.

She nods. "I'm on Nash and Paisley's sofa. I had a rental in place, but it fell through."

"The apartment above the bar is empty. It can get a little noisy, but you're welcome to take a look if you're interested."

"I thought Ryder lived above the bar?" Paisley asks, her eyebrows pulled together in confusion.

"He did. He moved out last week. He's bought a house on Carter Street."

She frowns. "How did I not know that?"

"It's always busy at the bar. There's never time for much small talk."

"I guess."

I look back at Taylor, who's watching me.

"How much is the rent?" she asks.

"A thousand a month, excluding bills."

"Is it one bedroom?" I nod, and she bites her bottom lip. "Could I see it?"

"Sure. I can show you tomorrow if you're free. I'll be working anyway."

"That would be great. Thanks." She looks across at Paisley, an excited smile on her face.

"No problem."

"So, what have you been up to, Seb? No one's seen you in weeks," Cade asks.

"Yeah, it's not like you to pass up on Mom's Thursday roasts," Ashlyn adds.

I shift uncomfortably in my seat when everyone looks at me, and I swallow thickly. "Just work. You know how it is."

"You've never been too busy for food before. Are you sure you're not seeing someone and that's why you have no time for us?" Ash asks.

I look across at her and she wriggles her eyebrows. Despite the grilling I'm getting, I can't help but smile. Ashlyn has never had a filter and often says exactly what she's thinking. It's what I love most about her.

"There's no one I'm seeing, Ash."

"Like you'd tell me anyway," she mutters, rolling her eyes.

"Are you working next weekend?" Cade asks.

"I work every weekend."

"Can you get next Saturday night off?" He shifts his gaze to Sophie and smiles softly at her. "The house is finally fixed up after the fire and we're having a get-together on Saturday night to celebrate."

"Please say you'll come, Seb," Sophie says.

Her eyes meet mine, and I know I can't say no. I should, if only to save myself from more heartbreak, but I'm done avoiding everyone. My family means too much to me.

"Of course I'll come. I've given Ryder this weekend off work, so I'm sure he'll be happy to cover my shift on Saturday night."

She smiles and turns to Taylor. "You'll come too, won't you, Taylor?"

"I'd love to. Thanks," Taylor says, a hint of surprise in her voice.

Before anyone can say anything else, Mom appears at the living room door.

"Dinner's ready. Henry, can you come help me?" she asks, disappearing back into the hallway. My dad quickly follows her, and I hang back as everyone makes their way into the dining room. Wyatt waits too, placing his hand on my shoulder when we're alone.

"How you doing?" he asks, raising his eyebrows in question.

He knows how I've been. He's been calling me a few times a week. I'm sure he's got better things to be doing than checking on me all the time.

"I'm good, Wyatt."

"Really?"

I shrug. "I'm just getting on with things. It's not like I have much choice." I give him a reassuring nod and try to move the conversation on. "How's the season going? That was a good win last game. The Cowboys definitely weren't on form."

He punches me not-so-gently on the shoulder. "I know you're trying to change the subject and that's fine, but you seem to be implying that the Cowboys should have beaten us."

His voice is full of humor, so I know he's joking, and I smile. "Well... on paper, they *are* the better team. I guess you just got lucky."

"Asshole," he mutters as he walks off, leaving me standing alone in the living room.

I chuckle and follow him into the dining room where everyone except my parents is already seated. My usual seat is next to

Ashlyn and opposite Cade, but it's a little different this year with three extra people to squeeze around the table. Taylor is in my usual seat, but there's a spare seat next to her, so I sit down, smiling as she turns to look at me.

"Is this how you always celebrate Thanksgiving?" she asks, gesturing to the impressive spread in front of us. "It looks amazing."

I look at the large bowl of mashed potatoes, green beans, corn, and cranberry sauce. "Yeah. Mom goes all out at Thanksgiving. You didn't celebrate?"

"We did, but it was only ever me and my mom growing up. Our Thanksgiving was nice, but nothing like this."

"Paisley told me of your mom's passing, Taylor. I'm sorry for your loss."

"Thanks, Seb."

Our conversation is interrupted when my dad walks into the dining room carrying the largest turkey I've ever seen.

"Wow," Taylor whispers, leaning in close to me. "We're not going to eat all of that, surely?"

I laugh. "Wait and see. We can usually pack away a fair amount," I whisper back.

Her eyes sweep over me and her cheeks flush pink before she looks away. Despite being wrapped up in my feelings for Sophie, I can appreciate how beautiful Taylor is. Although I don't know her well, I get the feeling she has no idea just how beautiful she is.

"This looks incredible, Tessa," Paisley says.

"It really does, Mom," Ashlyn agrees.

She waves off their praise. "You know how I love to cook. Especially on Thanksgiving. Cade, are you going to carve?" she asks my brother.

"Sure."

He brushes a kiss on Sophie's cheek before standing and walking to the head of the table. Dad always used to carve the turkey on Thanksgiving, but the last few years, as the oldest sibling, Cade had taken on the role. I steal a look at Sophie, who's watching Cade with a large smile on her face. She looks so happy. She always loved it when we all got together for a family meal, and I know how much being here with us all will mean to her. I look away before she realizes I'm staring and catch Paisley watching me. She gives me a small smile, and I smile back before lowering my eyes to the table, my fingers playing with the edge of my napkin. Despite being apprehensive about seeing Sophie and Cade together, it's easy to see how happy they are. They belong together, even if admitting that to myself hurts my heart a little.

CHAPTER FOUR

Taylor

It's the day after Thanksgiving, and I wake up on Nash and Paisley's sofa with a pounding head and a mouth that feels like I've eaten a bucket full of sand. I drank far too much yesterday, and I'm definitely paying for it this morning. I groan as I remember drinking at least two bottles of wine with Ashlyn. Paisley drank a fair amount too, and I can't help but wonder if she's feeling as bad as I am this morning.

I sit up and swing my legs off the edge of the sofa, my stomach rolling. I drag in some deep breaths. The last thing I want is to throw up at Nash's place after everything he's done for me.

"Urgh," Paisley groans as she walks into the living room and flops down onto the sofa next to me. "I feel like shit! How much did we drink last night?" she asks, dropping her head onto the back of the sofa.

"Too much. Ashlyn is a bad influence. I'll have to remember when we have our girls' night out that I can't keep up with her."

Max bounds into the room and jumps onto the sofa between the two of us. I drop my head onto his fur and pull him close against me. Nash appears and chuckles when he sees the state we're both in.

"It looks like you're feeling as bad as Paisley, Taylor."

"I'm blaming your sister," I tell him, releasing Max and dropping my pounding head into my hands.

"She does love a drink. How does bacon and egg sound, with a side of Tylenol?"

Paisley stands from the sofa and throws her arms around his neck. His arms circle her waist as he pulls her against him.

"That sounds like the perfect hangover cure," she tells him, brushing a kiss on his cheek. She steps out of his embrace and turns to me. "You want some bacon and eggs, right, Taylor?"

"I would love some, Nash. Thank you." My stomach chooses that moment to rumble loudly, and Nash laughs.

"I'll get right on it," he says, beckoning for Max to follow him.

When he's left the room, Paisley sits back down on the sofa.

"You've got a keeper there, Paisley. I wish I had someone to make me bacon and eggs when I'm hung over."

She bumps her shoulder with mine and smiles. "Well, you can share Nash today, but I'm not sure about next time."

"Next time! I'm never drinking again."

She laughs. "I'll remind you of that on our night out."

I turn on the sofa to face her. "Are you busy today?"

"No, why?"

"Would you come with me to look at the apartment above Seb's bar."

"Sure. What time do you need to go?"

"He said any time is good. I was thinking lunchtime, before it gets too busy."

"Sounds good. Maybe we could get lunch while we're there."

"Yeah, okay."

~

A few hours later, after eating what tasted like the best bacon and eggs I've ever had, I'm showered, dressed, and feeling a little more human than when I first woke up. I'm on the sofa, watching a movie while I wait for Paisley and Nash to get back from walking Max. When I hear Max barking from the entryway, I turn the television off and go to them.

Paisley is trying to take Max's leash off when I get into the entryway, and I can't help but laugh when I see him jumping all over her.

"Having fun?"

"I swear this dog is crazy. We've just been for an hour-long walk and he's still got endless amounts of energy."

"Where's Nash?" I ask as I pull on my Converse, seeing that she's finally managed to get the leash off Max.

"He went to Sophie and Cade's place to help move some of their heavier furniture. They're hoping to move in completely over the weekend, and with Sophie being pregnant, she can't help with any of the lifting."

"If they need any help, I'm happy to pitch in."

"Thanks, Tay. Ready to head to Eden?"

I nod and follow her out of the front door and onto the driveway. I wait while she locks up and we walk arm in arm through Hope Creek toward town. When we reach Eden, we head inside and straight to the bar. Seb's working, and he tips his head in acknowledgment of us while he finishes serving a couple of women their drinks. I watch him as he tosses a cocktail shaker in the air, catching it and emptying the contents into a glass. The women he's making the drinks for are equally enthralled, and I can't say I blame them. He looks hot.

"Hey, what can I get you both to drink?" he asks, wiping his hands on a cloth as he makes his way over to us.

"Just a Diet Coke, please," I tell him, hoping he didn't catch me staring at him.

"Same for me," Paisley says. "I had enough alcohol yesterday to last me a lifetime."

Seb laughs while he pours our drinks. "Don't say that too loud in here. I kind of hope people keep coming back for the alcohol." He winks as he slides the drinks across the counter to us. "Take a seat and I'll grab the keys to the apartment."

There's only us and a couple of other people in the bar, so there are plenty of tables to choose from. We decide on one of the booths and I slide into the seat, Paisley sitting next to me.

"How's work?" she asks before taking a mouthful of her drink. "Do you have anything going on at the moment? I haven't seen you with your laptop since you got here."

Suddenly feeling warm, I pull my sweater over my head and toss it onto the seat next to me. "I have a couple of things scheduled for next week, but I purposely left this week free thinking I'd be settling into my new place."

"Hopefully the apartment is good and you can move in over the weekend."

"Hopefully." I take a swig of my drink before putting the glass down heavily on the table. "Shit! I never asked Seb if the apartment comes furnished. If it doesn't, I have nothing."

"It does come furnished," a voice says from behind me, and I turn in my seat to see Seb. He looks hotter than ever this close up, and now that he's not behind the bar, I can see he's wearing dark jeans and a tight black t-shirt, the Eden emblem sitting on his chest. His inked arms bulge from his t-shirt, and my eyes drop to them, tracking over his tattoos. "I might need to get a new mattress," he says, pulling me from my perusal of him. "Ryder always complained it was uncomfortable, and I never really took much notice. I thought he was being a pussy. Bring your drinks and we can have a look." He gestures to our half-drunk sodas.

I nod and stand, picking up my drink. Paisley does the same, and we follow Seb through the bar and down a hallway marked, *staff only*. I've only been in Eden a handful of times, and never out the back. This place is way bigger than it looks from outside. Seb stops in front of a set of stairs and turns to face us.

"This is it," he says.

I pull my eyebrows together in confusion and look up the stairs. "There's not a separate entrance?"

He points to a door at the end of the hallway. "You don't have to go through the bar. That leads outside, where there's a parking space if you have a car."

"I don't have a car right now, but I was going to look at getting one, so that's good to know."

He starts to climb the stairs, and I follow him, trying not to check out his ass. When he reaches the top, he opens the door and stands to one side, letting me and Paisley go in first. My eyes widen when I take in the space, and I glance at Paisley, who's having the same reaction. The doorway opens onto an open-plan living room, with a small kitchen off to the right. The walls of the apartment are painted white, making it look even more spacious than it already is, and dark wooden floors are laid throughout. My eyes go to the pale gray kitchen cabinets and the bright white countertops. Despite not seeing the rest of the apartment, I'm already in love with it and know for sure I want to live here. A large gray corner sofa sits in the middle of the living room with an entertainment center housing a large flat-screen television on the wall opposite. There are a couple of small tables dotted around the space, but that's it for furniture. It's enough for me, though, and I can feel my excitement building as I continue to look around.

"This is the living room and kitchen, as you can see," Seb says from behind me. "The bedroom and bathroom are through that door." I turn to see him gesturing to a closed door on the other side of the room. "The only bathroom is off the bedroom."

He crosses the space and opens the door. I follow him into a good-sized bedroom, where a double bed sits against one wall and a nightstand on either side. On the opposite wall is a large dresser, and next to that is a door, which I'm guessing leads into the bathroom. I leave Seb in the bedroom and push open the door, finding myself in a large bathroom with a freestanding tub and a separate shower.

"Seb! This is incredible," I exclaim, the words dying on my lips when I poke my head back around the doorjamb to find him lying on the bed.

"I'm glad you like it," he says, patting the space next to him on the mattress. "Come and lie down. See if this is comfortable. It feels okay to me, but I can get a new one if you don't like it."

"Okay," I say quietly, willing my cheeks not to flush with heat.

I cross the space and sit down on the edge of the bed, bouncing up and down slightly.

"It feels good," I say, my back to Seb.

"Lie down. You can't tell from sitting on the edge."

I slowly scoot backwards and lie down. It's not a huge bed, and my bare arm brushes Seb's as I lie next to him. Tingles of electricity shoot up my arm and my gaze snaps to his. I can't read his expression, despite his gaze holding mine.

"What do you think?" he asks, looking away and bouncing his body up and down on the bed. I squeal as his sudden movements almost cause me to fall off.

"Well, it's… bouncy," I tell him, laughing. He smiles at me, and I have no idea if it's comfortable or not. I don't seem to be able to string a sentence together when he's this close, let alone know whether the mattress is comfortable.

"What's going on?" Paisley asks, appearing in the doorway. I drag my gaze off him to look across at Paisley. I groan internally when her eyebrows rise in surprise and a smile forms on her face. "You two look cozy."

"We're just seeing if the mattress needs replacing," Seb says, jumping up.

"And does it?" she asks.

"Does it what?"

She rolls her eyes. "Does the mattress need replacing?"

"No. It's fine," I tell her, climbing off the bed. She's still grinning, and I discreetly shake my head, knowing she'll try and play matchmaker at even the slightest hint at something between Seb and me.

"I can leave you two looking around if you want," Seb says, making for the bedroom door. "I should get back to the bar."

"I don't need to look around anymore," I tell him. "I love it. It's perfect."

He smiles. "Great. I'll get the contracts drawn up. When do you want to move in?"

I screw up my nose. "Now?"

His eyes widen. "Now?"

I nod. "I can pay a couple of months up front and a security deposit."

"That won't be necessary, Taylor. I don't think you're going to be throwing wild parties and trashing the place."

I laugh. "No. My wild party days are long behind me."

"If you're happy to move in before signing the contract, that's fine by me. I'll get it drawn up as soon as I can."

"I don't know how to thank you, Seb. This place is even better than the original rental I had in place."

"Everything happens for a reason, Tay," Paisley says. "This place is perfect. In fact, it's so perfect, why don't you live here, Seb?"

"I did for a while when I first bought the bar."

"Why did you move out?"

"I needed to separate work and home life. As good as my staff are"—he winks at Paisley—"I knew if I continued to live above the bar, I'd never switch off, even when I wasn't working."

"That's true. You are a bit of a control freak," Paisley says, her voice deadpan.

"Hey! I'm not a control freak," he says, feigning hurt.

"Really? So moving away from the bar worked and you don't come in on your days off?" She grins at him and he laughs.

"Okay. Okay." He throws his arms in the air. "I still come in on my days off. I *am* a control freak." She bursts out laughing, and he rolls his eyes. "Do you two want some lunch before you leave?"

"Smooth change of subject," Paisley says, linking her arm with mine as we walk through the apartment and down the steps to the bar.

"Your keys, Taylor," Seb says, handing me the keys to the apartment. "Ask Paisley to give you my number in case you need anything when I'm not at work. Welcome to Eden."

I grin as I take the keys from him. I knew moving to Hope Creek had been the right decision, but when things started to go wrong before I'd even gotten here, I did begin to question if I was making a mistake. Those doubts have gone now, though, and all that's left is excitement at what's to come.

CHAPTER FIVE

Seb

It's been a few days since Taylor moved into the apartment above the bar, and even though I've been at Eden every day since then, I haven't seen her. I guess it's not a big surprise. When I'm not serving, I'm stuck in my office doing paperwork, so it's possible I've missed her.

I'm in the office, tackling some ordering, when my stomach rumbles and I realize I've missed lunch. I close down the laptop and head to the bar. It's Wednesday, and it's always quiet midweek, but I notice a few regulars are in. Ryder's off today, but Alex is behind the bar, and I've got one server, Trudy, out on the floor.

"Hey, Alex. How's it going?"

"Pretty quiet. Just a regular Wednesday. I did meet the new tenant, though."

"Taylor?" I ask, frowning. He nods. "She was in the bar?"

"She still is." He gestures to one of the high tables across the room. Following his gaze, I see her engrossed in whatever is on her open laptop, a glass of red wine on the table next to her. "You never said she was gorgeous."

I ignore his comment and watch as her fingers fly over the keyboard on her laptop, her bottom lip pulled between her teeth. Her long blonde hair is piled on top of her head in a messy bun and black-rimmed glasses sit on her nose.

"How long has she been here?"

"A couple of hours."

I'm still staring when she looks up. Her eyes meet mine and she smiles, raising her hand in a wave. I leave Alex behind the bar and walk over to her.

"Hey, Taylor. Are you all settled in?"

"Hi, Seb. Yes. Almost. I have a desk on order, but sitting on the sofa to work is killing my back, so I've come down here for a couple of hours. I hope that's okay."

"Of course it is." I gesture to her half-drunk glass of wine. "Do you want a top-up?"

"I'd better not. One glass is my limit when I'm working. Any more and I'll be making mistakes." She giggles, and I smile.

"What is it you do? I don't think Paisley ever said."

"I'm an editor."

"What do you edit?"

"Romance books. Erotica mainly."

My eyes widen in surprise, and I sit down on one of the high chairs. "Really?"

She laughs. "Yes, really. You sound surprised."

"I guess I am."

"Why?"

I shrug. "You just seem a little shy, that's all. I didn't have you down for enjoying mommy porn."

Her mouth drops open. "Mommy porn? I'm editing it, not acting it out. Have you ever read an erotic romance?"

"Well, no..."

"I can recommend some if you're interested."

"I'm more of a thriller type of guy."

"You do read, then?"

"Occasionally, if I have some downtime."

She holds my gaze before grinning. "Wait here. I'll be right back."

She jumps off the chair and starts to cross the bar. "Where are you going?" I shout after her. She ignores me and disappears out of sight.

Unable to stop myself, I move out of my seat and into the one she's just vacated. My eyes widen as I start to read the words on the screen. I quickly look over my shoulder to make sure no one is watching me before looking back at the screen.

"This pussy is mine, Eva," he whispers in my ear, his fingers circling my clit before pushing roughly inside me. I gasp at the sudden intrusion and arch my back, silently asking for more. "I'm going to fuck you until you can't walk and you're begging me to let you come all over my cock. No other man will ever know what it's like to be inside you. Only I get that pleasure." His fingers continue to pound into me and my legs begin to shake at the intensity of his words. "Do you understand? No one else will ever see you like this."

I can't form the words to answer him, too lost in my pleasure. Suddenly, his fingers still.

"Answer me, Eva." His tone sounds desperate, but I must be hearing him wrong. James Campbell doesn't lose control. He's the epitome of control.

"Eva," he warns when I still don't answer him. "Do you want to come?"

"God, yes!" I whimper, my whole body on fire.

"Then answer me," he bites out. "Do. You. Understand?"

"Yes! I'm yours. No one else will see me like this. Please, just please..."

I trail off as his fingers begin to move again, and in an instant, he's between my legs, his breath hot on my skin. He pulls my clit into his mouth and sucks hard. My hands go into his hair and I hold him against me as he eats me like I'm his favorite dessert.

"Enjoying that?" a voice asks, and I jump up, heat flooding my face.

"Taylor! I... erm... I just..."

She laughs. "Still think it's *mommy porn?*"

I step in closer so the few people in the bar with us can't hear what we're saying. "How can you sit in public and read that? Doesn't it get you... hot and bothered?"

She laughs again. "Are you asking me if it turns me on?" I hesitate before nodding. "Sometimes. It depends what it is and how invested in the characters I am. Other times, it's just work." She raises her eyebrows. "Did it turn *you* on?"

I try to ignore my semi-hard cock in my jeans while I think about how to answer her without admitting that it did. "I've never read anything like that before."

"That's not an answer," she says, calling me out. "You've watched porn, right?"

My eyes widen, and I quickly glance around the bar, hoping no one is listening to our conversation. "You're not as shy as I thought you were," I tell her, shaking my head.

"I have no idea why you thought I was shy, and you've avoided my question again."

A smile pulls on her lips and I sigh. "Fine. I was turned on reading it, and yes, I've watched porn. Show me someone who hasn't."

"I've watched it, but I prefer reading it."

I grin. "So, you admit that it is porn?"

"No. It's erotica. Erotica that plays out like porn in my head. Tell me you weren't imagining that scene while you were reading it."

I move awkwardly from one foot to the other. This is definitely not a conversation I expected to be having when I came over here. I like sex as much as the next guy, although the next guy is probably having a lot more of it than I'm getting lately. I just don't know how comfortable I am talking about it in the middle of Eden.

"Sure. I guess."

She tosses me a book I didn't notice she was holding. "Try this."

I look down at the half-naked man on the cover and frown. "Why does the guy have no clothes on?"

She shrugs and sits down in front of her laptop. "Sex sells, Seb."

I turn the book over and skim-read the back cover. "This guy's a teacher who falls for his student? That's messed up."

She rolls her eyes. "He's a young college professor who falls for a student in his class. They're both legal."

"And it's... erm... hot? Like that one?" I nod my head toward the laptop.

"It's hotter than this one."

"Oh. Okay. I'll take a look. If I have time."

She smiles. "Sure. Let me know what you think. If you have the time to read it, of course."

"Did you edit this one?" She nods. "I'll let you know if I find any spelling mistakes."

"You do that."

I leave her chuckling and head back to the bar, where Alex is watching me. I round the bar and grab a bottle of Coke from one of the refrigerators.

"What's that?" he asks, gesturing to the book in my hand.

"Something Taylor suggested I read."

"Dude, there's a shirtless guy on the cover."

I hold it up. "Sex sells, Alex," I say, repeating Taylor's words.

I disappear out the back before he has a chance to say anything else, heading to the kitchen to order some lunch before going back to my office. I quickly finish off the ordering I was looking at earlier, just closing the laptop as Trudy knocks on the door with my lunch.

My eyes keep flicking to the book Taylor gave me as I eat my burger, and eventually, I give in and reach for it. I wasn't lying when I told Taylor I like to read, but on the odd occasion I do pick up a book, it's nothing like this one. Despite that, though, I'm soon engrossed in Peyton and Professor Clark's story and I can't put it down.

CHAPTER SIX

Taylor

It's Friday afternoon and I'm almost done unpacking the last of my things. I'm trying to get the apartment straight before Paisley and Ashlyn head over tonight to watch a movie and eat pizza. This isn't the girls' night Ashlyn planned during Thanksgiving dinner. Sophie and Ashlyn's friend, Bree, can't make tonight, so we're having a chilled one just the three of us before what I'm sure will be a messier night another time.

I ordered some prints to go up in the apartment to break up the stark white walls, and they've been delivered today. I haven't asked Seb if I can hang things in the apartment, but I guess I'd better make sure I can before I put holes in his walls.

I grab my keys and lock the apartment door, jogging down the stairs and into Eden. It's busy, but there's only Ryder serving. Making my way to the bar, I sit on one of the high chairs and wait for him to finish.

"Hi, Taylor," he says when he spots me. "What can I get you?"

"I'm looking for Seb. Is he working today?"

"Yeah. He's in his office out back. You can go through if you want. It's the second door on the right."

"Thanks, Ryder."

When I get to Seb's office, I knock lightly on the door. After a minute or so, there's no answer, so I try again, a little louder this time.

"Come in," Seb shouts, and I push open the door. "Hey, Taylor. Everything okay?" he asks when I walk in.

"Sorry to bother you," I say as I close the door behind me and walk toward his desk. "I just wanted to ask if I could put some pictures up in the apartment?"

"Sure you can. You don't need to ask. If you want to paint any of the rooms, I'm more than good with that too. I know white isn't everybody's first choice."

"Really? That would be great. I was thinking a little color in the bedroom might be good."

He nods. "I trust you, Taylor."

"Thanks." My eyes drop to his desk where the copy of the book I lent him sits open but facedown as though he put it down when I knocked on the door. It looks like he's almost finished.

"How are you finding it?" I ask, gesturing to the book.

"I think I owe you an apology," he says sheepishly.

"What do you mean?"

"I thought erotica would be just sex, but it's more than that. I mean, don't get me wrong, there is a *lot* of sex in it, but there's a story too and I wasn't expecting that."

"So you like it?" I ask with a smile.

He chuckles. "Yeah, I like it. I probably shouldn't read it at work, though. Not when it gives me blue balls all day."

"Fuck!" My mouth drops open. "I think that's a little too much over-sharing, Seb." My eyes track over his broad chest, and I find myself wishing he wasn't sitting behind his desk so I could see the full effect the book is having on him.

"Shit! Sorry. I don't know why I said that."

I laugh and wave off his comment. "It's fine. I've heard far worse. It's a hazard of the job. I have plenty more when you're done with that one, though. If you want to keep reading, just let me know."

"Thanks. I might just take you up on that."

"Oh, one more thing. You wouldn't have a hammer I could borrow, would you? Like an idiot, I ordered the hardware to hang the pictures but nothing to actually hammer them into the wall with."

"Sure. I think there's one around here somewhere. It's probably in the storeroom. I'll see if I can find it and bring it up to you."

"Thanks, Seb."

I leave him in his office and head back upstairs. It will be good to be able to decorate and put my own stamp on the place. Maybe I'll ask Paisley and Ash if they want to help. We can have a painting party.

Fifteen minutes later, there's a knock on my door. I put down the picture I'm holding, cross the space, and open the door.

"What's that?" I ask when all I can see is Seb's inked arms holding a large box.

"No idea. It's just been delivered downstairs. Didn't you say you were waiting on a desk?"

"Ooh, yes! Come in." I take hold of his arm and guide him into the apartment, knowing he won't be able to see anything because of how big the box is.

"Where do you want it?" he asks.

"Anywhere is good. I haven't decided where my workspace is going to be yet. I can move it around once I've figured out how to build it."

He places the box on the floor and heads back to the door.

"I found the hammer. I couldn't carry it with the box, so I'll go back down and grab it."

While he's gone, I rip off the packaging and pull out the white wooden pieces of the desk. There's what looks like a million nuts and bolts, and I frown as I pick up the instructions and flick through them, thinking they might as well be written in a different language.

"How can there be this much hardware?" I tear open the clear plastic bag that's holding them, cringing as they scatter all over the wooden floor. "Fuck," I say, scrambling to grab them all.

"Having fun?" Seb asks from behind me.

"Urgh, I knew buying unassembled was a mistake. I'm going to be working in the bar forever if these instructions are anything to go by."

"Let me take a look."

"Oh, no. I didn't mean for you to help. I know how busy you are. Maybe Paisley or Ash can help."

He laughs. "Paisley, maybe. Ashlyn, definitely not. She's the least practical person I know."

"Wait until you know me better. I'll be vying for that title!"

"Pass me the instructions."

"Don't you have stuff you need to be doing?"

"Yes, but I've already wasted half the day reading that book you gave me. What's another hour?" he says, stepping forward and picking the instructions up off the floor before I can stop him.

"Thank you. Do you want a drink?"

"Sure. What do you have?"

I walk into the kitchen and open the refrigerator. "Water, soda, or wine."

"Are you having wine?"

I look over my shoulder at him. "Sure. It's Friday, right? Is red okay?"

He nods, and I pour us both a glass from the already open bottle I have. "Do you have a screwdriver set?" he asks, setting the pieces of wood into piles and sitting down next to them.

I smile triumphantly. "Yes! I ordered some. They came yesterday. I haven't opened them yet. Hang on, I'll grab the box."

I place both drinks on the breakfast bar and disappear into my bedroom, coming back with two boxes. I'd ordered a ton of things from Amazon earlier in the week and I have no idea which box the screwdrivers are in. I sit on the floor next to him and tear into the first box. I reach inside and blindly pull out what I think is the screwdriver set. My face floods with heat when I look down at the large, hot-pink rabbit vibrator I completely forgot I'd ordered in my hand.

"If that's the screwdriver set, they sent the wrong thing," Seb says with a chuckle. I groan internally, wanting the ground to open up and swallow me. "Is that what I think it is?"

Despite the fact that the hottest guy on the planet is asking me if I've bought myself a sex toy, I decide to own it. I'm a grown woman with needs and I've got nothing to be ashamed about, even if my face feels like it's on fire.

"Yes. It's a vibrator. You've seen what I do for a living. Sometimes I need some… relief."

He raises his eyebrows, his eyes going from the vibrator to me and back again. I'd love to know what he's thinking, and if I'd had more wine, I'd be tempted to ask, but I'm pretty sure we've shared enough today.

I shove the vibrator back in its packaging and grab the unopened box, going through in my head what I ordered in the hope that whatever's inside this box isn't quite as embarrassing. I'm cautious once the box is open, and I peek inside, breathing a sigh of relief when it's the screwdriver set. Why couldn't I have opened this box first?

"Here they are," I say, pulling the set out and passing it to him.

He takes it from me, his gaze fixed on mine. "That's a shame. I was looking forward to seeing what other naughty things you might have bought."

He winks at me, and heat pools in my stomach. Is he flirting with me, or am I imagining it? It's been so long it's hard to know.

"You sure like pink," he says with a chuckle. "I don't think I've ever seen a pink screwdriver set."

"I have a few pink *things*," I tell him, trying to flirt back.

His eyes flash with what I think is heat, and he swallows thickly. "I'm going to need my drink," he says, his voice low.

"Sure thing."

I stand up and turn my back on him as I make for the breakfast bar. I drag in a deep breath, and what feels like a million butterflies take flight in my stomach. Despite being confident and outgoing, all that confidence disappears when I like a guy, and I do like him. I didn't expect to, even though I'd noticed how hot he was when I first visited Hope Creek. Now that I'm beginning to get to know him, I'm seeing there's more to him than just what he looks like, and I find myself wanting to know everything.

It takes about an hour for Seb to put the desk together, and we spend that time talking, laughing, and drinking almost a whole bottle of wine. He's so easy to talk to and he tells me about his family and the things he used to get up to with Wyatt as a child. There's no more flirting, and I put it down to whipping out a sex toy in front of him. I guess any guy would have the same reaction.

"There, done," he says, standing up and picking the desk up off its side and righting it. "Where do you want it?"

I stand too and look around the apartment for the perfect place, finally deciding on under the window. "How about there?" I tell him, pointing to the spot.

He nods and maneuvers the desk in place before standing back to admire his work.

"Looks good. I can imagine you sitting there all day editing your naughty books."

I laugh. "Says you who's now reading one of those *naughty books.*"

"I'm almost done with the one you've lent me."

"I saw. The question is, are you going to want to borrow another one?"

He turns to the pile of books stacked up the wall behind the sofa. I haven't gotten a bookcase for them yet, but I'd unpacked the box before I realized I had nowhere to put them. "Yeah, I think so." He walks toward them and kneels down to get a closer look. "Are these all the ones you've worked on?"

"God, no! I wish. A handful are. The rest are some authors I like."

"Do you have any where the main characters don't end up together?"

I raise my eyebrows. "As in where one of them dies or something?"

"Not necessarily. Just where they have a relationship and then things don't work out and they go their separate ways. You know, like *real life.*"

"Real life?" I ask in confusion. I can't help but wonder why he thinks relationships don't work out in real life. Two of his brothers are proof they do.

"Yeah. Surely you can't think books like the one you gave me portray actual relationships. All that 'happy ever after' shit. That's definitely not real life."

"Okay…" I say slowly, walking over to him. "I think Nash and Paisley and Sophie and Cade might disagree."

He shrugs and drags his hand through his hair. "They probably would, but look at all the heartache they had to go through to get it."

"I'm willing to bet they'd say it was worth it."

"Maybe. It's not going to be something that's in my future, though."

"Why?"

"It just won't. I won't let it." I start to ask him what he means, but he's crossed the room and opened the door to the apartment before I can. "I'd better get back," he calls over his shoulder, disappearing out of sight before I can even thank him for building my desk.

I'm left standing alone in my apartment, wondering what just happened and who the hell broke Seb Brookes' heart. No one writes off love like that unless they've been so badly hurt it destroyed them. If that is what happened, he's putting on a good show of being okay.

CHAPTER SEVEN

Seb

I've been in my office all night, trying to catch up on the work I should have done when I was reading the book Taylor gave me. I could blame the hour it took me to assemble her desk as the reason I'm behind, but it's definitely the book. I've done nothing the past couple of days other than read, and now that I've finished the book, all I can think about is that fucking pink vibrator from earlier and what Taylor might be doing with it.

"Fuck," I say, pushing down my wayward thoughts. While thinking about Taylor is a welcome distraction from thoughts of Sophie, she's Paisley's best friend and my tenant. It's complicated. I'm not looking for anything more than friendship or a hook-up at best. Taylor definitely isn't someone I can have meaningless sex with. What I said to her earlier was true. Falling in love isn't in the cards for me. I've experienced it once and all it gave in return was heartbreak. I don't need that, and especially not with Taylor. Sure,

I'd noticed how beautiful she was at Thanksgiving. I'd have to be blind not to, but it must be all the sex in this damn book she lent me that's giving me all these crazy thoughts. It has to be that. Lust and nothing more.

"I need a drink," I mutter, pushing down thoughts of sex and Taylor.

When I walk out of the office, the noise from the bar hits me. With my door closed, I somehow manage to tune the noise out, and it always takes me by surprise just how loud it is when I step outside. I'm expecting the bar to be busy. There's a singer playing tonight, and it's always packed when there's live music.

"Hey, boss. The singer's a hit," Alex shouts over the music as I join him behind the bar.

I look out into the crowd. He's not wrong. It's four or five deep at the bar, and there isn't a free inch of floor space. I tip my head to Ryder who's at the other end of the bar. All thoughts of grabbing a drink disappear when I see how busy it is, and I spend the next hour serving. When the singer ends her set, people start to leave, and it finally slows a little.

"God, that last hour was crazy," Ryder says, collecting a bunch of empty glasses and loading them into the countertop dishwasher.

"I think we deserve a drink," I tell him. "You more than me." I grab three bottles of beer and pass him one. "Alex," I shout. He's down the other end of the bar. "Drink." I hold up his bottle and he walks toward me, taking it from my outstretched hand.

"Thanks, man. I need this."

He takes a pull before serving a group of women who ask for cocktails. I offer to help when they all order something different. When they finally have their drinks, I turn to find Taylor standing at the end of the bar. She's wearing tiny sleep shorts and a tank that puts her perfect body on display. My eyes sweep over her and I know every jackass in the place is going to be looking at her dressed like that. When she looks up, her eyes find mine, and she smiles.

"You know you're in the bar in your pajamas, right?" I tease as I make my way to her. "Your very small, very tight pajamas."

She laughs. "Yes, I know. I'm drunk and I couldn't be bothered to get dressed to come down here."

"You're drunk?"

"Yep! Not as drunk as the last time I saw Ashlyn, although the night isn't over yet." She wriggles her eyebrows. "That's why I'm here. I need shots!" She waves her arm dramatically, and I chuckle.

"You *need* shots? Ash sent you down here, didn't she?"

She nods. "She said if she came down here, you wouldn't give her any. You know that she's a grown woman, right?"

I smile. "Yes, Taylor. I'm aware she's a grown woman. She's also my baby sister. How drunk is she?"

She rolls her eyes. "Never mind. Alex will give me some if you won't."

She's already moving along the bar to where he is.

"Taylor. Wait."

"Alex," she shouts, ignoring me. "Can I get some shots?"

"Hey, Taylor. Sure," he replies. "What do you want?"

"Hey, darlin'. You're a little underdressed, aren't you?" a guy asks, sliding up next to her and wrapping his arm around her shoulder. She tries to move out of his hold, but he doesn't let her. "Come and dance with me."

"No, thanks. I'm good," she says, trying to shake off his embrace.

"Aww, you're just a little tease, aren't you?"

"Get your hands off her!" I bite out. "She's not interested." I'm beyond pissed that some random guy has his hands on her. He's got one chance to step away or I'm going to make him.

"Fuck off! No one asked you," he shouts.

"Wrong answer!" I round the bar in seconds and drag him off Taylor.

"What the hell—"

"Get out! You're barred," I tell him, dragging him through the crowds of people and tossing his ass onto the sidewalk.

"You can't do that!" he cries, scrambling to stand up.

"I just did. It's my bar and I can do what the hell I like. Have some fucking respect. She said no!"

I leave him on the sidewalk and head back inside. Taylor's waiting by the door for me.

"Are you okay?"

She nods. "Thanks, Seb. I guess now I know why you're so protective of Ash."

"Guys like that are assholes. I see far too many of them in here disrespecting women. I don't want that for Ash or you."

"I'm an idiot. I should have at least put on a sweater before I came down here. I guess I was asking for trouble. Drunk *and* half dressed."

"It shouldn't matter what you wear, Taylor. No man has the right to put his hands on you if you don't want him to. That's not to say it isn't a little… distracting." Her cheeks flush pink, and I chuckle. "Go back upstairs. I'll bring the shots up. What do you want?"

"Are you sure?"

"Yes."

She smiles. "Tequila, please. Two each."

"Two each?"

She nods and pushes a couple of twenties into my hand. "They're on me, Taylor," I tell her, giving her back the twenties.

"No, Seb. I can't let you do that."

"You can. It's just a few shots."

She holds my gaze before going up on her tiptoes and pressing a kiss on my cheek. "Thank you."

I watch her as she crosses the bar, weaving drunkenly through the crowd. My eyes drop to the curve of her ass that peeks out from the bottom of her ridiculously short shorts. She's a fucking walking wet dream, and I know from the glances she's getting from guys in here that I'm not the only one to think that.

Taylor

"You've been gone ages!" Ash cries as I walk into the apartment, finding her and Paisley on the sofa where I left them. "Hey! Where are the drinks?" she says as she looks down at my empty hands. "Seb wouldn't serve you, would he?" She jumps up from the sofa. "I'm going down there. He's such a jackass!"

"Seb's bringing them up. Some guy got handsy and he had to throw him out. I can't believe I went downstairs wearing this."

She sits back down, and I spin around as if they haven't already seen me in my sleep shorts and tank.

"You look hot," Paisley slurs. "Did Seb like your outfit?"

"What?"

"Seb. Did he like your pjs?"

I screw up my nose and drop down onto the sofa between Paisley and Ash. "He said I was distracting. What the hell does that even mean?"

"It means he likes you," Ash says, dropping her head onto my shoulder.

"He doesn't."

"How do you know?"

I shrug. "I just do."

After our conversation earlier, it's crystal clear that as hot and sexy as Seb Brookes is, he's not looking for anything remotely like a relationship. It's just my luck that I'm attracted to someone who's emotionally unavailable.

I giggle as I remember a different conversation with Seb, and Paisley looks at me.

"What's funny?" she asks, a smile pulling on her lips.

"Seb saw my vibrator earlier."

"Your what?" she screeches.

"My vibrator."

"You have a vibrator?" I nod. "I wanna see."

"Why?"

"I've never seen one."

"You've never owned a vibrator?" Ashlyn asks, her voice etched with surprise.

"No. Do you have one?" Paisley asks.

Ashlyn laughs. "More than one. Girl, you're missing out."

"I doubt it. Nash is pretty talented, especially with his mouth."

"Oh my God! That's my brother, Paisley."

"Yep. Your hot, sexy-as-fuck brother."

"I need more alcohol!" she groans, standing and stumbling into the kitchen.

"I think you've grossed out Ash," I tell Paisley.

She waves off my comment. "She'll get over it. Please will you show me, Tay?" Paisley begs, and I chuckle.

"Okay. Wait there."

I go into my bedroom and reach under my bed for the small box I know is hiding there. I open it and pull out the toy.

"Here you go," I shout, holding it in the air as I walk back into the living room. My eyes widen and my face flushes with heat as Seb stands in the kitchen with the tray of tequilas. I quickly hide it behind my back.

"You should really stop showing me that, Taylor. It's already burned into my memory as it is," he says, placing the tray on the countertop.

"Hi, Ash."

"Hi, Seb."

Paisley giggles from the sofa. "It's my fault. I asked her to get it. I've never seen one before. Pass it here, Tay."

She holds her hand out and I glance at Seb before reluctantly bringing my hand from behind my back and passing her the vibrator.

"What's this bit for?" Paisley asks, flicking the rabbit ears on the clit stimulator.

My cheeks flush hotter as I realize I'm going to have to explain how it works in front of Seb.

"That's for your clit, Paisley," Ashlyn says from the kitchen.

"Okay. I should go," Seb says, glancing at me before shaking his head and making for the door. "Is Nash picking you two up?" he asks, looking from Paisley to Ashlyn.

"Yep. I've got to call him when we're done," Paisley says.

He nods. "I'll see you all at Sophie's place tomorrow night."

"Night, Seb. Thanks for the shots," Ashlyn calls from the kitchen.

Paisley waves her hand in the air, too engrossed in studying the vibrator to do more. I cross the room and go to him at the door. "Thanks for the drinks. Sorry about…" I trail off, not wanting to say the word out loud in front of him.

He laughs. "It's fine, Taylor. Have fun tonight," he whispers, winking before he turns and jogs down the apartment stairs. I stare at the empty stairwell long after he's out of sight. Did he mean fun with Ash and Paisley, or fun on my own after they've left? I wish I'd had the guts to ask.

CHAPTER EIGHT

Taylor

I smooth my hands down my electric-blue cami and flick my freshly curled hair over my shoulder. It's the get-together at Sophie and Cade's place tonight, and I've opted for black skinny jeans and a top. Dressy, but casual. I take one last look in the full-length mirror in my bedroom, happy with my outfit choice, before slipping on my heeled pumps and picking my purse up off the dresser.

I'm not drinking tonight. After the wine and tequila shots last night, my liver needs a break. I've warned Ashlyn, and after she threw up before she and Paisley left, she's in agreement.

After slipping on my jacket and locking up, I head downstairs and into Eden. It's early evening, but there's already a decent crowd gathering. It looks like it's going to be another busy night.

"Hey, Taylor," Alex calls from behind the bar. "You look beautiful."

I watch as his eyes sweep over me, and my cheeks flood with heat. "Thanks."

"Hot date?"

I laugh. "No. A party."

He nods and continues drying the glass in his hand. "Can I take you out for a drink sometime?"

I'm taken aback by his question and have no idea how to respond. I've only spoken to him a couple of times. He's always been so confident but seems nervous as he waits for my answer. He's cute, there's no doubting that. He's tall and well built, with messy blond hair and blue eyes, but there's no ink on his arms and his jaw is free of stubble, unlike Seb's. It's not fair to compare them, but I can't help it. As cute as he is, I'm just not attracted to him.

"As flattered as I am, I'm not dating at the moment. I've had some personal stuff going on and I'm just taking some time for myself."

I hope a little white lie to save his feelings is okay on this occasion. I guess it's a half-truth. I *have* had some personal stuff going on, but if the right guy asked me out, there's no way I'd say no.

"Sure. I get that. Maybe when you're ready, then?"

"Yeah, maybe. Have a good night, Alex."

"You too, Taylor."

I walk quickly out of Eden, grateful for the blast of cold air that hits me when I reach the sidewalk. I haven't been asked out in a really long time. I dated a guy for almost a year before my mom got sick, and while I loved him, when I had to cancel dates to care for my mom, he soon lost interest and ended things within weeks. I later found out he went back to his ex who he'd been hung up on for a while. I was upset at the time, but I soon realized I had a lucky escape. A guy like that was never going to stick around when things got tough. I was better off without him.

It's dark as I leave Eden, and I'm beginning to wish I'd taken

Nash up on his offer of a ride. I didn't, knowing Sophie's place is only around the corner for him and Paisley. I didn't want them coming out of their way to pick me up. I pull my jacket tightly around myself and walk a little faster. I jump a few minutes later when the roar of a motorcycle pierces the silence. The driver rides past me before slowing and turning around. My heart thunders in my chest as the motorcycle comes to a stop next to me, cutting the engine. I continue to walk, quickening my pace.

"Taylor, wait! It's me," someone shouts, and I stop, recognizing the voice.

I breathe a sigh of relief when I turn and Seb's sitting on his bike with his helmet in his hand. I know he rides a motorcycle, but in the dark, I had no idea it was him.

"Shit, Seb. You scared me."

"Sorry. What are you doing walking in the dark?"

"I'm going to Sophie and Cade's party."

"I know that. Why didn't you ask me for a ride?"

I frown. "You weren't at work this afternoon. I didn't think you'd want to come all the way back to Eden just to pick me up."

"It's a five-minute ride, Taylor. I wouldn't have minded. Get on. You can have my helmet."

I shake my head. "Oh, no! I can't get on that."

"Why?"

"I just can't. You, you're perfect for it, but me… no. I can't. No."

He laughs. "Are you still drunk?"

"What?"

"You're rambling."

"I am not."

He holds my stare and my stomach dips. He looks so fucking sexy straddling his bike. Why couldn't it have been Seb asking me out instead of Alex?

"What did you mean when you said I was perfect for the bike?" he asks.

I bite my bottom lip. "Just that you look… like that." My eyes sweep over him. "Your tattoos and… stuff."

"You don't like tattoos?"

"Oh, no. I like them. I like them a lot…"

I stop talking and groan internally. I might as well have told him outright that I'm attracted to him.

A smile pulls on his lips. "Do you have any?"

"Any what?" I ask, distracted by how much of an idiot I'm making of myself.

"Tattoos, Taylor."

"Actually, I do."

"Where? I've seen you in the tiniest of pajamas and there was no hint of any tattoos."

I smile. "You can only see it when I'm naked." His eyes widen, and he opens his mouth as if to say something before closing it again.

"Shit," I say. "I forgot Sophie's flowers."

He shakes his head and blows out a breath. "Okay, get on the bike. I'll take you back to Eden and you can grab them." He holds the helmet out to me and I hesitate. "You'll be safe. I promise."

I nod and slip the helmet over my head. Taking a deep breath, I climb on behind him.

"Should I hold on to you?"

"Yep. Unless you want to fall off." I slide my arms around his waist and hold on to him tightly. "I still need to breathe, Tay."

"Sorry." I loosen my hold and smile against his back when he calls me *Tay* instead of *Taylor*. Even over the top of the sweater he's wearing, I can feel how toned his stomach is, and I wish I could slip my hand underneath and brush my fingers over his skin.

"Do you have tattoos everywhere?" His stomach moves under my hands as he laughs.

"Not quite everywhere, but honestly, I don't think it's fair you've seen mine and I haven't seen yours."

"I haven't seen *all* of yours."

"True, but I haven't seen *any* of yours."

"Show me one I haven't seen and I'll think about showing you mine."

I'm not sure where my confidence has come from. Maybe it's because I'm behind him with his helmet on and I know he can't see me. Whatever it is, I love this flirty banter that's between us. I don't think it's going to lead anywhere, but I love it all the same.

"You're a tease, Taylor Jacobs. Hold on tight."

Before I can answer him, he's firing up the bike and pulling away from the sidewalk. I let out a little scream and hold on to him, pressing my head against his back. I feel his hand rest on my thigh before he squeezes gently.

"You okay?" he shouts. I tap his stomach, not able to lift my head and answer him. "I'm going to need actual words, Taylor."

"I'm good," I shout, hoping he can hear me when I'm talking into his back.

He squeezes my leg in acknowledgment, and it's only when he pulls up at the back of Eden that I realize he never moved his hand. I climb off the bike and tug the helmet off, handing it to him.

"I'll just be a sec."

Minutes later, I'm back outside, a large bouquet of flowers in my hand. I frown as I look from the flowers to the bike.

"I didn't think this through. I'm not sure how I'm going to hold on to you and the flowers. Maybe I should walk."

"Nah, I'll make it work. Pass them to me."

I'm skeptical, but within minutes, I'm back on the bike with both arms wrapped around Seb and the flowers in front of him. I'm sure having a bunch of flowers in his face while he tries to drive isn't ideal, but the roads are quiet, and it isn't long before we're pulling up outside Sophie and Cade's place.

Despite being terrified at the idea of being on the back of his bike, it wasn't as bad as I thought. "Thanks for the ride," I say as I climb off. "I hope I haven't made you late."

He waves off my comment. "It's fine. I guarantee Ash will be later than us."

I hand him the helmet, which he puts next to his bike, and I attempt to fluff my hair with my free hand.

"Do I have helmet hair?" I ask him, trying to see my reflection in the window of Cade's car.

"You look beautiful, Taylor."

I turn to find him standing right behind me.

I tilt my head back to look at him, his six-foot-three frame towering above me, even with my heeled pumps on. "Thanks. You look good too."

And he does. He's wearing dark jeans pushed into black boots and a dark-colored hoodie. His hair is styled like he's spent the day running his fingers through it and the ever-present stubble is on his jaw. He looks sexy as hell.

"We should go inside," he says, his voice low.

I nod before hearing him sigh as he drops his eyes from mine and takes a step back. I follow him up the porch steps, wondering if we've just had a moment or whether I'm imagining things.

CHAPTER NINE

Seb

It's been almost a week since Cade and Sophie's party. Despite my apprehension about going, I had a good night. I forced myself to speak to Sophie, and it seems every time I see her, it gets a little easier and hurts a little less. I figure if I want to get our friendship back, I need to let go of any feelings I have for her.

Maybe it didn't hurt so much because I spent most of the night talking to Taylor. She's so easy to talk to, and we seem to have this energy between us that I can't explain. I know for sure that us talking didn't go unnoticed. Nash even called me the next day to ask if something was going on between the two of us. I assured him there wasn't and that we're just friends. I'm not sure he believed me. Even though friendship is all I can offer, it doesn't stop me from thinking about her all the time and where that damn tattoo is.

It's Friday lunchtime, and I've just brought a case of beer up from the cellar.

"I asked her out," Alex says to Ryder as I walk behind the bar. "She's not dating right now."

"Did she say why?" Ryder asks.

Alex shrugs. "Something about some personal shit she's got going on."

"Who are you talking about?" I ask, placing the crate of beer on the bar.

"Taylor."

I spin around to look at Alex. "You asked Taylor out?" He nods. "When?"

"Saturday night. She was leaving for that party at Cade's place." He frowns. "You look pissed."

"I'm not. I just didn't know you liked her." I turn my back on him and begin to stock the refrigerator with the Coronas I just brought up. I shouldn't care he's asked her out, but somehow, I do.

"She's gorgeous. You can't tell me you haven't noticed."

"I've noticed." When neither Alex nor Ryder comment, I turn around. They're both grinning at me. "What?" I ask, looking between them.

"You like her," Ryder says.

"Sure I like her. As a friend."

"I don't mean as a friend," he says. "For what it's worth, I think she likes you too." He turns to Alex. "Sorry, man, but I've seen the way she looks at him."

Alex shrugs. "Plenty more fish in the sea," he says, and I roll my eyes, focusing back on Ryder.

"She doesn't look at me any way," I tell him, my stomach suddenly churning with nerves, although I've no idea why. "Since when did you become an expert on attraction?"

"I work in a bar. I see people flirting *all* the time. You get good at noticing these things. People who are into each other, people who aren't. You should take a look when you're behind here."

I look at him like he's lost his mind. "I'm too busy making drinks to notice who's getting it on and who isn't. As long as they keep buying drinks, I don't care."

"I've watched people and I've watched you two."

I shake my head. "Well, you've got it wrong this time, Ryder. Dead wrong."

"You keep telling yourself that and I'll be here to tell you *I told you so* when you end up together."

"You have a vivid imagination."

I turn my back on him and continue to restock the refrigerator. I might have pushed down his theory, but if I'm completely honest with myself, I know he's right, even if I don't want to admit it aloud. I like her, but I shouldn't. I'm pretty sure she likes me too. I've caught her watching me more than once, and whenever we talk, there's always an undertone of attraction. It doesn't change anything, though. I was friends with Sophie before I realized I liked her, and there's no doubt my feelings for her have strained our friendship, even if she has no idea. It changed things for me, and I don't want the same to happen with Taylor. When feelings are involved, it confuses everything.

∽

I haven't seen Taylor all week. I know after speaking to her at Cade and Sophie's place she was chasing a deadline for the book she was editing. I'm guessing that's kept her busy and she's been working nonstop.

I'm not expecting to see her tonight, and when she walks into Eden, my breath catches in my throat. She looks fucking stunning, and I can't take my eyes off her. Her long blonde hair falls around her shoulders in waves, and the black dress she's wearing hugs her body in all the right places. The tight material falls mid-thigh, and as my gaze sweeps over her, I groan internally as I see the black, heeled shoes she's wearing, making her legs look like they go on forever. I can't help but wonder who she's meeting dressed like that.

"Hey, Seb," she says as she nears the bar, and I finally drag my eyes up to meet hers.

"Hey," I reply, smiling at her. "Night out?"

"It's girls' night."

An unexpected wave of relief washes over me knowing she's meeting the girls and not some guy.

"Should I get more tequila from downstairs? Is it going to get messy?" I tease.

She screws up her nose, making her look even more beautiful. "Not for me. I still haven't finished my edits, and the deadline is Monday."

"So, sodas all night for you, then?"

"Well… I was thinking maybe one glass of wine would be okay."

I smile. "Is it me you're trying to convince or yourself?"

"Urgh, you're no help. I'll take a large red wine."

"Coming right up."

I grab a wineglass and fill it to the top before handing it to her.

Her eyes widen. "Are you trying to get me drunk, Seb Brookes?"

"If you're only having one, then you may as well fill the glass."

"You're a bad influence, you know that?"

I chuckle. "What time are the girls getting here?"

"Eight. I'm a little early. I was desperate to get out of the apartment and away from my laptop."

"You should come and work down here again for a couple of hours. Get a change of scenery."

"Yeah, maybe I will tomorrow."

"Wait there and I'll grab you a seat. You can sit at the bar while you wait for the girls."

"It's okay. I'll just grab a table. You're busy."

"It's fine. You don't want to sit on your own. You can keep me company."

I move out from behind the bar, reaching for a reserved sign as I go. I place the sign on one of the booth tables before picking up a chair from a free table and bringing it to where she's standing.

"Thanks, Seb," she says with a smile as she slides onto the chair. My eyes drop to her toned and tanned legs as she crosses them and her dress rides up. I know for sure if she were to sit alone in one of the booths while she waits for the others, there would be some guy hitting on her in minutes. I don't know why the idea of that bothers me so much, but it does.

There's a steady stream of customers, and I chat to Taylor in between serving them. There have been a few guys who have hit on her when I've had to serve, and I watch out of the corner of my eye, unwanted jealousy swirling in my stomach that the next guy who approaches her is one she'll end up wanting to talk to. I'm down the other end of the bar making a cocktail and stealing glances at her when Ryder bumps his shoulder with mine.

"She looks hot, doesn't she?" he says quietly.

"I hadn't noticed," I lie, pouring the fruity drink I've made into the cocktail glass and sliding it across the bar.

"I call bullshit! There's no way someone as hot as Taylor is going to be single for long. You should ask her out."

"Not going to happen."

"You won't mind if I go and talk to her, then."

"Knock yourself out. She's already warded off a couple of guys who've tried it on while she's been sitting there. If you think you can do any better…" I take payment for the cocktail and turn my back on him, putting the money in the register. I know he's fucking with me and he's not going to hit on her. That doesn't mean every other guy in the place won't try.

I hear her laugh and I make my way over to them.

"Oh, God!" she says, covering her mouth with her hand. "I can't believe people do that in a public bathroom."

"What's funny?" I ask with a smile, her laugh infectious.

"Ryder's just telling me about the couple you found going at it in the bathroom last night. Does that happen often?"

"You'd be surprised."

"What were they doing?" she asks, her eyes wide.

A smile pulls on my lips. "They were having sex, Taylor."

She rolls her eyes. "Well, I figured that much! Were they in one of the stalls? What did they say when you asked them to leave?"

I laugh. "Yes, they were in one of the stalls. The guy asked me if he could finish first."

Her eyes widen. "What did you say?"

"I said no!"

"Spoilsport!"

Her eyes flash with heat and I hold her gaze. "I'll be sure to let the next couple finish before I throw them out. Surely stuff like that happens in your naughty books?"

"Naughty books?" Ryder asks, a smirk on his face.

She shakes her head, a smile on her lips. "It's erotica."

"You read erotica?" Ryder asks, looking from me to Taylor.

"Read it, edit it, lend it to friends." She winks at me, and Ryder grins before punching me on the arm.

"*You're* reading erotica?" His tone is laced with surprise.

"Hey, don't knock it until you've tried it." I look at Taylor. "I never did swap the book you gave me for another one."

She smiles. "Come up whenever you want. You can choose the next one."

"Taylor," a voice shouts, and I look up to see Paisley, Ashlyn, and Bree walking toward us.

"Hey," Taylor says, standing and pulling each of them into a hug.

"You look hot, Taylor," Ashlyn says as she steps out of the embrace. "That dress is incredible."

"Thanks. You look good too. Where's Sophie?"

"She's not feeling great, so she decided to stay at home," Ash says, leaning over the bar and pressing a kiss on my cheek.

"Is she okay?" I ask as she steps back.

She nods. "She felt dizzy earlier, so Cade wanted to keep an eye on her."

My heart squeezes in my chest knowing she's sick. I hope she's okay.

"I thought you weren't drinking tonight?" Paisley asks Taylor, pulling me from my thoughts.

Taylor catches my eye and grins.

"Seb made me have one."

"Trying to get her drunk, Seb?" Paisley says before I can respond.

"I'm joking. I'm just having the one. Seb just made it a very large one."

Paisley introduces Taylor to Bree, and when they all have a drink in their hand, they head to the table I reserved. Despite worrying about Sophie, my eyes gravitate to Taylor more than they should. Occasionally she sees me watching her, a smile forming on her face when she does. I know I should stop, but I seem powerless to.

There's music playing, and it isn't long before all four of them are up dancing. Within minutes, there are a couple of guys hanging around them. Paisley and Bree are oblivious to the attention, but Ashlyn seems to be lapping it up. I watch as she crooks her finger toward one of the guys, who doesn't hesitate to pull her against him. His friend approaches Taylor and my fist clenches at my side as he says something to her and winds her arms around his neck.

"Told you," Ryder says as he walks past me and looks out into the crowd.

"Fuck off, Ryder. I'm going on my break. Keep an eye on them for me."

He chuckles. "Sure thing, boss."

I toss the cloth I'm holding onto the countertop and make for my office. Jealousy swirls in my stomach. Even though I know I can't hold her in my arms like that, it doesn't mean I don't want to. Maybe I should have reserved them a table at the back of Eden and away from the bar. At least that way I wouldn't have to watch. It's going to be a long-ass night.

CHAPTER TEN

Taylor

I've had the *best* night with the girls. I already knew how amazing Paisley was, but Ash and Bree are incredible too. I couldn't ask for a better group of friends. It's made me realize how lonely I was in Pittsburgh. I had Paisley, but because of her ex, we never did girls' night. Connor would never have let her.

We've danced all night and my feet are killing me. I sit in the booth and slip my shoes off, rubbing my sore feet with my hands. I look across the bar to see Brandon, the guy I danced briefly with, watching me. I felt a little awkward when Ashlyn asked him and his friend to join us, but I didn't want to be rude, so when he asked me to dance, I said yes. I'd seen Seb watching me a couple of times, and I don't know if it was the buzz from the wine, but every time my eyes met his, my heart raced and my stomach dipped. I'm sure he's just watching out for me like he would for Ash and Paisley, but I swear there was something in his stare.

"Nash is here," Paisley announces, waving her phone in the air. There's a slight slur to her voice and I know from the amount of wine she's had she's a little drunk. I didn't stick to my one-glass-of-wine rule and ended up having another. Drinking Coke when everyone else is drinking alcohol is no fun. I'm almost done with the manuscript I'm working on, though, so I know I'll meet my deadline on Monday.

"I've had a great night. We have to do it again and soon," I tell the girls as they each hug me goodnight.

"Definitely," Bree says. "A night out these days is rare, so count me in for sure."

"You know it's a yes from me," Ashlyn says with a giggle. "I'll just go and say bye to Seb. See you soon, Taylor."

"I'll call you tomorrow, Tay," Paisley says, pulling me in for another hug.

I wave them off and sit back down in the booth. I've still got a little of my wine left and I pick up the glass, sipping the red liquid. I look out into the crowd of people still dancing, chatting, and having a good time. My eyes fall on Brandon, and he smiles when he sees me. Groaning internally, I drink down the last of my drink and push my aching feet back into my shoes. I don't want to get into another conversation with him and decide to call it a night.

I stand from the booth and head to the bar. "Night, Seb," I call out, seeing he's busy serving.

He looks up, his eyes finding mine. "Oh, night, Taylor. Did you have fun?"

I nod. "I had the best night."

He smiles. "Good. I might see you tomorrow if you decide to work in the bar for a while?"

"Sure. See you tomorrow."

I raise my hand in a wave and make my way to the *staff only* hallway that leads to my apartment. I dig in my purse for my keys as I climb the stairs to my front door. I've just unlocked the door when I hear movement behind me. I turn around, fear prickling up my spine.

"What are you doing? You can't be back here."

"Is this your apartment?" Brandon asks, moving closer toward me.

"You need to leave."

"I saw you watching me before. Why don't I come in and we can get to know each other better?"

"No. You need to go." He's still a couple of steps away from me and I take my chance, hoping I can get inside the apartment and close the door before he reaches me. As soon as I make the move, I know I've made a mistake. He's by my side in seconds and pushing his way into the apartment.

"Get out! I don't want you in here!" I back away from him, trying to put some space between us. He's fast, though, and he grabs my arms and pushes me down on the sofa before I know what's happening.

"No! Get off me!" I cry, struggling to get out from underneath him. Panic swirls in my stomach and I have no idea how I'm going to get away from him. My eyes search frantically for my purse, which holds my cell phone. If I can just get to that, I can try and call for help. I can't see it, though, and my skin crawls when I feel his hands all over me.

"No! Stop! Please." Tears fall down my face as the realization of what's about to happen hits me.

"What the fuck!" a voice shouts and a wave of relief washes over me hearing Seb.

Seconds later, Brandon's weight is lifted off me, and I scramble off the sofa and into my bedroom. I just need to get as far away from him as possible. My whole body's shaking, and I lie on the bed, curling my body up as small as it will go.

I don't know how long I've been lying on the bed, but it can't have been long when Seb appears in the doorway.

"Taylor," he says, his voice laced with concern. "Are you okay?"

"Is he... is he gone?"

"Yeah, he's gone. Ryder's calling 911. Did he hurt you?"

I shake my head. "You got here just in time. How did you know to come up?"

He sighs and sits down on the edge of the bed. "I saw you come back here and then I saw someone follow you. I got up here as quickly as I could. I just wish I'd gotten here sooner."

The shock of what's happened suddenly hits me and I burst into tears. Within seconds, Seb's on the bed and I'm in his arms. I tense as he pulls me against him before realizing he's nothing like the man who just attacked me.

"It's okay. It's over. Don't cry," he whispers.

I sag against him, my fingers clinging on to his t-shirt as he holds me. He somehow lays us both down on the bed without letting me go, and I cry into his chest. One of his hands strokes my hair, and eventually, my tears stop.

After a few minutes, I lift my head from his chest, my tears leaving a mascara-stained mark on his t-shirt.

Looking up at him, I smile apologetically. "I'm sorry about your t-shirt," I tell him, dragging my fingers over the wet patch.

"I don't care about my shirt. Are you okay?"

I shrug and drop my head back onto his chest.

"Why does someone think they have the right to try and..." I trail off, unable to say the words.

He increases his hold on me and blows out a breath. "I don't know, Tay. He's a fucking asshole. No one has the right to *ever* do what he did."

Before I can say anything, I hear a voice from the living room.

Panic rises in my chest again, and I know Seb can feel my body tense in his arms.

"Seb," the voice says again. "It's Jackson."

"It's the police, Tay. Jackson works with Nash. I'm guessing they want to talk to you. Do you feel up to it?" I nod, knowing I have to talk to them at some point. I just want it over so I can curl up in bed and forget about it all. "We'll be right out, Jackson," Seb shouts.

I sigh before sitting up and wiping my tearstained face. I swing my legs to the side of the bed and stand.

"Do you need to get back to the bar, or can you stay?" I ask hesitantly. There's no reason why he would stay, but I don't want to be on my own.

"I can stay." He takes out his phone, his fingers flying across the screen. "Ryder can close up."

"Thank you," I whisper.

Taking a deep breath, I walk out of the bedroom.

"Hi, Taylor. I'm Officer Jackson Adams."

"Hi."

"Are you hurt? Do you need me to call the EMTs?"

I shake my head. "No. He didn't hurt me."

He gestures for me to take a seat, and I sit down. I look over to Seb, who's followed me out of the bedroom, and he sits next to me.

"Can you tell me what happened?" Jackson asks.

I spend the next thirty minutes reliving the night from when we first met Brandon to when Seb pulled him off me. It feels like I've said the same thing over and over again, but I guess he needs to know my side of things.

"What happens now?" I ask when I think he's done with his questions.

"We've arrested Mr. Murphy and he'll be questioned in the

morning. So far, he's saying you invited him in and what happened was consensual."

"What?" I ask, my head swinging around to look at Seb. "That isn't what happened!"

"I had to drag the bastard off her, Jackson. I *heard* her say no."

He holds up his hands. "I know, and that's why I need to ask you if you're happy to give a statement as a witness, Seb?"

"Yes! Of course."

"Okay. I'll leave it for now as it's late, but if you can come down to the station in the morning, someone will take your statement." He stands and gives me a small smile. "Don't worry, Taylor. With Seb witnessing what happened, it's doubtful he'll get away with what he's done."

"I've never seen him before," Seb says. "I don't think he's from Hope Creek."

"He's not," Jackson confirms. "He was just passing through." He makes his way to the door. "Someone will be in touch soon to let you know what's happening."

I stay on the sofa while Seb goes to the door. "Thanks, Jackson." He shakes his hand before letting him out. When he's closed the door behind him, he comes back to me on the sofa.

"How you doing?"

"I'm okay. He didn't actually do anything. It's just what could have happened if you hadn't shown up."

"You're safe now."

"I know. Thank you."

"You don't need to keep thanking me, Taylor."

I give him a small smile. "I need to take a shower. I feel like his hands were everywhere." I shiver in my seat.

"Fucking bastard," Seb mutters, his hands fisting in his lap.

I bite my bottom lip. "I feel stupid asking, but would you stay here tonight? I'll go on the sofa. You can have the bed. I don't want to be on my own. I'd call Paisley, but she was drunk and she'll be asleep now. If you don't want to, that's okay."

He reaches for my hand and squeezes gently. "Breathe, Taylor." I close my eyes, knowing I'm rambling like an idiot. "Of course I'll stay. I just need to go downstairs and check that Ryder's okay. Do you want to come down with me?"

"No. I'll be okay. I'll take a shower while you're gone. Will you take my keys and lock the door?"

He smiles sadly. "Yes. I'll lock the door. I won't be long."

I watch as he leaves the apartment, hearing him lock the door behind him. I'm so grateful Seb's here. I know it's unfair to ask him to stay, but I don't want to be on my own. I'm angry someone thought they could just come into my apartment and make me feel unsafe in my own home. I love Hope Creek, though, and I love my apartment. As unsettled as I feel right now, I refuse to let anything change that.

CHAPTER ELEVEN

Seb

I've no idea how I managed not to punch that asshole when I found him on top of Taylor. After she'd said goodnight, I watched her go out of the bar and through to the *staff only* area. It was only when I turned to grab a bottle of Bud from one of the refrigerators that I saw someone follow her. I didn't get a good look at them and thought it was one of the servers. It was only when I saw the server out on the floor a couple of minutes later that I knew it couldn't be them. There was always the chance she'd invited someone back to her place, but surely if that were the case, they would have gone up to her apartment together. Something felt off, so I'd gone to check. I'm glad I did.

I lock her apartment door behind me and jog down the stairs. There's still an hour until closing, and while I know Ryder can manage, Alex isn't in tonight and I want to check everything is okay.

"Is Taylor okay?" Ryder asks as soon as I get behind the bar.

I told him briefly what happened when I brought the guy downstairs and asked him to call the cops. A couple of guys I know who were drinking in the bar had kept hold of him until Jackson showed up and he was put in the patrol car. "She's shaken up. I'm going to stay with her. Are you okay to close?"

"Sure. Things have quietened down anyway."

"If people leave, just close early. Don't worry if you don't get everywhere cleaned up. I'll do it tomorrow. I'd better get back to her. Thanks, Ryder."

I grab an unopened bottle of Jack Daniel's before leaving the bar and taking the stairs to her apartment two at a time. I have no idea if she wants a drink, but I know I could do with one. I've only been gone for five minutes, so I'm expecting her to still be in the shower. When I unlock the door, I'm met with an empty living room. Her bedroom door is open slightly and I can hear the running water of the shower. Not really knowing what to do, I pace the room until I hear the shower turn off.

A few minutes later, her bedroom door opens. Even though I know what she's just been through, when she appears in the living room, I can't take my eyes off her. She's wearing tiny, black silk sleep shorts and a matching tank. Her hair is wet from the shower and she's braided it over her shoulder, which has left a wet patch on her top. She's not wearing a bra, and I force myself to look away when her nipples pebble under my gaze, pushing against the thin material.

"Feeling better?" I ask, reaching for the bottle of Jack I'd put on the kitchen countertop.

"Yeah, a little."

"Drink? It might help you sleep."

She lifts her shoulder in a shrug. "Sure. Why not?"

I watch her as she walks toward me and goes into the kitchen. Going up on her tiptoes, she reaches up to one of the cupboards, her tank riding up and giving me a glimpse of her skin. I close my eyes and shake my head. After everything that's happened tonight, I shouldn't be checking her out. I need to be her friend and nothing more.

She pulls down two glasses and places them on the countertop.

"You're having one too, right?"

I nod and pour us both a measure. I pass her a glass and she takes a sip, screwing up her face. I chuckle.

"Not a fan of Jack Daniel's?"

"Yeah, but with Coke. I've never had it neat."

"I can run down and grab you a Coke."

She shakes her head. "This is fine."

She walks past me and flops down onto the sofa. I have no idea what I should say to her. All I want to do is pull her into my arms and hold her, but I know I can't do that. Instead, I sit down next to her.

"I guess this is the second time you've rescued me from some jerk. I owe you."

"You don't owe me anything, Taylor. Those guys are the exception, not the rule. I promise."

"It doesn't feel like that right now. I feel so needy, asking you to stay with me," she says, leaning back into the sofa and tilting her head to look at me.

"You're not needy. I'd be worried if you were telling me you were fine."

She suddenly downs all of her drink and holds her glass out to me. "Can I have another one?"

I hold her gaze. "Are you sure?" She nods. "Okay."

I fill her glass and she drinks that down too, closing her eyes and shaking her head as she swallows. There's no way I'm letting her get drunk on Jack Daniel's, and I'm glad when she puts her glass down on the side table and folds her legs underneath her.

"How come you're single?" she asks, turning her body toward mine.

I smile. "What?"

"How come you're single?"

"I told you why."

She waves her hand. "I'm not talking about falling in love. Surely you date?"

"Not really."

"Why the hell not?"

"I'm busy with the bar."

"Too busy for sex?"

My eyes widen. Clearly the two shots of Jack have relaxed her, which is what I was hoping for, but I wasn't counting on this conversation.

"Who says there's anyone offering me sex?"

Her eyes flash with heat before sweeping over me. "You're telling me no one ever hits on you. I find that hard to believe."

I chuckle. "Why?"

"Why what?"

"Why is it hard to believe no one hits on me?"

"No one *ever* hits on you?" she asks again, ignoring my question.

I stare at her. I'm damn sure if she hit on me twelve months ago, I wouldn't have said no. I can't lie to her. I get hit on all the time. It's a hazard, and sometimes a perk, of the job.

"I work behind a bar, Tay. I get hit on every night."

Her eyes widen and she grins. "I knew it! And you never flirt back?"

"Sometimes."

"You're not giving anything away, are you?"

I smile. "I'm not exactly sure what you're asking. If you're asking if I date my customers, then the answer is… occasionally."

"What about me? If you didn't know me and I hit on you, what would you do?"

Images of me fucking her over my desk flash through my mind, and I drop my gaze from hers. There's no way I can tell her that and I don't trust my face not to give away how much I want her. She must take my silence as something else and stands before I can answer.

"Ignore me. I've no idea why I asked you that. We should sleep. I'll get the spare comforter. You can take the bed."

"Taylor—"

"I'll be right back."

She rushes into the bedroom and I follow, standing in the doorway. "Taylor."

She ignores me as she pulls a comforter out from under the bed and grabs one of the pillows.

"I'll just brush my teeth."

"Stop." She finally looks at me. I walk toward her and take the bedding from her arms, tossing it on the bed. "If you'd hit on me, I'd probably think you were joking. You're way out of my league."

"Out of your league?"

"You're beautiful, Taylor, and stunning in that dress you were wearing tonight. You're equally as beautiful with no makeup and your pjs on. There's no way I would ever think you'd be hitting on me."

"Oh," she whispers, her cheeks flushing pink.

"I'll take the sofa." I reach for the bedding, but she stops me.

"No way. *I'm* on the sofa."

"Tay—"

"No," she says, cutting me off. "I've asked you to stay. The least I can do is offer you a comfy bed. There's no way you'd fit on my sofa anyway."

Before I can argue, she's picked up the bedding and disappeared into the living room. There's no way I'm letting her sleep on the sofa. I'll wait until she's asleep and then carry her in here. I'll go on the sofa then.

"Night, Seb," she shouts from the living room.

"Night, Taylor."

I sigh and strip out of my jeans and t-shirt, leaving me in my boxers. After using the bathroom, I slide under the comforter and stare at the ceiling. Taylor's perfume is on the sheets and it invades my senses as I lie in her bed. I'm grateful that I'll be bringing her in here when she's asleep. There's no way I'll be able to sleep with her scent all around me.

About half an hour passes when I hear the bedroom door open. The light from the living room streams in and I turn over. Taylor's standing in the doorway and it looks like she's been crying.

"Are you okay?" I ask, the comforter falling away as I sit up.

"I can't sleep. Every time I close my eyes…" She trails off as tears streak down her cheeks.

My heart squeezes in my chest when I see her crying, and I climb off the bed and go to her.

"Come here." I close the door and take her hand, guiding her to the bed.

"What are you doing?" she asks quietly as I gently pull her to sit down.

"Holding you. Is that okay?" She's silent for a minute before she nods. I scoot backward. "Lie down." When she does, I open my arms to her. She hesitates for a second, then places her head on my chest, pressing her body against mine. I wrap my arms around her and hold her close before tugging the comforter over us.

"Thank you," she whispers. "I'm glad you're here."

I brush a kiss on her head and hold her tighter. I'm blurring the lines between us and that's unfair on Taylor, but the need to comfort her is overwhelming.

CHAPTER TWELVE

Taylor

I lie on the sofa in the living room, willing myself to fall asleep. I'm desperate to close my eyes and forget everything that's happened tonight. Instead, when I close my eyes, all I can see is Brandon's face. I can even feel the weight of his body still on top of me and I start to panic. When I can't stand it any longer, I go to Seb. I'm not sure what I was expecting when I went to him, but it wasn't that I'd end up in his arms.

My heart thunders in my chest as he holds me, and despite knowing he held me earlier before the cops arrived, this time feels different somehow.

"You okay?" he asks into my hair.

I lift my head and nod. My eyes fall to his lips and I want him to kiss me more than I've ever wanted anything. I know he won't, though. He's already made it clear he doesn't do relationships. Right now, I don't care about that. I'm attracted to him. I always have been, and I just want his hands on me. I want him to make me forget how Brandon made me feel.

I swear his eyes flash with heat as I stare at him, and finding a confidence I didn't know I had, I lean into him and brush my lips against his. I pull away when he doesn't respond.

"I'm sorry," I whisper, rolling out of his embrace and onto my side, feeling mortified that I've read him wrong.

In seconds, his strong arms have rolled me onto my back and his body hovers over mine.

"Are you sure this is what you want? I can't give you anything more than tonight, Taylor."

"I know, Seb. I want this, even if it's just for tonight."

His eyes search mine for a few seconds before he lowers his head and kisses me. The kiss starts softly, and I reach up, winding my fingers into his hair. His teeth bite my bottom lip and I open up to him, moaning into his mouth as his tongue collides with mine. Despite him not touching me yet, my body's on fire for him. If this is just what his kiss does to me, I can't wait to see how it feels when he does touch me.

His lips pull away from mine and he peppers kisses along my jaw and down my neck. The stubble on his face feels incredible on my skin, and his mouth makes its way down my neck, his fingers skating under my tank.

"This needs to come off," he mutters against my neck, pulling his lips away briefly to remove my top. He slides his fingers into the waistband of my sleep shorts, stilling as his eyes find mine. "Are you sure?"

"Yes," I tell him, lifting my hips and giving him permission to remove them. He pulls them down my legs and tosses them on the floor with my tank, leaving me naked.

"Holy fuck, Taylor," he says, his eyes sweeping over me. "Fucking perfection."

My cheeks flush with heat as I watch him. The room's dark, but my eyes have adjusted, so I know he can see me.

"I'm pretty sure that exact phrase describes you," I say, dragging my hands up his toned and inked chest, resting them on his shoulders.

He smiles before kissing me again, leaving me breathless. His mouth finds my pebbled nipple and he sucks it into his mouth, my back arching off the bed. One of his hands tweaks and pinches my other nipple between his fingers, making my clit pulse with need. I involuntarily lift my hips off the bed, shamelessly grinding my clit against his leg, desperate to dull the ache that's building there.

"What do you need, Taylor?" he asks after releasing my nipple from his mouth.

"Touch me, please," I say, too far gone with pleasure to care that I'm begging.

His hand slides down my body, his fingers sweeping through my folds.

"You're so wet."

All I can do is moan in response as his fingers brush against my clit. His touch is featherlight and I need more. I try to push against his fingers but he pulls his hand away, making me wait. His mouth continues kissing around my stomach and he stops when he gets to my hip.

"Fucking hell," he mumbles against my skin. "I think that's the sexiest thing I've ever seen."

I sit up slightly and look down my body, knowing he's found the peony tattoo on my hip bone. It had hurt like crazy to get it done, but peonies were my mom's favorite flower, and when she died, I got it to remember her by.

"You think?" I ask him. "I haven't had it for long."

"It's perfect."

He bites gently on the area, eliciting a gasp from me before soothing the skin with a kiss. His mouth kisses lower until he sits up, lifting my leg as he does. He brushes kisses around my knee, edging his way toward the inside of my thigh, his stubble tickling my skin. Despite panting and squirming on the bed, I'm suddenly nervous. I'm not a huge fan of oral sex. I never seem to be able to relax enough to enjoy it. He must feel my apprehension when he suddenly stops.

"Are you okay? You've tensed up," he asks, lifting his head.

"Erm..." I trail off, embarrassed to say what I'm feeling.

He sits up. "If you've changed your mind—"

"God, no!" I cut him off. "I just don't really like oral." I can feel my cheeks flush with heat and I drop my head back onto the bed. He moves out from between my legs and brings his body over mine.

"You don't have to feel embarrassed to tell me what you like and don't like, Taylor. I want this to be good for the both of us." He drops his head and kisses me, snaking his tongue into my mouth. After a minute or so, he pulls out of the kiss. "Can I ask why you don't like your pussy being eaten?"

"Seb!" I drop my eyes from his and squirm uncomfortably beneath him.

He chuckles. "You read about guys going down on women *every day*, Taylor."

"That's different."

"I don't see how. You should always be able to tell a guy what you want. So why don't you like it?"

I blow out a breath. He's right. I should be able to tell a man what I like. I don't know why I feel so uncomfortable doing it.

"It's just never felt that good. I can never relax enough to enjoy it. Not that there's been anyone in quite a while…"

His hand cups my neck and his lips find mine again. My body hums with desire, and I can't imagine anyone making me feel the way he does when he kisses me.

"You've been with the wrong guys, Taylor," he whispers against my lips.

"I have?"

He nods. "Let me try. If it doesn't feel good, I'll stop."

Despite my initial apprehension, my clit pulses at the thought. I've never been as turned on as I am right now. Maybe he's right and the guys I've been with in the past just haven't taken the time to make it good for me.

"Okay."

He smiles. "Okay?" I nod, and he kisses me again before butterflying kisses down my neck and over my chest. He picks my leg up again and continues where he left off, brushing featherlight kisses around my knee and on the inside of my thigh. The ache building between my legs feels almost unbearable, and when he blows gently on my clit, I moan and raise my hips off the bed. My hands go into his hair, and I tug gently, urging him closer. Just when I think I can't take it anymore, his tongue swipes through my folds and I swear I nearly come off the bed. It feels incredible and like nothing I've ever felt before.

"Oh, God!"

He laps at my clit before sucking it into his mouth. I feel him push two fingers inside me and I gasp, pulling on his hair. His fingers pump in and out of me as his mouth works me over. When his fingers hit a spot inside, I drop one of my hands and fist the sheet, my legs clamping around his head. My orgasm is right there, and when he reaches his free hand up and pinches one of my nipples, I come hard, crying out his name. My entire body shakes as my orgasm crashes over me in waves and it feels like it's never going to end. No one has ever been able to get my body to react like that, and as his fingers and mouth pull every last drop of pleasure from my body, I flop back onto the bed, breathing hard.

He gently removes his fingers and kisses slowly up my body

until his lips reach mine. I kiss him hungrily, tasting myself on his lips. When he pulls out of the kiss, he rests his forehead on mine.

"Fuck, Seb. That was… wow. Just wow."

He chuckles and kisses me again. "I'm glad you enjoyed it. It's not over yet, though. I can't wait to see you fall apart again."

He leans back, and I stare at him with wide eyes and shake my head. "There's no way. I've never…" I trail off, worried I'll sound like an idiot.

He raises his eyebrows. "You've never what?" he asks, lowering his head and kissing around my jaw, nibbling on my earlobe. I can't concentrate when he's kissing me, so I don't answer, too lost in him to form a sentence. "You've never what, Taylor?" he asks again, pulling his lips from my neck and staring into my eyes.

"I've… never come more than once, and never… during sex."

"Another case of the wrong guy, but I've got you, Tay." I start to ask him what he means, but he cuts me off with a kiss. "Don't overthink. Just feel."

My body is still humming from my orgasm, and it's as though *all* I can do is feel.

"I want to touch you," I tell him, placing my hands on his hard chest and pushing gently. He chuckles and rolls onto his back. I lie next to him and drag my fingers slowly over his chest. When I brush a nipple, I roll it between my fingers, pinching gently. He inhales sharply and reaches for me, pulling me on top of him. My legs straddle his hips and I can feel his erection through his underwear.

"Happy to see me?" I ask him with a smile.

His hands rest on my waist and he squeezes gently. "Something like that."

I lean down and kiss his lips, my tongue pushing eagerly into his mouth. One of his hands skates up my side and tangles in my hair. I roll my hips against his, eliciting a moan from him as I grind over his cock. He's rock hard and I can't wait to feel him inside me. Not yet, though. I want to taste him first. I pull my lips from his and kiss around his jaw and down his neck. His hands roam my body as I kiss him, and heat pools in my stomach again at his touch. My tongue licks and nibbles his skin as I make my way down his body. His whole chest is covered in tattoos with large angel wings over his pecs. There isn't an inch of his chest that doesn't have ink.

"God, you're sexy," I tell him, dragging my lips from his skin and tugging his underwear down his legs. He smiles as he lifts his hips, and I toss the material over the side of the bed. I can't take my eyes off him. The perfect V that I thought only existed in books is an actual thing and is right in front of me. The only thing better than that is his long, hard cock that's sprung free from his underwear and is hitting his stomach.

"You're staring," he says, his voice husky.

"Sorry," I mutter, lowering my eyes. He sits up and places his fingers under my chin, tilting my head until my eyes meet his.

"It's hot, Taylor. I like it."

"Oh," I whisper.

He leans in and kisses me, stealing my breath. I smile against his mouth and push him back down onto the bed. I hold his gaze as I move down his body, my fingers grazing his chest as I go. When I reach his erection, I take him in my hand and pump his length. His eyes close and he drags in a shaky breath. I lower my head and take him in my mouth. My tongue circles his head before I sink down onto him. His hands go into my hair and his legs begin to shake as my head bobs up and down.

"Fuck, Taylor," he moans, pulling gently on my hair. "That feels… incredible."

I take him to the back of my throat and swallow, a moan escaping his lips. I continue to work him over, my clit pulsing with need. When his breathing becomes labored, he reaches for me, pulling my mouth off him.

"Is something wrong?"

"God, no!" he says, tugging me up his body and into his arms. He kisses me as he rolls me onto my back. He pulls out of the kiss and stares down at me. "I was going to come, and I want to be inside you for that."

The ache that's been building between my legs intensifies at his words and I bite my lip.

"Do you have a condom?"

He nods and climbs off the bed, reaching for his jeans that he must have taken off earlier. He pulls out his wallet and takes out a condom. I watch as he kneels on the bed and rolls it down his length. His eyes never leave mine, and in seconds, he's settled his body between my legs.

"You're sure about this?" he asks, lowering his head to kiss me again.

"Mmmm," I mutter against his lips, and he chuckles.

I wind my arms around his neck and kiss him like I never want to stop. I'm breathing like I've run a marathon when he pulls back and slips his hand between us, circling my clit with his fingers. I'm on fire for him again and lift my hips, pushing against his fingers. I whimper when he removes his hand, pulling his mouth to mine. He lines his erection up with my entrance and I gasp into his mouth as he pushes inside me.

"Are you okay?" he asks against my lips, stilling when he's all the way in. I nod as I take a second to adjust to his size.

"I just need a minute," I mumble. It's been a while and there's a little discomfort. Despite that, I've never felt so full. He drops his head to my shoulder and brushes kisses over my skin, licking over the pulse point on my neck.

"Relax, Taylor. I've got you," he whispers in my ear.

I take a deep breath, feeling the pain start to ebb away as I do. When all I'm left with is pleasure, my body craves him. I roll my hips, and he groans. He pulls out and slowly pushes back inside, his jaw tense as he tries to hold back. I don't want him to hold back, though. He feels incredible and I want more.

"Harder, Seb. Please."

His movements increase and I cling to his shoulders as he fills me. Despite never reaching orgasm through sex alone, I can feel something building in the pit of my stomach with every movement and I find myself chasing that pleasure. No one has ever made me feel like this and I never want it to end.

"You feel so good, Tay," Seb moans. "You're so tight."

His words turn me on even more, and when his fingers slide between us and he pinches my clit, I know I'm almost there.

"I can feel your walls fluttering around my cock. Come for me, Taylor," he demands, circling my clit over and over again. When my orgasm crashes over me, I cling on to him, shuddering in his arms. If possible, it feels even more intense than earlier and it seems to last forever. My release must trigger his, and he comes on a cry, dropping his head into my shoulder.

We're both panting hard and our bodies are slick with sweat. I hold him against me as our breathing evens out, and I can't help but wonder what happens now. I know he doesn't want anything remotely like a relationship, but after how incredible that was, I've no idea how I'm going to be able to keep my hands off him. I hope we haven't just fucked everything up.

CHAPTER THIRTEEN

Seb

When my breathing has evened out, I lean up and brush my lips against Taylor's. "I'll just clean up," I tell her, noticing how beautiful she looks with her face flushed from her orgasm.

I gently pull out of her and climb off the bed. Crossing the room to the bathroom, I close the door behind me. After getting rid of the condom, I grip the vanity, staring at my reflection in the mirror.

"You're a fucking idiot," I mutter to myself. "You've ruined everything because you couldn't keep your hands off her." I shake my head and drop my eyes from the mirror. Despite knowing I shouldn't have touched her, now that I have and I know how incredible sex with her is, I've no idea how I'm going to be able to go back to how we were. I know how she tastes and I know what she looks like when she comes. I want more. She deserves the world, though, and I know I can't give her anything close to that.

"Is everything okay?" Taylor calls from the bedroom. I take a deep breath and drag my hand through my hair.

"Be right out," I shout, taking one last look in the mirror before opening the door.

She must have turned the lamp on that sits on the nightstand and my mouth goes dry as she lies naked on the bed, her face and chest still flushed with heat. My cock jumps, and despite only just finishing, I want her again.

"I should get dressed and go back on the sofa," she says, sitting up and reaching over the side of the bed for her pajamas. She slips on her sleep shorts and tank and stands.

Something shifts in my chest and there's no way I want her back on the sofa. Somehow, her disappearing like that cheapens what we've just done, and I don't want that. "Like hell you will."

"What?" she asks, her eyebrows pulled together in confusion.

"You're sleeping with me, Taylor. I've just tasted every inch of you. I think we can share a bed."

"Oh," she mutters. "Okay. If you're sure."

I reach down for my boxer shorts and pull them on. "I'm sure. Come to bed."

I climb into bed and watch her as she hesitates before slowly sliding under the comforter. I'm probably giving her mixed signals. I've told her tonight is all I can give her, but then I demand she sleeps in the bed with me. If tonight is all we can have, though, I want to make the most of it.

"How are you feeling?" I ask, rolling onto my side and propping my head up on my elbow so I can look at her.

She mirrors my stance and smiles. "Honestly?" I nod. "I'm feeling pretty good."

I chuckle and hold her gaze. "Good. I'm glad I could put a smile on your face."

"You did more than that."

"We should get some sleep," I tell her as she lets out a yawn. I roll over and turn off the light, plunging the room into darkness. When my eyes adjust, I turn onto my side to find her watching me.

"Are things going to be weird between us now?" she asks quietly.

"There's no reason they should be," I tell her, despite thinking the same thing in the bathroom. "We're both consenting adults who happen to have had incredible sex."

She smiles. "You thought it was incredible?"

"Yes. You didn't?"

"No! I did! It was the best I've ever..." She trails off and giggles.

I smile. "The best ever, hey?"

I reach across and tickle her waist. She laughs and squirms, rolling onto her back and away from my hands. I bring my body over hers and stare down at her as she catches her breath. She's so fucking beautiful. I shouldn't be doing this, but I can't seem to stop myself.

"It's still tonight, right?" I ask, my eyes dropping to her lips. She nods and reaches her hands up and around my neck, pulling my mouth to hers. I'm soon lost in her again, all thoughts of this being a bad idea chased away by having her in my arms.

~

I wake up to someone banging on the apartment door, and it takes me a second to realize where I am. Taylor's bed. She's wrapped in my arms, her head on my chest, and our legs tangled together. What happened last night comes flooding back, and my cock jumps as I remember how good it felt to be inside her. It's then I realize we're both naked. The pounding on the door starts again and I have no idea who it could be. Whoever it is must have a key to Eden.

"Taylor, there's someone at the door," I say softly, dragging my fingers gently up and down her arm, enticing her to wake up.

"Tell them to go away," she mumbles sleepily, pushing her naked body closer to mine. My semi-hard cock brushes against her thigh, and she stills before slowly lifting her head. "Shit. We fell asleep with no clothes on."

I chuckle. "You wore me out and I couldn't be bothered to get dressed."

Her cheeks and neck flush pink as she untangles herself from around me and sits up, pulling the comforter with her. As she does, the comforter slides off me, exposing my rapidly hardening cock. Her eyes flick to where it's standing proud before she slowly backs off the bed. The banging on the door continues, and I stand and pull on my boxers.

"I'll get it. You get dressed."

"Taylor! Are you in there?" a voice shouts through the apartment door.

"Fuck! It's Paisley!" Taylor rushes around the room, snatching up her sleep shorts and tank.

Shit. I drag my hand through my hair and blow out a breath. I wasn't expecting anyone to see me at Taylor's place and especially not half dressed. I know exactly how things will go if Paisley realizes I spent the night in Taylor's bed.

"Tay, maybe we don't tell anyone what happened between us last night. Paisley will only start playing matchmaker and we both know that's not how things are between us. What do you think?"

A look flashes across her face, but it's gone before I can process what it was, and she schools her features. "Suits me," she says. "Would you get the door? I need to pee."

She disappears into the bathroom, and I jog through the living room. I think maybe I've hurt her by wanting to keep what happened between us a secret. I'll have to speak to her about it another time. Right now, I think Paisley might tear the door down if I don't open it.

"Taylor... oh," she says when I swing the door open. Her eyes track over me before she grins. "What are you doing here and why do you have no clothes on?" She looks past me into the empty apartment.

"I stayed the night. Taylor's in the bathroom."

I step aside to let her in and she walks past me, her eyes fixed on mine. "Stayed the night? Like *stayed* the night?"

I close the door and move to the sofa, picking up the comforter that Taylor used before she came in to me. "If by, *stayed the night*, you mean slept on the sofa. Then yeah, I stayed the night."

"Why?"

Before I can answer her, Taylor appears in the bedroom doorway.

"Hi, Paisley. What are you doing here?"

Paisley rushes across the apartment and pulls Taylor in for a hug.

"Are you okay? I heard what happened last night. Why didn't you call me?"

Taylor's eyes find mine before she looks away. "I'm okay. I didn't call because you were drunk and I knew you'd be asleep."

Paisley frowns and takes Taylor's hand, tugging her to sit down on the sofa. "That wouldn't have mattered. I would have come anyway."

"I know, but I didn't want to bother you."

"Bother me? You're my best friend, Taylor."

"I'm okay, really."

"If you're okay, why did Seb stay the night?"

Taylor blows out a breath. "Fine. I wasn't okay last night, but I am now. I just want to forget *everything* that happened last night and move on."

I look at her, but she won't meet my eye. When she says she wants to forget everything, does she mean what happened between us too? I know for sure now that I've upset her.

"Actually, I didn't sleep on the sofa," I blurt out. Paisley looks at me before looking at Taylor.

"Okay," she says slowly.

"Seb," Taylor warns.

"I slept in Taylor's bed and we had sex. Twice."

"What the fuck! What are you doing?" Taylor asks, standing from the sofa and pushing me backward into her bedroom. "I'll be right back," she says to Paisley over her shoulder before closing the door behind us.

She prods me sharply in the chest, forcing me backward and farther into the room. "What are you doing? Why did you tell her that?"

"Because I should never have asked you to keep what happened between us a secret. I was being selfish. I didn't want people playing matchmaker, but I don't want you to think I'm ashamed about us sleeping together because I'm not. I think that might be how you took it, though. Am I wrong?"

Her face, which is clouded in anger, softens at my words. She opens her mouth to say something, then closes it.

"Tay," I prompt when she doesn't answer.

"Okay, okay. Maybe I did think that, but you don't owe me anything. You made it clear what last night was. I'm the idiot for feeling hurt."

"No. You aren't."

"Yes, Seb. I am." She shakes her head. "I should get back to Paisley. She's going to have a million questions."

I chuckle. "We're good though, yeah?"

She nods. "We're good. Thanks again for last night." I grin and she rolls her eyes. "I mean getting that guy off me and staying here."

"Oh, right. Yeah, that."

She smacks my chest. "I'll leave you to get dressed."

"Do you want a ride to the station? I need to go home and shower, then I was going to head there."

"I think I might walk. Get some fresh air."

"Okay. I might see you later, then?"

"Yeah. You might."

She hesitates before going up on her tiptoes and brushing a kiss on my cheek. Then she turns and walks out of the bedroom, closing the door behind her. I frown as I stare at the closed door. She says we're okay, but I'm not so sure. Despite reassuring her last night that things wouldn't be weird between us, I'm not convinced I was right.

CHAPTER FOURTEEN

Taylor

I leave Seb to get dressed and go back into the living room. Paisley greets me with wide eyes.

"You slept with Seb?" she says excitedly. "I *knew* you liked him."

"Shhh," I tell her, glancing back to the bedroom door. "Lower your voice."

She frowns. "Why? He knows I know. He was the one who told me."

"He doesn't know I like him," I mumble.

She laughs. "You slept with him, Tay. I think he's got a pretty good idea you like him."

I shrug off her comment. "It was just sex. It won't be happening again."

"What? Why?"

"Because he doesn't want it to happen again."

"Well, what do you want?"

"Does it matter?"

"Of course it matters."

Before I can reply, the bedroom door opens and Seb walks out.

"I'll see you later, Paisley. You're working tonight, right?" he says, crossing the room and making for the door. She nods and I stand, walking to the door to see him out. "If you change your mind about a ride to the station, text me."

I nod, and he bends down, kissing my cheek.

"Bye, Seb."

I close the door behind him and groan internally as Paisley stares at me.

"You *really* like him, don't you?"

I'm beginning to realize why Seb didn't want to say anything about us sleeping together.

"Yes, I really like him, not that it matters." I bite my bottom lip. "Do you know what happened in his last relationship?"

She frowns. "He hasn't been in a relationship the whole time I've known him. Why?"

I shrug. "Just something he said."

"What did he say?"

"That being happy with someone wasn't in his future. Why would he say that?"

She sighs. "I don't know, Tay. Maybe he's been hurt and he's scared to open himself up again. I'm sure if he met the right person, he'd feel differently."

I shake my head. "I don't think so. He seems pretty closed off."

"Don't write things off with him. He's a great guy."

"Yeah, I know. Let's talk about something else." I go into the kitchen and move the bottle of Jack Daniel's that Seb brought up with him off the breakfast bar. "Do you want pancakes?"

I busy myself getting the ingredients out to make the batter, only stopping when Paisley comes behind me and takes the bowl out of my hand.

"Sit down. I'll make them."

"I'm okay—"

"Sit down, Tay." I accept defeat and sit at the breakfast bar. "I won't mention Seb again, but tell me what happened with that guy last night. All I know is when Nash got on shift this morning, there was a guy in the cells and he was there because he'd attacked you. Did he hurt you?"

I shake my head, and while she makes pancakes, I spend the next ten minutes telling her what happened.

"What a fucking asshole. I'm so glad Seb followed him up."

I shiver. "I can't even think about what would have happened if he hadn't." She pushes a stack of pancakes in front of me. "There's syrup in the cupboard," I tell her, gesturing to one of the kitchen cabinets. She grabs it and sits next to me.

"It hasn't put you off living here, has it?"

"No. I love living here. I'll just be a little more aware next time I come up from the bar drunk and alone."

She takes my hand and squeezes gently. "I hate that he's made you feel like that."

I shrug. "Me too. Will you come to the station with me in a bit? One of the officers came over last night, but I need to go in and give my statement."

"Of course I will."

After eating breakfast, I leave Paisley in the living room while I take a shower. As the hot water washes over me, my mind wanders to Seb and when I'll see him again. I'm setting myself up for heartbreak, but I *really* like him. Sleeping together just cemented that for me. I know I'd do it again in a heartbeat, even though he doesn't want a relationship. I guess that makes me stupid or desperate, maybe both. All I know is there's a tiny flicker of hope that maybe, just maybe, he'll change his mind and realize how good we could be together.

~

*I*t's late Saturday afternoon, and a week since I gave my statement to Nash at the station. Brandon was charged with assault, but because of his clean record up until then, he got away with a fine. It was a large fine, but I was pissed he wasn't getting punished more for what he'd done, or at least what he would have done given the chance. I had to put it behind me, though. Brandon was gone. Back in LA and thousands of miles away. As long as I never had to see him again, I was good with that.

I'm on the sofa watching a movie. I have the worst period cramps and I feel like shit. My periods have always been awful, and cycle-wise, all over the place. This month is no exception. I usually take Tylenol and have a heating pad attached to my stomach for the first couple of days, but this is my first period since moving here and I can't find my heating pad, even though I was sure I'd brought it with me from Pittsburgh. I'd ordered one online, but it hasn't been delivered yet. I hope it comes soon. I could cry from the pain.

My phone vibrates on the arm of the sofa with an incoming message, and I reach for it, smiling when I see it's from Ash. She'd been upset when she'd heard about what happened with Brandon. She'd asked him and his friend to dance and blamed herself. There was no way she could have known what Brandon was going to do. It wasn't her fault, but she'd either stopped by the apartment or messaged me every day this week to check I was okay. Swiping the screen, I pull up her message.

Ashlyn: Hey, Taylor. Ivy and I are meeting in Eden for a drink tonight. Pais-

ley's out with Nash. Do you want to come?

There's no way I can go out tonight. I just want to keep my sweats on and eat chocolate. My fingers fly over the screen as I type out a reply.

Me: Rain check? I have horrible period cramps and just want to stay on the sofa. Say hi to Ivy for me.

I haven't met Ashlyn's best friend yet. She's been out of town visiting relatives. Ash has talked about her enough that I feel like I know her, though, and she sounds great. She must be if she's Ash's best friend.

My phone vibrates with another message.

Ashlyn: Ahh that sucks, Taylor. Feel better soon. Do you need anything?

Me: Nah, I'm okay. Thanks, though. Have a great night.

Even if I didn't have period cramps from hell, I don't think I'd be up for a night in Eden. I haven't seen Seb since last weekend. I'm not exactly avoiding him, but I'm not seeking him out either. I've got a replacement bottle of Jack Daniel's I need to give him. I drank the rest of the bottle he left here last weekend, so I can't avoid him forever. He's messaged me a few times over the week to see if I'm okay, but they were hardly long conversations. Maybe he feels as awkward about seeing me as I do him.

I decide to have a bath, hoping the hot water will help my cramps. I'm running the water when a knock sounds on the door. I make my way across the apartment and use the peephole to see who's knocking. My heart stutters. It's Seb. I swing the door open just as pain explodes in my lower stomach and I double over, clinging on to the door.

"Fuck! What's wrong?" Seb asks, his voice not hiding his concern. The pain is coming in waves and I can't answer him straightaway. "Should I call Cade?"

I shake my head and hold my index finger up, silently telling him I need a minute. When the pain's subsided a little, I stand.

"Come in," I tell him, making for the sofa and sitting down.

Seb kneels in front of me, his forehead furrowed in concern. "Are you okay?"

"It's cramps."

"Cramps?"

"Period cramps."

"Oh. I didn't know they could be that bad."

"They're not for everyone. I guess I'm unlucky, plus I can't find my heating pad, which always helps."

"I'll get you one. Do you need Tylenol?"

My eyes widen in surprise. "You don't need to do that. I'm sure you're busy. I've ordered one online. It should come soon."

"Taylor, you're in pain now. Do you need Tylenol?" he asks again.

"No. I have some. Thank you." He smiles at me and stands. "Shit!" I say. "I've left the water running. I was going to take a bath when you knocked on the door."

"I'll get it. You stay on the sofa." He disappears into the bedroom before returning a minute later. "Did you want to get in the bath while I'm gone? I can take your key and let myself back in."

"No. I'll wait. It'll give the water a chance to cool a little."

"Okay. I won't be long."

"Thanks, Seb."

He waves off my thanks as he walks out, closing the door behind him. I drop my head back on the sofa and close my eyes, willing the pain to let up a little. Even the Tylenol isn't working, and I have another couple of hours before I can take some more.

The constant pain is exhausting and I close my eyes as I wait for Seb to come back. I must fall asleep, waking with a start when a knock sounds on the door.

When I open it, Seb stands on the other side with a large grocery bag.

"What did you buy?" I ask, eyeing the full-to-bursting bag.

He walks in and across the apartment to the kitchen, placing the bag on the countertop.

"I got you a few extra things. I also spoke to Cade."

"Why?"

"Because clearly the Tylenol isn't working. He said you can take Advil in between the Tylenol. I didn't know if you had any, so I picked some up."

I watch in disbelief as he empties the brown bag. Along with the Advil, he pulls out a heating pad, a box of chamomile tea, and bar after bar of chocolate, along with candy and chips.

"I didn't know what chocolate or candy you liked, so I got a bunch of different stuff. If there's something I've missed, I can go back out." He gets down a glass and fills it with water before handing it to me along with two Advil. "Take these and go and sit back down. I'll make you a chamomile tea. I heard it was good for cramps. I'll bring the heating pad over too."

"I don't know what to say," I whisper. "Thank you."

Tears fill my eyes, and before I make a complete idiot of myself, I head to the living room and curl up on the sofa. The tears soon fall, though, and I try to wipe them away as quickly as they come. It's the hormones making me cry, but as well as that, no one has taken care of me like this for years. I'd almost forgotten how good it feels.

"Here you go," Seb says, placing a steaming cup of chamomile tea on the side table. He plugs the electric heating pad into the nearest outlet and passes it to me. I take it from him and press it to my stomach. "Are you crying?" He sits down next to me and places his hand on my leg, squeezing gently.

"No," I lie, looking anywhere but at him.

"You are. Come here." He opens his arms and I bite my bottom lip. "It's just a hug, Taylor. It looks like you could use one."

"I could," I tell him, my voice cracking.

"Come here."

I hold his gaze as I scoot across the sofa, melting into his embrace. He takes the heating pad and presses it against my lower stomach.

"Is that helping?" he asks.

"A little. It can take a while sometimes."

I thought it might feel weird for him to hold me after what happened last time we were together, but it doesn't. It just feels right.

After a few minutes of lying in his arms, I raise my head. "I'm sure you didn't come up here to do… this." He looks down at me. "Why were you looking for me?"

"Oh shit! I'd forgotten why I'd come up when I saw you were sick." He repositions me in his arms and digs in his jeans pocket. "This is for you." He presses a small black fob into my hand.

I look down in confusion. "What's this?"

"I was hoping to show you. Do you feel like a walk downstairs and I can explain?"

I screw up my nose. "I'm not really dressed for the bar," I tell him, gesturing to my sweats and tank.

"We're not going into the bar, just to the bottom of the stairs."

"Okay. I'll grab my sweater."

I untangle myself from his arms and head to the bedroom. I'm a little torn. I want to see whatever it is he wants to show me, but I also want to stay wrapped in his arms. I've no idea if he'll hold me like that again, but I do know it didn't last nearly as long as I'd have liked.

CHAPTER FIFTEEN

Seb

I blow out a breath as I wait in the living room while Taylor gets her sweater. When she'd opened the door earlier and nearly collapsed on top of me, my stomach rolled knowing she was sick. I'd been seconds from calling Cade when she assured me she was okay. I didn't believe her. Her face was pale and I could see from her expression that she was in pain. While a chamomile tea and a bunch of candy won't take her pain away, I hope it helps a little.

"Okay. I'm ready. I hope we don't see anyone. I'm a hot mess."

My eyes sweep over her. She might be wearing sweats and a loose hoodie, her hair piled on the top of her head and not a scrap of makeup on, but she's *not* a hot mess. She looks beautiful, like she always does.

"You're about as far from a hot mess as you can be, Taylor." I shake my head. "Come on. Let's go."

"Oh. Hang on. I got this for you."

She walks into the kitchen and picks up an unopened bottle of Jack Daniel's.

"What's that?"

"I drank the bottle you left last weekend. This is the replacement."

My eyes widen knowing we only had a couple of shots out of it. "You drank the whole bottle?"

She smiles sheepishly. "It helped me sleep."

"You had trouble sleeping? Why didn't you tell me?"

"You're busy with the bar. What would you have done, anyway?"

"I could have come over."

She laughs. "You do remember what happened last time you came over?"

I hold her gaze. As if I could forget. It's all I've been able to think about since I left here last week. It's mainly why I've stayed away for the past few days. I wasn't sure I'd be able to stop myself from touching her if I'd seen her. I guess having her in my arms on the sofa five minutes ago suggests I couldn't.

"I remember." She holds the whiskey out to me, but I shake my head. "Keep it."

She frowns. "I can't."

"Why not?"

"I don't drink Jack Daniel's."

I chuckle. "Really?"

She laughs too. "Okay. I don't *normally* drink Jack Daniel's. Please, take it."

"Keep it, just in case. I'll have it back if you haven't opened it in a couple of weeks."

"You'll be getting it back. I won't open it." She turns away from me and places it back on the countertop. "So, what is it you want to show me?" she asks as she turns back around.

"Do you have the fob?" She grabs it from where she left it on the arm of the sofa and holds it up. "Come on, then."

She follows me to the apartment door and down the stairs. When we reach the bottom, I turn, and her eyes go wide as she notices the new door at the entrance to the staff area.

"You had a door put on?" she asks, her voice not hiding her surprise.

I nod. "What happened last weekend made me realize just how shit the security is in this place. Anyone can get back here, and honestly, I'm surprised no one has tried over the years. Pass me the fob and I'll show you how it works. It's pretty simple." She passes me the fob and I walk to the small gray box on the wall by the door. "There's one of these panels on either side of the door and you'll need the fob to get in and out. Hold it against the panel and the door will open." I demonstrate and pull the door open.

When I let the door close, I turn around and she throws her arms around my neck. I don't hesitate in pulling her against me, winding my arms around her waist. She's up on her tiptoes and her head rests on my chest.

"Thank you," she says quietly. "You don't know how much safer I feel knowing no one can get back here."

I increase my hold on her, hating that she's been scared. "Is that why you haven't been out of the apartment all week?" I ask softly, inhaling the vanilla scent of her shampoo. When she doesn't answer, I lean back out of our embrace.

She screws up her nose. "Maybe."

I sigh. "I wish you'd called or messaged me."

"I felt stupid."

"So you got drunk instead?" I tease, tickling her waist.

She giggles and pushes my hand away. "Not drunk exactly. Just relaxed enough for me to fall asleep."

She drops her arms from around my neck and I reluctantly let her go.

"I want you to feel safe, Taylor. I hate that you don't."

She gestures to the door. "This makes me feel a hell of a lot safer, Seb. Thank you."

I smile at her. "You already thanked me."

"Well, I'm thanking you again."

Pain suddenly clouds her face and her hand goes to her stomach.

I frown. "You okay?"

She nods. "I think I'm going to go and take that bath. Hopefully that'll ease it, and I have my chamomile tea to drink." She winks, and I laugh.

"I hope the bath and the tea work."

"If not, I have a ton of chocolate and a full bottle of Jack Daniel's. I'm in for a good night!"

I smile. "Feel better, Tay."

"Bye, Seb."

I watch as she walks up the stairs to her apartment and unlocks the door. She turns and gives me a small wave when she sees I'm still watching her. I wave back before she closes the door and disappears into the apartment. I groan internally. I know exactly what she looks like naked, which is both a blessing and a curse as I try and fail not to imagine her wet and soapy in the tub.

∽

Saturday night in Eden is busy like usual and I'm trying to serve as well as keep my eye on Ashlyn and Ivy. After what happened to Taylor last weekend, I'm being extra vigilant. I've even hired more security on the weekend. I want Eden to be a safe space for everyone and I'll do whatever it takes to make that happen.

There's a live singer on tonight, and like always, when they've finished their set, the bar empties out a little and things begin to slow. Ashlyn and Ivy wait until the crush at the bar is gone before heading over.

"Hey, Seb," Ash says. "Can we get two vodka lemonades?"

"Sure. You having a good night?" She nods. "No Paisley or Bree tonight?"

"Nope. Oliver is teething, so Bree is exhausted, Paisley's out with Nash, and Taylor's sick, but after last week, I'm wondering if she's just avoiding a night out."

I slide two vodka lemonades across the bar. I know Ashlyn blames herself after inviting that jackass and his friend to dance with them last week, but what happened isn't her fault.

"She's not avoiding a night out. I saw her earlier. She really is sick."

"Being a woman sucks sometimes," Ivy says, reaching for one of the drinks and swallowing a mouthful.

"I brought her a ton of chocolate and some chamomile tea. I hope it helped."

"Oh my God!" Ashlyn cries, a huge smile on her face.

"What?"

"You *like* her!"

I roll my eyes. "Of course I like her. She's my friend."

"You like her as more than a friend. You brought her chocolate while she was on her period."

"So?" I ask in confusion.

"So... you like her. Like, *really* like her. Guys don't go to that much trouble for their friends."

"You need to get some better male friends because I can assure you, they do."

She lets out a sarcastic laugh. "Male friends? I should be so lucky. I have four overpowering brothers who won't let a guy get anywhere near me, friend or not!"

"You're exaggerating, Ash. We're not that bad."

"Really? I have to date in secret because you guys are so over the top."

I frown. "You're dating?"

"Urgh. Thanks for the drinks."

She picks up her drink and links her arm with Ivy's, disappearing across the bar before I can question her more. I guess we are a little overbearing, but it's only because we care.

I catch Ryder's eye and flick my eyes to the back, letting him know I'm going on my break. He nods in acknowledgment, and I head to my office. As I close the office door behind me, my phone vibrates in my pocket with an incoming message. I smile as I reach for it, Taylor's name on the screen.

Taylor: Thanks again for earlier. Feeling better after the tea and the chocolate. I meant to ask, how did you know the tea would help? Was it Cade?

I glance at the time on my phone. It's almost midnight. I can't help but wonder if she's having trouble falling asleep again.

Me: Glad you're feeling better. Cade didn't tell me about the tea. I Googled what might help. Can't you sleep again?

I watch the screen as three dots appear, telling me she's typing out a reply. When the dots disappear, I wonder if she's fallen asleep. Seconds later, they flash up again. Eventually, my phone vibrates with another message.

Taylor: You Googled what would make me feel better? Why?

I chuckle before typing out a reply.

Me: Because I wanted you to feel better. Is that so hard to believe?

Taylor: No... what else did Google say?

I hesitate. The other things Google suggested are not things that should happen between friends. Definitely not between friends who've already crossed the line and slept together. I wouldn't mind crossing the line again, though, even if I know I shouldn't.

Me: There were a few things I didn't think you'd want me suggesting or trying.

Taylor: Sounds intriguing. Like what?

I go with a relatively safe one first.

Me: A massage.

There's a pause between messages, and I can't help but wonder what she's thinking. I perch on the edge of my desk as I wait for her reply.

Taylor: I wouldn't have said no to a massage... would it have been one with a happy ending?

"Holy fuck!" I mutter as I read her message. Images of her flushed face as she comes on my tongue flash through my mind. I shake away my thoughts and type out a reply. I avoid answering directly. I don't trust myself not to say something I shouldn't.

Me: Funnily enough, that was one of the things Google suggested.

Taylor: A massage with a happy ending???

I burst out laughing.

Me: No. An orgasm, Taylor. It helps with the cramps... apparently.

Taylor: Mmmm. Maybe I'll try it tonight. It might help me sleep too.

She adds a winking emoji onto the end of her message, and I groan out loud. I know what I'm going to be thinking about for the rest of the night. Part of me wants to find out if she needs any help, but I know I can't. Sleeping together had been inevitable. If it hadn't happened last week, it would have happened eventually. The sexual tension that had been building between us *had* to come to a head at some point. We can't keep sleeping together, though. Not when it can't lead to anything. I don't want to hurt her, and I can't mess up another friendship by letting feelings get involved. Knowing I have to shut down the conversation, I type out a reply.

Me: Enjoy. I hope it helps.

Taylor: Night, Seb.

Me: Night, Taylor.

I push my phone into the pocket of my jeans and head back to the bar. I'm distracted for the rest of the night, though, and even when I get home, I can't fall asleep. Damn you, Taylor Jacobs, and your naughty texts.

CHAPTER SIXTEEN

Taylor

It's Thursday morning and I've just turned on my laptop when my phone rings in my pocket. I slide it out and smile when Paisley's name flashes up.

"Hello," I say as I press the phone to my ear.

"Hi, Taylor. It's me. What are you up to?"

"Not much. I'm working. What about you?"

"How busy are you?"

"I've just started a new edit, why?"

"Wyatt called. He's playing in Phoenix tonight and he's got some tickets. Do you want to come?"

I screw up my nose. "I know nothing about football, Pais. I won't know what's going on."

"Me neither, but we get to meet the team afterwards and, trust me, some of them are hot! Please come."

I chuckle. "I didn't know you were into hot football players."

"I'm not! I was thinking for you."

I roll my eyes. "I'm not looking for a guy, Paisley."

"Come anyway. It'll be fun."

"Okay. Why not? Nash will have to explain what's going on, though."

She laughs. "Pack a bag. We're staying overnight. We'll pick you up in an hour."

"Wait!" I shout before she can end the call. "Staying overnight?"

"Yep. It'll be too late to drive back after the game."

"Where are we staying?"

"Wyatt's booked us into a hotel. There's a pool, so bring a swimsuit."

"Okay."

"See you in an hour."

I end the call and power off my laptop. Excitement swirls in my stomach as I think of a night away. I'd become a little withdrawn after the incident with Brandon, and despite Seb making the staff area more secure, I'd lost some of my confidence. A night in Phoenix might be exactly what I need to pull me out of my funk.

An hour later, I'm showered, dressed, and packing the last of my stuff into an overnight bag when my phone chimes with a message.

Paisley: We're here.

Me: I'll be right down.

Not knowing if we're going to any kind of after-game party, I throw in an electric-blue pencil dress and some heeled pumps, just

LAURA FARR

in case. I don't want to be underdressed if we end up in a bar or a club. Grabbing my purse, I zip up the case before heading downstairs. Eden isn't open yet, but Ryder's behind the bar.

"Hey, Taylor. Off somewhere nice?" he asks when he sees my bag.

"Phoenix, to watch Wyatt play."

"Nice! Have a great time. I'll let you out." I follow him to the entrance and wait while he unlocks the door.

"Thanks, Ryder."

"See you later."

When I get out onto the sidewalk, Nash's truck is parked across the street. I can see Nash in the driver's seat, and I raise my hand in a wave. He climbs out when he sees me, brushing a kiss on my cheek. He takes my bag from me, and I open the back door, surprised to see Seb on the back seat.

"Oh, hi. I didn't know you were coming."

He scoots across the seat so I can climb in. "Not disappointed, I hope?"

"Of course not. Paisley just never said, that's all."

I meet Paisley's eye as she turns in her seat and flashes me a grin. Clearly, she had no intention of telling me Seb was coming. After she found out we slept together a couple of weeks ago, she kept her promise not to ask me about it that morning, but she's tried multiple times since then. I ended up telling her he was the best I'd ever had, which wasn't a lie. I assured her we were friends and nothing more, though. It was the truth, even if I wish it wasn't.

"How are you feeling now?" Seb asks as Nash pulls away from Eden.

"I'm good, thanks. Until next time, anyway."

I grimace and he gives me a small smile. "You should speak to Cade. There might be something he can give you."

"Yeah, maybe."

"Did the Google suggestion help?"

"Google?" I ask, frowning in confusion.

He leans across the back seat. "An orgasm. Did it help with the cramps?"

"Oh," I mutter, heat flooding my cheeks. "It might have."

His heated eyes widen, and he grins. I hold his gaze, wondering what he's thinking. Paisley starts singing loudly to the song playing on the radio, pulling me from my Seb haze. She's not a good singer, and Nash laughs from the driver's seat.

"Sorry about the in-truck entertainment."

"Hey!" Paisley exclaims from beside him. "My singing is not that bad!"

"Baby, I love your singing," Nash says.

"Sounds like it."

He reaches his hand over and tangles his fingers with hers. He leans over and whispers something in her ear, her cheeks flushing pink. She smiles and brushes a kiss on his jaw.

"Looks like he's managed to dig himself out of the hole he fell into with that comment," I mutter to Seb, gesturing with my head to the front of the truck.

"Yeah, looks like it. He was right, though. Her singing sucks," he whispers.

I smack him gently on his arm. "Shhh, she'll hear you."

He laughs. "Have you been to a football game before?" he asks.

I screw up my nose. "Maybe once or twice in high school."

"You like football, though?"

"Not really."

He chuckles. "So, Paisley's made you come, then?"

"Something like that."

"She's come to see all the hot football players," Paisley says from the front of the truck.

I flick my eyes to Seb, who's watching me.

"I hope that's not the reason you're going," Nash says to Paisley, tickling her side.

She giggles and pushes his hand away. "I have a sexy cop. Why do I need a football player?"

"Right answer," he says.

"I'm not going for the hot football players. I've no idea who any of them are, other than Wyatt." I steal another look at Seb, who's still watching me.

"I'm messing with you, Tay," Paisley says over her shoulder. "I know you're not interested." Her gaze goes to Seb, but he doesn't notice, his eyes still fixed on me. I wish I knew what he was thinking, but his expression gives nothing away.

"Well, I hope you're all up for explaining the rules of football because I have no idea."

"Seb's your guy," Nash says. "I watch football, but Seb used to play alongside Wyatt."

I raise my eyebrows in surprise. "I never knew that! You played professionally?"

"I played college football."

"What happened?"

"I fucked up my knee. Tore my ACL and my MCL."

"Were you going to play professionally?"

He nods. "I was waiting to be drafted."

I frown and reach across and take his hand. "I'm so sorry, Seb. I had no idea. That must have been so hard."

He shrugs. "It feels like a lifetime ago."

"Is it hard to watch Wyatt play?"

"Not anymore. It used to be. Wyatt was always the better player, though. He was always going to go further than me."

"You were just as good, Seb," Nash says from the front. "Don't put yourself down."

"What position did you play?" I ask, my fingers still tangled with his.

He smiles. "Would you know if I told you?"

I laugh. "Probably not. Tell me anyway."

"Quarterback."

"Like Tom Brady?"

He chuckles. "I might have known you'd know who Tom Brady is."

"Who doesn't?"

"What position does Wyatt play?"

"He's a linebacker."

I screw up my nose. "I have no clue what that is."

The two-hour drive to Phoenix is spent with Seb and Nash trying to explain the rules of football. With terms like offence and defense, time-outs, end zones, and downs, by the time we get there, I'm more confused than ever. I pretend to understand what they're saying. I don't want them to think I'm an idiot. It's only a football game. It can't be that difficult to understand. I hope when I'm watching, I'll know what they've been talking about.

"Are you both okay with checking into the hotel and then meeting Wyatt for lunch?" Paisley asks as Nash parks in the hotel parking lot. "I think there'll be some time for some last-minute Christmas shopping after lunch and before the game."

"Sounds good to me," I tell her.

"Lunch sounds good. I might pass on the shopping," Seb says.

"Don't tell me you've got all your presents for everyone?" I ask in surprise, knowing most guys leave Christmas shopping as late as possible.

He groans. "No. I never know what to buy."

"I'll help you. I *love* Christmas shopping."

"Can we find a bar along the way?"

"I second that!" Nash says from the front seat.

Paisley and I laugh, and I look out of the window at the impressive-looking hotel. I'd flown into Phoenix twice in the past few months, but I'd only ever seen the airport. I'm excited to see a little of the city and even more excited to spend some more time with Seb.

CHAPTER SEVENTEEN

Seb

"Just so you know, this isn't how normal people watch a football game," Seb says, walking around the private loft space Wyatt has hired for us.

After checking into the hotel and meeting Wyatt for lunch, we spent a few hours shopping in Phoenix, much to Nash and Seb's dislike, and now we're at the stadium, waiting for the game to start.

I chuckle. "Normal people?"

"People who aren't related to the players and have to sit in the *regular* seats. Usually it's a hard, plastic chair, a huge foam finger, and a hot dog."

"That sounds like a true fan experience," I tell him, walking through the lavish space and out onto the balcony that gives an impressive view of the field. He follows, and I turn to him. "You can't complain about the view, though."

"No. These are definitely some of the best seats in the stadium."

The balcony has large recliner seats facing out over the field, and I sit in one, sinking into the plush material.

"Do you want a drink?" he asks. I look over my shoulder to where Nash and Paisley are investigating what drinks the enormous refrigerator holds. There's also food laid out on the countertops, even though we ate not long ago.

"Is all that food for us?" I ask, standing and following him inside.

"Yeah. I think so."

"It must have cost Wyatt a fortune to hire this place."

He laughs. "Don't worry. He can afford it. What do you want to drink?"

"What is there?"

"I think it would be easier to tell you what there isn't," Paisley says with a chuckle. "Do you want some champagne if I open a bottle?"

My eyes widen in surprise. "Champagne?" She nods. "Sure."

When we've all got a drink in our hands, we head back outside onto the balcony. There's some time before kick-off, and we all sit on the comfy loungers, sipping champagne.

"Does anyone else feel like this is a little surreal?" Paisley asks with a giggle. "Have you been in one of these lofts before?"

Nash laughs. "No. We're usually in the stands. I'll be expecting these seats every time now." He looks from Paisley to me. "Did Paisley talk to you about Christmas, Taylor?"

"I haven't yet," Paisley says. "I haven't had a chance."

"Christmas?" I ask, looking between them.

"My parents want you to come over for dinner on Christmas Day," Nash says.

I glance at Seb, who smiles. "They do?" I ask. Nash nods.

"Your mom can't be cooking again for everyone, surely? She just did it at Thanksgiving."

Seb laughs. "She loves it. You should come."

I hadn't let myself think about what I might do at Christmas. It will be the first Christmas without my mom, and I'd assumed I'd be spending the day on my own. I thought I might see Nash and Paisley in the evening if they weren't busy, but now it seems I get to spend all day with them. "I'd love to. Will you thank her for me?"

"Sure," Nash says. "She'll be pleased you're coming."

While we've been talking, the stadium has come alive with people of all ages, talking, laughing, and taking their seats. I stand from my seat and walk to the edge of the balcony, looking out over the field.

"They're coming out," I shout, pointing to where the teams are emerging. "What color is Wyatt wearing?"

"Red and white. The LA Rams are in blue," Seb says from behind me.

"And what number is Wyatt? They all look the same from up here."

"Eleven. That's him." Seb points into the distance and my eyes go to where he's pointing.

"He looks so different in his uniform."

"Lycra will do that to you," Nash jokes, he and Paisley coming to stand next to us.

We watch as the cheerleaders perform a routine, and the crowd goes wild. It's a hive of activity on the field while the players warm up, and despite not really knowing what's going to be happening during the game, I love the atmosphere and the excitement in the air.

"What's happening now?" I ask as the cheerleaders leave and a woman with a microphone walks into the middle of the field.

"It's the national anthem," Seb explains.

Everyone in the stadium stands as the woman belts out "The Star-Spangled Banner," and the cheerleaders run back on, holding an enormous American flag. When she's finished, the crowd erupts into cheers and the field empties as the players take their places.

Three hours later, and no one is more surprised than me to find that I loved watching the game. As play went on, with some pointers from Seb, I think I understood a little about what was happening. The Cardinals have won, albeit by a close margin, but winning has made the atmosphere in the ground electric.

"I think I'm a converted football fan. That was amazing. When can we come again?"

Nash laughs. "I'm sure Wyatt can get you a ticket whenever you want, Taylor."

"I'd love that."

"Well, they won, so I guess that means the team will be out celebrating. Can we go and meet them?" Paisley asks excitedly.

When we'd met Wyatt for lunch earlier, he explained that if the team won, the players went for celebratory drinks at one of the clubs in Phoenix. They had a VIP section upstairs, and he promised to put our names on the guest list.

"Did you bring anything to wear to a club, Taylor?" she asks me, linking my arm as we walk inside.

"I did bring a dress. Just in case."

"Me too!"

"Looks like we're going to the club," Seb says with a chuckle as he and Nash follow us inside.

"Seems that way," Nash agrees. "Wanna head back to the hotel and get changed? I'll message Wyatt and get the details of the club."

"This is going to be such a great night," Paisley squeals, and I laugh.

"Yeah, I think it is."

Seb

We've been back at the hotel for about an hour. I was ready to go out ten minutes after we got here, but Paisley and Taylor seem to be taking forever to get ready. Nash and I are in the hotel bar having a drink while we wait for them.

"Does Paisley always take this long to get ready?"

Nash laughs. "Yeah. Usually. She's worth the wait, though." He wriggles his eyebrows and I roll my eyes. "How are... things?" he asks, taking a pull of his beer.

"Things?" I ask, raising my eyebrows in question.

"You know. Sophie?"

"Things are good."

His gaze holds mine and I know he doesn't believe me. "Really?"

"Really," I assure him. "I'm happy they're happy. They belong together."

It's the truth. I am happy for Cade and Sophie, and the more time that passes, the more okay I am about my feelings for her.

"What about Taylor?" he asks.

My eyes widen in surprise. "What about her?" I wonder if Paisley told him about finding me half undressed at her place the night after she was attacked. I wouldn't be surprised if she had. I'm sure they tell each other everything.

"I've seen the way you look at her, man. You like her."

"Sure I like her. As a friend."

"It seems like it's more than that. Sophie was always out of reach, but Taylor, she's right in front of you, Seb."

I shake my head. "I'm not like you and Cade. What you have isn't in the cards for me."

He frowns. "What do you mean?"

"The big love like you have with Paisley. While I'm happy for you guys, I know that isn't something I want."

"Why the hell not?"

I shrug halfheartedly. "Love complicates everything. I don't need the hassle."

"Hassle?" He shakes his head. "Sounds like you're scared of putting yourself out there. I get that. I knew I was in love with Paisley way before we got together, but she was running scared and I never knew if, after everything she'd been through, she'd ever want to open her heart again. She took a chance, though, and look at us now."

"That's different. Anyone can see you two are made for each other."

"You can have that, Seb. Hell, you might have already met that person and you're just too terrified to acknowledge it."

"No, Nash."

"I think you're in denial."

"You don't know what you're talking about." My voice is tinged with annoyance, and I know Nash hears it when he raises his hands.

"Okay. Okay." He takes a pull of his beer before placing the empty bottle on the table. "So, if Jackson asked me to give Taylor his number, you'd be okay with that?"

My jaw clenches, and the hand that isn't holding my beer balls into a fist.

"*Did* he ask you to give her his number?"

"Yes. He's spent the last week asking me questions about her."

"What did you tell him?"

He smiles knowingly. "Not much. I don't know a lot about her. Why are you bothered?"

"I'm not," I lie.

It's not as though I can say Jackson is an asshole. He's not. He's a great guy. I've known him for years and we're friends. He grew up in Hope Creek and drinks in Eden sometimes. I don't want him to go out with Taylor, though, but that's not my decision to make. We're not together. She can do what she wants.

"I'll give her his number, then."

"You do that."

"You're an idiot, Seb."

"Thanks! Do you want another drink?" I ask, trying to move the conversation along.

"No. Looks like the girls are ready."

He's looking past me, and I follow his gaze. My heart thunders in my chest and all the air rushes from my lungs as I watch Taylor walk toward us. She's wearing an electric-blue pencil dress that falls a few inches past her knees. The material hugs her body in all the right places, and she looks nothing short of incredible. The dress has a deep V at the front, and I can't take my eyes off the swell of her breasts that are escaping the material. I swallow thickly as my mind takes me back to how it felt to roll and pinch her nipples between my fingers. Despite the material of the dress covering her, I know exactly what's hidden underneath, and it's etched into my mind no matter how hard I try to push it away. It's always there. Front and center.

"All of Wyatt's teammates are going to be falling over themselves with her looking like that," Nash mutters as Taylor and Paisley stop in front of us. I have no idea what Paisley's wearing. It could be a trash bag for as much notice as I've taken. I can't drag my eyes off Taylor long enough to look. Out of the corner of my eye, I see Nash pull Paisley into his arms, leaving Taylor standing alone.

"What do you think?" Taylor asks, spinning in a circle, her curled hair fanning out as she turns.

I can't get my brain to function enough to pull a sentence together, so I continue to stare at her.

"Is it that bad?" she asks with a giggle.

Her laughter pulls me from my daze. "God, no! You look beautiful, Tay."

Her cheeks flush pink. "Thank you."

I can't help but think Nash is right. I've been out with Wyatt after a game enough times to know how his teammates act around women. Although it's normally the women falling over themselves to get close to the players, Taylor won't be like that. I know for sure guys will be hitting on her, though, especially in that dress. I'm going to need more alcohol.

CHAPTER EIGHTEEN

Taylor

"I can't believe how busy it is for a Thursday night. I'm glad we don't have to wait in line," I say, shivering as we walk past a huge crowd of people waiting to get inside.

Seb chuckles. "Getting used to the VIP treatment already?"

I laugh. "I'm just cold. I should have brought a jacket."

"I'd give you mine if I had one."

"It's okay. We'll be inside soon."

I'm surprised when he slips his arm around my waist and tugs me against him. I look up at him with wide eyes. "I'm just keeping you warm," he says, holding my gaze.

"Thank you," I tell him quietly.

A few minutes later, his arm slips from around me as Nash gives over his name to the guy at the door and we're shown into the club. It's dark and loud inside, with people drinking and dancing.

"It's up here," Nash shouts over his shoulder, pointing to a staircase in front of him. He takes hold of Paisley's hand and guides her up the stairs.

"Have you met the players before?" I ask Seb as we walk side by side up the stairs.

"A couple of times. I don't get to as many games as I'd like."

When we reach the top of the stairs, there's a security guy blocking the way.

"We're with Wyatt Brookes," Nash shouts over the noise of the music.

"Name?"

"Nash and Seb Brookes," he says, gesturing over his shoulder to Seb.

He gives a swift nod of his head and steps to one side to allow us to pass. Wyatt must have told him we were coming. As we walk into the crowd, everyone seems to be congregating around one of the booth tables.

"Hey! You made it!" Wyatt says as he sees us and stands from the booth, moving a woman who is sitting in his lap. There are around eight guys with him, most of them with a woman draped over them. I don't recognize any of the guys he's with, but that's no surprise. I had no idea who Wyatt was when I first met him. He pulls Nash in for a hug and kisses Paisley on the cheek before turning to Seb.

"What did you think of the game?" he asks, hugging him.

"It was great, and I think we might have a new football fan in Taylor."

He turns to me and grins. "You liked the game?"

"I loved it! Well done on the win. When can I come again?"

He laughs and presses a kiss on my cheek. "Anytime you want, sweetheart. Let me know when you're free and I can hook you up with a ticket. You can stay at my place."

"Let's get a drink," Seb says from the side of me, slipping his hand in mine and tugging me away from Wyatt before I can reply.

"What are you doing?" I ask, pulling back on his hand.

He looks over his shoulder. "Getting a drink."

"But we were talking to Wyatt."

I look behind me to see Wyatt watching us, a grin on his face.

"And now we're getting a drink."

When we reach the bar, he drops my hand, gently maneuvering me so that I'm standing in front of him, my back to his chest. His large, inked arms rest on the bar either side of me, caging me in. He's not actually touching me, but it feels intimate somehow, and my pathetic, needy brain wonders if he got jealous when I was talking to Wyatt.

"What do you want to drink?" he asks, dropping his mouth to my ear. His breath is hot on my skin, and I close my eyes, dragging in a shaky breath.

"Red wine, please," I mutter.

"Should I get Paisley the same?"

I nod. He gives over the order to the guy behind the bar, who asks where we're sitting. Seb points to Wyatt's table.

"I'll bring them over," he tells Seb.

"We'll wait."

Taking a deep breath, I turn around, tilting my head back to look at him.

"Is everything okay?"

"Yes. Why wouldn't it be?"

"You just seem a little… pissed at me."

His face softens. "I'm not pissed at you, Taylor."

I raise my eyebrows. "But you are pissed?"

He drags his hand through his hair and shakes his head. "No. I'm not." He reaches past me and picks up my drink.

"Thanks," I tell him, taking it from him.

"Can you carry Paisley's drink and I'll get the beers?"

"Sure."

He steps away from me, and it's only now that I feel like I can catch my breath. We walk side by side as we head back to the table, and when everyone has a drink in their hand, Wyatt asks us to join him and his teammates in the booth. I sit down first, scooting around the table. Paisley sits next to me, with Nash and Seb on the end.

"Who are all the girls?" I whisper to Paisley before taking a sip of my wine.

"I think some of them are the cheerleaders and others are groupies who follow the team around. They seem pretty desperate to me," she whispers back.

I glance around the table, my heart pounding in my chest as I see one of the girls eyeing up Seb. She's wearing a tiny cheerleader outfit that looks like it's been painted on. She moves from the other side of the table, and without even speaking to him, sits down on his knee.

"You must be Wyatt's brother," she gushes, dragging her hot-pink nail up and down his arm. "I've heard a lot about you." I try not to watch, but I can't take my eyes off them.

"Seb, this is Kristie. She's head cheerleader for the team. Kristie, this is Seb," Wyatt says.

"Nice to meet you, Kristie."

"I've always had this fantasy about being with twins. Do you think you and Wyatt might be up for fulfilling that fantasy?"

She bites her bottom lip and pushes her chest into his face. My stomach rolls, and I want to drag her off his lap and scratch her eyes out. It's irrational when we're not together and never will be, but I can't help how I feel.

"Fucking hell!" Paisley whispers into my ear. "Did you hear what she just said?"

"Yeah." I pick up my drink and swallow down a large mouthful. If I've got to sit and watch some half-naked woman flirt with Seb all night, I'm going to need more wine.

"Some of the women who follow the team around are a little over the top," the guy sitting next to me says. "Kristie more so than most."

"A little over the top is a bit of an understatement," Paisley says from the side of me.

He chuckles. "I'm Lewis."

"I'm Taylor, and this is Paisley," I tell him.

"How do you know Wyatt?"

"Paisley's dating his brother."

His eyes widen. "Not his twin brother, I'm guessing."

I laugh. "No. His older brother, Nash." I glance at him. He's about the only guy around the table who doesn't have a girl draped all over him. He's good-looking, so I wonder if he's married or gay. "Are you not looking for a hook-up tonight with one of the cheerleaders?" I groan internally when he raises his eyebrows. "Shit, sorry. I think I've drunk my wine too quickly," I tell him, holding my empty wineglass up.

He puts his hand on my arm and laughs. "It's fine, Taylor, and no, I'm not looking to hook up. I've only come for one drink to celebrate the win. My wife's at home with our newborn daughter. I'm actually itching to get home to them."

"Congratulations! What's your daughter's name?"

"Lila. Do you want to see a picture?"

"I'd love to."

He reaches into the pocket of his pants and pulls out his phone. He scoots closer and holds the phone out for me to see. A tiny baby fills the screen, and I smile.

"She's beautiful, Lewis. I can see why you can't wait to get back to her."

He scrolls through a few more pictures, and in a couple of them, he's holding her, looking like the proud father.

"You know what?" he asks, slipping his phone back into his pocket. "I think I'm going to go home."

"I don't blame you. It was nice to meet you, Lewis."

"You too, Taylor."

"Actually, I need to use the restroom. Can you point me in the right direction?"

"Sure. I'll show you on the way out."

I turn to tell Paisley where I'm going, but she's deep in conversation with Nash. I glance at Seb, seeing Kristie's still on his lap, and now she has her arms wrapped around his neck. Jealousy creeps up my spine as his eyes meet mine. I give him a small smile before turning back to Lewis, who is asking his teammates on the other side of him to let us out. I scoot along the seats, standing when I can. The VIP area is busier than when we arrived, and I follow Lewis, weaving through the crowds.

"The restrooms are just through there," Lewis says, pointing past the staircase we came up earlier. "Bye, Taylor."

"Bye."

He jogs down the stairs, and I wait a few minutes before following him. The need for some air wins out over the restroom, and I push through the crowds until I'm out on the sidewalk. It shouldn't matter what Seb does and who he does it with. My head seems to have gotten the message; my heart, not so much.

CHAPTER NINETEEN

Seb

Kristie's talking nonstop but I've no idea what she's saying. I'm not listening. My eyes are fixed on Taylor as she talks to Lewis Wright, the quarterback for the team. He laughs at something she says and puts his hand on her arm. Jealousy swirls in my stomach and I pick up my beer, draining the bottle. Lewis takes his phone out, and I can't help but wonder if she's giving him her number.

"Are you listening to me?" Kristie asks, her hands snaking up my chest and over my shoulders. I drag my eyes off Taylor to look at her.

"Sorry. What were you saying?"

She repeats herself, but I'm still not listening. When I look back at Taylor, she's watching me. She gives me a sad smile before she turns and leaves the table with Wright. I gently take Kristie's arms from around me and push her off my lap. Her lips form into a pout as I do.

"Not a fan of threesomes, then?" she asks with a giggle, her laugh setting my teeth on edge.

"No. I don't share, and definitely not with my brother." My eyes follow Taylor across the room until I lose her in the crowd.

She shrugs. "Your loss."

I very much doubt that. Sure, she's hot. I'm not blind, but I'm guessing she's with a different guy after every game.

"Do you know where Taylor went?" I ask Paisley, interrupting her conversation with Nash.

She flicks her head to where Taylor was sitting before looking back at me. "No idea. She was here a second ago."

"I saw her leave with one of the players."

Her eyes widen in surprise. "Maybe she's gone to dance or to the bar."

"Yeah, maybe." My eyes go to Taylor's empty wineglass. "I'm going to head to the bar. Do you want anything?"

They both say no, so I slip away from the table, using needing a drink as an excuse to see where she is. I've got no right to be jealous. We're not together and I made it clear we never could be, but that doesn't stop me going to look for her. I push my way through the crowd, heading in the direction I saw her last. When I get to the top of the stairs, I look over the railing and spot her at the bottom of the stairs. She makes her way across the bar toward the exit. I frown and look for Wright. I don't see him, but is she leaving with him? My stomach rolls at the thought.

I jog down the stairs and take the same route she did out of the club. When I get outside, I look left and right, frantically searching for her. The sidewalk is full of people, but I don't see her. I glance across the street and breathe a sigh of relief when I find her sitting on a bench opposite the club. She hasn't seen me yet, and I take a second to watch her. I won't be surprised if Lewis

Wright has hit on her. She's stunning, and I know I won't be the only guy to think it. Suddenly, she looks up, smiling when she sees me.

I cross the road and sit down on the bench next to her. "What are you doing out here? Is everything okay?"

"I just needed some air."

"Where did Wright go?"

"Wright?"

"The guy you were talking to."

"Home to his wife and newborn baby." My face must give away my surprise, and she laughs. "Why do you look so surprised?"

"I… I thought…" I shake my head. "Never mind."

"You thought he was hitting on me?"

"I saw him get out his phone. I thought you were giving him your number."

"He was showing me pictures of his daughter."

"Oh." I feel like an idiot. I had no idea he was married.

"I didn't think you noticed who I was talking to. Not with Kristie on your lap," she says quietly, her eyes dropping from mine. "I guess if you're out here, you didn't like her suggestion of a threesome?"

"Fuck no! I thought Wyatt might try and set me up with someone, but I wasn't expecting that!"

"Why would he try and set you up?"

"He thinks I need to get laid." I don't tell her why he thinks that.

"Did you want to be set up?"

"No."

"Why did you follow me out here?"

I blow out a breath. "I thought you might have been leaving with Wright."

"And if I had been?"

I want to tell her that I'd have hated her leaving with him, but I can't. What good would it do? "I don't know," I whisper. She stares at me. "Why did you really come out here, Taylor?"

She shrugs. "Because I didn't want to watch you with Kristie." She shakes her head. "It's stupid, I know."

"It's not stupid." She shivers and wraps her arms around herself. "Do you want to go back inside?"

"I guess."

"We don't have to go back upstairs. We can get a drink with the regular people."

She laughs. "Okay. Being with the regular people sounds good."

I stand from the bench and hold out my hand to her. She slips her hand in mine and stands. With our fingers still entwined, we head back to the club, bypassing the line by giving over our names again.

When we've both got a drink, we move away from the crush of the bar to a quieter area of the club where comfy leather sofas are filled with people talking, laughing, and making out. There's one free, and Taylor grabs my hand.

"Quick! Before someone else grabs it," she says, tugging me across the room.

I chuckle and let her pull me along, sitting down with her when we reach the sofa. We're silent for a few minutes as we each nurse our drinks.

"Do you ever think about the night we slept together?" she asks quietly, her eyes fixed on her drink. I contemplate lying to her. The truth is, I've thought of nothing else since then, but telling her might complicate everything, and for what? I'm not sure I can lie to her, though.

"Yes," I whisper. Her head flicks up and her eyes find mine. "Do you?"

She nods. "More than I should."

Her tongue darts out to lick her lips, and I want nothing more than to kiss her again. I know I shouldn't. It's not fair when I can't give her anything more. I don't know if I can stop myself, though.

As if sensing my dilemma, she leans over and tentatively brushes her lips against mine. She pulls back, her eyes betraying her uncertainty. I put my bottle of beer on the table and take her wineglass out of her hand, placing it next to my drink. I hold her gaze for a few seconds before I slowly lean in and kiss her. She doesn't hesitate to kiss me back and reaches up, winding her fingers into my hair. I bite down gently on her bottom lip, silently asking for her to open up to me. When she does, her tongue collides with mine, and she moans into the back of my throat. My hand cups her neck and my thumb strokes her cheek as I kiss her. As much as I'm loving kissing her, I wish we weren't in a packed club and that I could strip her naked and put my mouth on every inch of her perfect body. Maybe it's a good thing we're not alone. I don't think I'd be able to control myself if we were.

I pull my lips from hers and pepper kisses around her jaw and up to her ear. My teeth bite down gently on her earlobe, and she moans again, the sound a direct line to my already swelling cock.

"God, Seb. I wish we were alone," she gasps.

I chuckle against her neck, thinking she pretty much read my mind. I continue to brush kisses along her skin until my mouth finds hers again. She tastes of red wine and Taylor, and I can't get enough. When I finally pull my lips away, I rest my forehead against hers, both of us panting hard.

"I know we weren't going to do this again, but I'm not going to lie. The sex last time was off the charts," she says, her breathing levelling off. "I want more."

My eyes widen in surprise, and I move back a little. "It was good for me too, Taylor…" I trail off and she frowns.

"I feel like there's a *but* coming."

"I just don't want to complicate things. I like you, I really do, but—"

"There it is," she interrupts. "The *but*."

"Taylor—"

"It's only complicated if we make it complicated. We're just two friends who enjoy sex with each other."

"Sex complicates things, especially if one person ends up wanting more than the other can give."

"Why are you so sure I want something you can't give me? Maybe I just like sex."

"I see the way you look at Nash and Paisley. You want that, and I can't be the guy to give it to you."

"You don't know what I want." She stands from the sofa and reaches for her glass. "Maybe we should go and find the others."

My resolve is hanging by a thread. I want more than anything to be with her again. She really has been all I've thought about this past week, but I'm trying to be the good guy here. I'm trying to do the right thing. I guess it's true when they say the nice guys never come out on top. If I didn't care about her, I wouldn't think twice about sleeping with her again, but I do care about her, and I don't want her to end up hurt and hating me. I couldn't bear that.

"Whoever broke your heart must have really done a number on you, Seb." She sounds sad, but she's right. The feelings I had for Sophie changed everything. Despite being on the other side of those feelings now, I can't deny they've changed me. I don't want to hurt like that again, and I don't want to be the reason someone else hurts like that either.

CHAPTER TWENTY

Seb

Taylor avoids me for the rest of the night, and I know I've upset her. I'm trying to do the right thing, but it seems I'm hurting her anyway. Kristie's thankfully taken my earlier hint and is currently making out with some guy on the dance floor. Rather him than me.

"Come to the bar with me," Wyatt says, squeezing my shoulder.

I stand and silently follow him through the crowd. When we get to the bar, he orders us both a bottle of Bud and hands me one.

"What's going on?" he asks before taking a mouthful of beer.

I frown. "What do you mean?"

"Taylor. You haven't taken your eyes off her all night, even when Kristie was on your lap. And don't think I didn't see how you reacted when I told her she could stay at my place next time she came to watch a game. What's going on?"

"Nothing." I take a pull of my beer and look away. I'm not exactly lying. Nothing is going on between us.

"You like her, don't you?"

"She's a friend."

He rolls his eyes. "I don't mean as a friend."

"I'm not looking for anything more than friendship."

"Why not? Is this because of Sophie?"

I groan internally, thinking this is just like the conversation I had with Nash.

"It's got nothing to do with Sophie." I drain my beer, suddenly needing something stronger. "Do you want a whiskey?"

He eyes my empty bottle and shakes his head. "No. I'm good. You know, I've seen her looking at you. I think she likes you too."

"What is it with everyone trying to set me up with Taylor? Why does everyone think they know what's best for me?"

Wyatt raises his eyebrows at my outburst. "I'm not trying to set you up. I'm trying to get you to see what's right in front of your face."

"You've been talking to Nash, haven't you?"

He smiles sheepishly. "He's just worried about you. Paisley too."

"I'm fine!"

"Don't let what happened with Sophie stop you from being happy, Seb."

"Nothing happened with Sophie."

"You know what I mean. Don't let how you felt for her stop you from moving on. You could have something good with Taylor."

I shake my head. "What if I let her in and then lose her, or worse, hurt her? I can't risk either of those things happening. It's just better if we don't start anything."

"Haven't you already started something?"

I sigh. "Paisley has a big mouth."

He chuckles. "She cares about you, Seb. She wants you to be happy."

"I am happy. Not everyone gets to have what she and Nash do, and I'm good with that." He goes to say something, but I stop him. "I'm good, Wyatt," I insist.

He holds up his hands. "Okay. I think you're kidding yourself, but I'll drop it."

I turn back to the bar and order a shot of Jack Daniel's.

"Let's head back," Wyatt says when I have my drink in my hand. "Everyone will wonder where we've gone."

I nod and follow him back to the table. Not for the first time tonight, jealousy rears its ugly head when I see who Taylor's talking to. "What's he doing here?"

"I've no idea," Wyatt says. "It's good to see him, though."

"Is it?"

His brow furrows in confusion. "Isn't it? I thought you and Jackson were friends."

"We are, I guess."

Nash stands from the booth. "I found Jackson in the bar downstairs. I had no idea he was coming to watch the game."

"He's gotten comfortable with Taylor pretty quickly," I say, my voice giving away my jealousy. He looks up, spotting Wyatt and me.

"Hey, guys," he says, maneuvering out of the booth and holding his hand out for first Wyatt to shake, and then me. "It was a great game, Wyatt."

"Good to see you, Jackson. You should have said you were coming to watch the game. You could have gone in the loft with these guys," Wyatt says, flicking his head toward me and Nash.

"I'm sorry to have missed that. I've been talking to Taylor

about how much she loved it. I've offered to bring her to the next home game if it falls on a day I'm not working."

My stomach twists. I know there's no way Taylor is going to say no to that. She loved the game and wants to come again.

"Let me know if you can make it and I'll hook you up with some seats. I can't promise one of the lofts again, but the stadium seats will be good," Wyatt says.

"Thanks, man. That would be great."

I glare daggers at Wyatt, who shrugs his shoulders. Not wanting to make small talk with anyone, I place my glass on the table and turn to Nash.

"I'm going to call it a night and head back to the hotel."

"Oh, okay." He leans forward and interrupts Paisley and Taylor's conversation.

"Seb's heading back to the hotel. What do you guys want to do? Do you want to stay or head back?" he asks.

"I think I'm ready to go," Taylor says, looking past Nash to me.

"Yeah, I'm good to go too," Paisley agrees.

"Looks like we're coming with you," Nash says when he stands up.

I nod and turn to Wyatt. "We're calling it a night. When are you back home?"

"Thursday."

"I'll see you at Mom and Dad's on Christmas Day, then."

He pulls me into a one-armed hug. "Think about what I said," he whispers in my ear before stepping out of the embrace. I give him a small nod before stepping back and waiting while Nash, Paisley, and Taylor each give him a hug. As they're saying goodbye, Jackson pulls me to one side.

"Hey, man. How's Taylor been since that asshole attacked her?"

"Erm... yeah, she's been okay," I tell him, taken aback by him asking.

He nods. "What do you think she'd say if I asked her out?"

My jaw tenses, and as much as I like Jackson, right now, I want to punch him. "I don't know. You'd have to ask her." I'm grateful when I see everyone has said their goodbyes and I can end the conversation. "I should go. Good to see you, Jackson," I lie.

"You too, Seb," he says, his attention going from me to Taylor. "Taylor, before you go, can I talk to you for a second?"

"I'll wait outside," I say to Nash, disappearing into the crowds before he can reply. It's got nothing to do with me whether she agrees to go out with Jackson or not, but I don't have to watch.

Once I'm outside, I pace the sidewalk as I wait for them. Nash appears first, followed by Taylor, who's laughing at something Paisley is saying. Nash sees me and walks over.

"Why did you rush off?"

"I just needed some air."

"Can we get a cab back to the hotel? My feet are killing me," Paisley says, coming up behind Nash and leaning against him.

He wraps his arm around her and presses a kiss on her head. "Sure, baby."

They walk together toward the line of people waiting outside the club for a cab, leaving Taylor to walk with me. It's a little awkward after earlier, and I hate that there's an atmosphere between us.

"Are we okay? After earlier, I mean," I ask, needing to break the silence.

She sighs. "We're good, Seb." I'm not sure I believe her, but what choice do I have? We don't have to wait long until we're at the front of the line. The drive to the hotel only takes a few minutes. I sit in the front with the driver while Taylor, Paisley, and Nash sit in the back. I pay the driver and climb out, opening the rear door. Paisley and Nash get out first, followed by Taylor. The girls must have removed their shoes in the back of the cab, both of them holding their heeled pumps in their hands.

"Stop!" Nash shouts, scooping Paisley up bridal-style into his arms. "There's broken glass on the floor."

I close the cab door and reach for Taylor, picking her up and holding her against my chest.

"What are you doing?" she gasps, her voice breathless.

"I don't want you to cut your feet."

"I could just put my shoes on."

"I thought your feet hurt?"

"They do."

"Then I've got you."

She drops her head on my shoulder. "Thank you."

I carry her silently through the hotel lobby toward the elevator, Nash and Paisley ahead of us. The elevator doors open as soon as Paisley presses the button, and Nash and I walk into the car, the girls still in our arms.

"I'd have taken my shoes off earlier if I'd known you'd carry me," Paisley jokes, and Nash chuckles.

"Like I need an excuse to have you in my arms."

Paisley grins at him and presses her lips to his.

"You can probably put me down now," Taylor says quietly, her head still on my shoulder.

"I'll take you to your room."

"Okay," she whispers.

When the elevator doors open, I follow Nash along the hallway, coming to Taylor's room first. I stop outside her door, gently putting her down. My room is next door, and Nash and Paisley's room is beyond that.

"Night, guys," Paisley shouts as Nash opens the door with one hand and they disappear inside before either of us can answer.

Taylor laughs. "I guess they were eager to get inside."

"Yeah, I guess they were."

I watch as she digs in her purse for the keycard. When she's unlocked the door, she turns and gives me a small smile.

"Night, Seb."

"Night, Taylor." I lean down and kiss her cheek.

I wait until she's inside and I've heard the click of the lock before I walk the short distance to my room and let myself in. I groan and flop facedown onto the king-size bed. My resolve to keep things firmly in the friend zone is diminishing by the second, especially after having her in my arms earlier. She was right when she said the sex had been off the charts. It had felt like that for me too. Could we really be together but just in a physical relationship? If we both know the score, then there's no reason for either of us to get hurt, right?

CHAPTER TWENTY-ONE

Taylor

I close the hotel room door and toss my shoes on the floor. Sighing, I reach behind me and twist my arm, trying to undo the exposed zipper on my dress. After a few minutes of contorting my body to try and get the zipper down, I give up.

"Fuck!" I shout in frustration, flopping down onto the bed. "The perfect end to a shitty evening," I mutter, knowing I made a complete idiot of myself with Seb earlier, throwing myself at him when he clearly isn't interested in anything other than friendship. His hot-as-hell kiss threw me for a loop, and I let myself believe he might want what I want.

A knock on the door pulls me from my thoughts and I sit up, wondering who it can be at this time of night. I stand and cross the room, my eyes widening when I look through the peephole and Seb is standing there. Swinging the door open, my eyes track over him as he stands in the corridor in just a pair of sleep shorts.

"Are you okay?" he asks, his face clouded with concern. "I heard shouting."

"I'm fine. I couldn't get the zipper down on my dress."

"Oh." His eyes sweep over me. "Do you want me to undo it for you?"

"If you don't mind. I'll be sleeping in it otherwise." I turn and walk into the room, Seb following me. I close my eyes when his fingers brush over my neck as he sweeps my hair over my shoulder. The zipper goes from the base of my neck to underneath my butt. The dress is tight, and I hold my breath, his fingers skating over my body when he pulls down the zipper. I'm not wearing a bra, and I know from how low the zipper goes, he'll be able to see the hot-pink thong I'm wearing underneath the dress.

He drags in a breath as the zipper goes over my butt, and I open my eyes, looking over my shoulder at him. His eyes are fixed on my back and his jaw is tense.

"Thank you," I whisper.

His fingers trace up my spine, and I close my eyes, goose bumps erupting on my skin where he's touching me.

"Have you any idea how much I want you?" His voice is low and husky, and I sigh, looking away from him.

"I have no idea what you want, Seb. You're giving me whiplash."

"I guess I deserve that, but God, I want to touch you."

"Touch me, then," I say, my voice barely audible.

He sighs. "I shouldn't..." He trails off, but his fingers continue to brush over my skin, setting me on fire.

"You're overthinking it."

"Overthinking what?"

Despite feeling like an idiot earlier, I want him, and as hard as he's fighting this pull between us, I think he wants me too. I turn to face him and bite my bottom lip. Taking a deep breath, I drop my dress, letting it pool on the floor at my feet. His heated eyes track over me and I reach for his hand.

"Sex, Seb. Wasn't it you who told me to just feel?"

He stares at me before smiling. "I guess it was. Right after I'd made you come on my tongue."

"Holy fuck," I mutter as he pulls me gently against his chest.

"I am guilty of overthinking, though," he says softly. "Fucking you again is *all* I can think about."

Heat pools in my stomach as his fingers trace up and down my spine again. "Your mouth on me is all I can think about," I whisper, my eyes closing as his hand tangles into my hair.

"Maybe I should make that a reality, then."

He tilts my head and presses his lips to mine. I lose myself in his kiss, and when he bites gently on my bottom lip, I open up to him, his tongue dueling with mine. I gasp into his mouth as my nipples pebble and brush against his hard chest. With his mouth still on mine, his hands go under my ass, and he picks me up, placing me gently on the bed. He lays me down and my legs fall open as his body moves over me. I can feel his erection pressing against the thin material of my panties, and I lift my hips, trying desperately to dull the ache that's building.

"Fuck, Taylor," he mutters as he kisses around my jaw and down my neck. Within seconds, his lips are on my nipple and his tongue circles the bud. I let out a breathy moan and arch my back, trying to get as close to him as possible. My hands go into his hair as I hold his head against me. With his mouth and fingers on my chest, it isn't long before my breathing becomes labored and my clit pulses with need. I whimper when he releases my nipple from his mouth and captures my lips again. I wind my arms around his neck and kiss him urgently.

"I need to taste you," he says against my lips. He pulls back and searches my eyes. "Is that okay?"

I hold his gaze. I'd been apprehensive about him going down on me last time, but I can't deny how incredible it had felt, and my body is aching for his mouth to be on me again.

I nod, and suddenly his weight is gone from on top of me and he's gently pulling me to the bottom of the bed, my ass on the edge and my legs dangling over the end. His fingers slide under the waistband of my panties, and I lift my hips as he removes them. He kneels on the floor and picks up one of my legs, resting it over his shoulder. He's so close to where I need him; I can feel his breath hot on my core. When he lowers his head, I gasp as his tongue swipes through my folds. He blows gently on my clit before sucking it into his mouth.

"Oh, God! Don't stop," I cry, fisting the comforter as my legs begin to tremble. His hands go under my ass, and he lifts me closer to his mouth as if he's devouring his favorite dessert. His tongue is relentless, and I can feel my orgasm building in the pit of my stomach. Moving his hands from underneath my ass, he pushes a finger inside me, and I moan. He adds another, and the combination of his mouth and fingers pushes me over the edge. I come hard, moaning and whimpering as he pulls every last second of pleasure from my body.

I sit up slowly, my cheeks flushing pink when my arousal coats his lips. He licks them, smiles, and holds out his hand. When I take it, he pulls me to stand, slipping his arms around my waist as my legs wobble.

"Take a shower with me?" he asks, kissing me softly.

"Okay."

He leads me into the bathroom, and with his hand still nestled in mine, he reaches into the walk-in shower and turns on the water. My eyes drop to his perfect ass, his toned and inked back flexing as he leans around the floor-to-ceiling shower screen. With the water running, he turns and places his hand on my hip, pushing me gently against the wall. His body presses against mine as he lowers his head and kisses me. I taste myself on his tongue, and despite just coming, the ache between my legs is building again as I think about where his mouth has just been. I also remember how good it feels when he's inside me, which is only adding to my arousal.

Pulling out of the kiss, I drag in some mouthfuls of air as his forehead rests on mine.

"Do you have a condom?" I ask.

"I have some in my room. I wasn't expecting…"

I smile. "Go and get some."

He raises his eyebrows. "Some?"

"If you think we're only doing this once, you're wrong. I'll be waiting in the shower for you. My room key is on the dresser. You can let yourself back in."

He grins. "I think I like assertive Taylor." He lowers his head and kisses me again, leaving me breathless. Pulling out of the kiss, he drops his hand from my waist. "I'll be right back."

I watch as he walks out of the bathroom and disappears from view. My heart thunders in my chest, and I drop my head back against the wall. I can't help but hope he doesn't change his mind now that he's not caught up in the moment. I know he's apprehensive about getting involved. I almost don't want to get into the shower until I'm sure he's coming back. I do, though, tilting my head back under the hot spray. I keep my eyes closed as the water washes over me. I haven't been standing under the water long when I jump, his arms circling my waist. I gasp as I'm pulled back against a hard chest, Seb's aftershave invading my senses.

"That was quick," I tell him, turning in his arms.

"I had something to rush back for," he whispers, dropping his lips to the crook of my neck. I tilt my head, giving him better access, and moan when he gently bites the skin below my ear before soothing the sting with his tongue. "Now, where were we?" he mutters against my neck.

Before I can answer him, his hands go under my ass, and he picks me up, pressing me against the wall of the shower. I gasp as the cold ceramic tiles hit my back, the chill soon chased away by the heat of the water and his body covering mine. I wrap my arms around his neck and my legs around his waist. He lowers his head and brushes kisses around my jaw and down my neck, stealing my breath. I can feel his erection, hot and hard against me, and he moans as I roll my hips.

"Fuck, Tay. I can't wait to be inside you," he says, his voice husky with need.

"Then don't," I mumble, rolling my hips again.

"I want you to come again."

He peppers kisses along my shoulder and my eyes widen in surprise. "Again?"

"Yes. Again."

He uses the wall to hold me up, removing one of his arms from around me and reaching his hand between us, circling my clit before gently pushing two fingers inside me.

"So ready for me," he says before capturing my lips with his. I kiss him like someone possessed, snaking my hands into his hair and tugging sharply. He growls into my mouth as his fingers find the sweet spot inside and my legs tremble around him. "Can you come like this?"

My cheeks flush, and I nod. "I think so."

He smiles when my eyes meet his, and I hold his gaze as his thumb circles my clit, his fingers still buried inside me. My orgasm builds like a tidal wave, and I close my eyes, dropping my head back onto the tiles.

"Your walls are gripping my fingers, Taylor. I can't wait to slide my cock into your wet heat," Seb whispers in my ear as he increases the pressure on my clit.

His words and fingers tip me over the edge, and I come hard, my head falling forward onto his shoulder as I ride out my orgasm.

Before I've fully come down to earth, he removes his fingers and replaces them with his cock, and I cry out as he pushes inside me. Everything is super sensitive after just coming, but as he pounds into me, I'm surprised to feel heat pooling in the pit of my stomach again. He feels incredible, and I never want him to stop.

My back scrapes against the tiles as he moves inside me, but I'm too turned on to care. With my fingers digging into his hair, I tilt his head and bring my mouth to his. I bite down on his bottom lip and he opens to me, our tongues sliding together. As my fingers slip out of his hair, my nails dig into his shoulder, and he growls into my mouth.

"Touch yourself, Taylor." He pants against my lips. "I'm close and I want you to come again."

"I can't… it's too much."

"You can. I want another one. Touch yourself," he demands.

I hold his gaze as I snake my hand between our bodies and circle my clit with my fingers. His eyes drop from mine as he looks down to where my fingers play.

"God, that's hot."

My fingers brush against his hard cock as he moves inside me and that familiar ache in the pit of my stomach starts to build again. Seb's breathing has become ragged, and his thrusts faster, telling me he's close. Knowing I am too, I increase the pressure on my clit, and when I feel him swell inside me, I come hard, Seb following my lead. My orgasm crashes into me, and it's a good thing he's holding me as there's no way I'd be able to stand right now.

I drop my head onto his chest, and he presses a kiss on my wet hair. When we've both caught our breath, I lift my head.

"I think you broke me," I tell him sleepily.

He chuckles and gently pulls out of me. "Can you stand while I get rid of the condom?" I nod and unfold my legs from around him. He lowers me to the ground, keeping his arms around me when my legs shake. "You good?"

"Yeah. I'm good."

He leaves the shower, and I watch him through the glass as he removes the condom and wraps it in a tissue before tossing it in the trash. His body is a work of art, and I can't drag my eyes off him. I might have told him earlier that whatever this is between us is just sex, but I'm beginning to wonder if I'm kidding myself. We have a connection, and not just a sexual one. I can't help but wonder if he feels it too and that's why he's reluctant to start anything. I know he doesn't do relationships. I hope I can keep my feelings for him in check. If not, I know for sure I'm going to end up with a broken heart because there's no way I can walk away now.

CHAPTER TWENTY-TWO

Seb

I can feel her eyes on me as I clean up. I can't deny how incredible having her in my arms felt, even though I know I shouldn't be here. I'm just blurring the lines of friendship but it seems I'm powerless to stay away. When I've tossed the condom in the trash, I go back to her, turn off the water, and scoop her bridal-style into my arms.

She giggles. "What are you doing?"

"Taking you to bed. I figured your legs might not carry you."

"I think you're probably right."

She shivers in my arms as the cool air of the bathroom hits her wet skin. I grab a towel off the heated rail and drape it over her. "Better?"

She nods. "Thank you."

When we get into the bedroom, I lower her to the ground next to the bed and take the towel, wrapping it around her. While she dries off, I go back into the bathroom and get a towel for myself. She's under the comforter by the time I get back, her eyes closed and her arm up and over her face.

"You've definitely broken me," she mutters. "I think I lost count of how many times you made me come."

I smile and sit on the edge of the bed. "Three, but I'll be going for four next time."

Her arm falls from over her face and she opens her eyes.

"Four!" She sits up, and the comforter falls off her, revealing that she's naked underneath. My eyes drop to her perfect tits and my cock twitches underneath the towel. "You're trying to kill me."

I laugh. "Death by orgasm. I guess there are worse ways to go."

She laughs too. "I guess there are." She looks down at the comforter, her fingers pulling on a loose piece of thread. "Are you... staying?" she asks, her eyes full of uncertainty when she finally looks up.

"If that's okay."

"It's okay." She pulls the comforter back and pats the space next to her. "We should get some sleep. I think Nash wants to head back first thing in the morning."

I stand and drop the towel, sliding into bed next to her. "Come here," I tell her, opening my arms. She hesitates for a second before moving across the bed and pressing her body against mine. I wrap my arms around her, and she drops her head onto my chest. My fingers track up and down her arm as I hold her.

"What did Jackson want earlier?" I ask quietly. I shouldn't be asking, but I can't stop myself.

She lifts her head and looks at me. "Umm... he asked for my number."

"Did you give it to him?"

She bites her lip and nods. "I couldn't think of a reason to say no, plus, I was mad at you."

Jealousy swirls in my stomach, and I push it down, swallowing thickly. "I'm sorry I made you mad."

She smiles. "I think you made up for it." She winks. "Three times."

I laugh and lean my head down, brushing a kiss on her lips. I want to ask her if she's going to go out with Jackson, but it's none of my business. She can date whoever she wants. It's not like we're together.

She pulls out of the kiss and lets out a yawn.

"We should sleep. Night, Taylor."

"Night, Seb."

She goes to move out of my arms, but I increase my hold on her. "Stay," I whisper, knowing I'm giving her mixed signals.

"Okay."

She relaxes against me with her head on my chest. Within minutes, her breathing has evened out and she's asleep. Despite loving having her in my arms, I can't push down the feeling that I'm fucking everything up. We can't be more than friends, but somehow, we already are. Once we've crossed that line, though, how do we ever go back?

I wake the next morning, my body tangled up with Taylor's. Her head still rests on my chest and my arms are wrapped around her. Although I know I shouldn't be holding her like this, I can't bring myself to move. Sighing, I drop a kiss on her head.

"Morning," she says quietly, her voice thick with sleep.

"Morning."

She tilts her head and smiles, pressing a kiss onto my jaw. "How did you sleep?" she asks.

"Good. You?"

"Yeah, good."

Her fingers trace circles over my chest, and when her touch begins to drive me crazy, I flip her onto her back and bring my body over hers. She gasps as I roll my hips, my erection pressing between her legs. I drop my head and kiss her, snaking my tongue into her mouth. As the kiss gets heated, a knock sounds on the door and I groan, pulling back.

"I bet that's Paisley," she whispers, her voice breathless.

"She has the worst timing. Do you think she has some sort of sixth sense?" I wriggle my eyebrows, and she laughs.

"I don't think so. Do you want to hide in the bathroom?"

My eyes widen in surprise. "You want to keep me a secret?" I tickle her side, and she squirms underneath me.

"Stop it." She giggles, pushing my hands away. "She'll hear us."

"You weren't saying *stop it* last night." I wink, and she rolls her eyes.

"She hasn't stopped asking me what's happening between us since she found out we slept together last time. Maybe your suggestion of keeping things between us wasn't the worst idea. I don't think she'd get the whole *friends with benefits* thing."

"What did you tell her?"

Her eyes drop from mine. "Nothing." There's another knock on the door.

"I'll go and hide."

I brush my lips against hers before climbing off the bed and walking naked across the room. I'm just at the bathroom door when Taylor whisper-shouts, "Seb! Your sleep shorts."

I turn to see her standing by the bed, a sheet wrapped around her. She tosses me my shorts and I slip them on. "Quick! Go!" she whispers, gesturing to the bathroom door with her hand.

I laugh and go into the bathroom, closing the door but not all the way. I want to listen to what she's saying to Paisley. I sit on the closed toilet seat, hearing Paisley as she comes into the room.

"Did I wake you?" she asks Taylor.

"Yeah, but it's fine. I need to get up anyway."

"Seb's not here, is he?"

"No!" Taylor says a little too quickly. "Why would he be?"

Paisley laughs. "I thought you might be getting more of the best you've ever had."

My eyes widen, and I grin like an idiot. So much for her telling Paisley nothing.

"I didn't say that!"

"Erm, yes you did. More than once."

"Yeah, well, he's not here. Isn't he in his room?"

"If he is, then he's not answering the door. Maybe he brought someone back with him."

"How drunk *were* you last night? The four of us came back together."

"I wasn't that drunk. He could have gone back out, though. That cheerleader was grinding all over his lap. Maybe he went back for her."

I grimace as I remember how over the top Kristie was. I know some guys would have loved it, but it would never have been a turn-on for me.

"I doubt it. He didn't seem that into her," Taylor says.

"Well, you'd know. You never took your eyes off him all night."

"I don't know what you're talking about. I'm sure Seb is just in the gym or something. I should shower and get ready. What time does Nash want to leave?"

"Hey. I didn't mean to upset you, Tay. I was only joking."

She sighs. "You haven't upset me. Seb and I are friends. That's all."

"I'm sorry. I'll quit teasing you about it."

There's silence for a minute or so, and I wonder if they're hugging.

"What about Jackson? Did he ask you out?"

Taylor laughs. "It didn't take you long to move from Seb to Jackson."

"It's not my fault you've got a bunch of hot guys after you."

"I do not have a bunch of hot guys after me."

"You don't think Jackson's hot?"

I stand and make for the door, pressing my ear to the wood as I wait for her to answer.

"Umm... well, yeah, I guess," Taylor says.

"You don't sound convinced."

"I'm not. I just don't think there's a spark."

"Maybe you should give him a chance. I know he's not Seb, but he's a good guy."

I frown at Paisley's words. While Taylor's telling me she's happy for a friends-with-benefits relationship, hearing Paisley makes me question how true that is. I don't know if I can walk away, though. Not now that I know how good she feels. I guess that makes me an asshole. I just hope to God neither of us ends up hurt.

CHAPTER TWENTY-THREE

Taylor

It's Christmas Eve, and I've worked nonstop since we got back from Phoenix. I'm trying to get the first read-through of the manuscript I'm working on finished so I can take some time off without feeling guilty. As good as watching Wyatt's game had been, I pretty much lost two days, and I need to catch up.

I've seen Seb every day since we got back, and he's stayed over a couple of times when he's been able to get away from the bar. It's a busy time of year for him, and he hasn't had much downtime in the last week. Everyone is coming to Eden tonight, though, and I know he's hoping to get a couple of hours off. It's another of the Brookes family's traditions to spend Christmas Eve together in the bar. Before this year, it's always just been the five siblings. It'll be a bigger crowd this year, with Sophie and Paisley now part of the family. Seb's asked me to come too, and I'm really looking forward to it. I'm quickly getting attached to the Brookes family, and I love how they've accepted me into their fold.

I've just stepped out of the shower when my phone chimes from the bedroom with an incoming message. I wrap a towel around me and pad through the room to the nightstand. I pick up the phone, and there's a message from Paisley.

Paisley: We're here. Are you coming down?

I quickly type out a reply.

Me: I'm running late. Just got out of the shower. Won't be long.

Paisley: I'll get you a drink.

Me: Thanks.

I toss the phone onto the bed and dry off. When I've dried my hair, I pile it into a messy bun on the top of my head, apply some makeup, and pull on some skinny jeans and a pink cami. I slip my feet into some heeled pumps and grab my purse. I'm only about thirty minutes late, but working nonstop meant I finished the edits and the manuscript is back with the author. It will probably be after Christmas when it comes back, giving me some much-needed time off.

When I finally get downstairs, Eden is packed with people dancing, drinking, and having fun. It's standing room only, and I can't see any of the Brookes clan, even though I know from Paisley that they're all here. I'm just about to head to the bar when I feel someone behind me, and a pair of hands come to rest on my waist. My body tenses until the person steps closer and my senses are overwhelmed by Seb. His aftershave envelops me, and his head drops to my ear, his breath hot on my skin.

"Hi," he whispers in my ear. "You look good enough to eat." His hands squeeze my waist, and I smile, turning to face him.

"Is that a promise?"

He chuckles. "You know it is."

"I'm going to hold you to that."

His eyes flash with heat, and he lowers his head, brushing his lips against mine. As surprised as I am that he's kissing me in Eden, I kiss him back, losing myself in him. He pulls away far too soon, leaving me wanting more.

"We should find the others," he says, his voice husky.

I take a deep breath and step out of his embrace before I drag him up to my apartment.

"I can't believe how busy it is," I tell him as he places his hand on the bottom of my back and leads me through Eden.

"It's crazy. I was hoping for a few hours off, but Alex has called in sick. I've managed to get one of the servers in to help behind the bar, but I'm going to have to serve too."

"I'm sorry, Seb. That sucks. I know how much you were looking forward to tonight."

"There'll be tomorrow to catch up with everyone."

His hand falls away from my back as we approach the table where everyone is. As we get nearer, Ashlyn and Ivy appear from behind us, and Ash quickly pulls me into a hug.

"Merry Christmas, Taylor," she shouts in my ear, grinning widely as she steps back.

I laugh. "Merry Christmas, Ash."

"This is Ivy," she says, turning to the beautiful brunette behind her.

"Hey. Good to finally meet you," I tell her.

"You too, Taylor."

"Paisley got you a drink," Ashlyn says. "Come and sit down."

Before I can, Wyatt stands and brushes a kiss on my cheek.

"Good to see you again, Taylor."

"You too."

I slide into the booth, smiling at everyone in turn. I pause when my eyes land on Sophie. She looks beautiful.

"How are you, Sophie? You look great."

She smiles, her hand dropping to her swollen stomach that I can just see above the table.

"I'm good, thanks. Really good."

Paisley told me how tough Sophie's pregnancy had been at the beginning and how sick she was. I'm happy everything's worked out for her and Cade.

I glance at Paisley, who's looking past me. I follow her gaze to see she's looking at Seb. Seb's watching me, and he smiles when our eyes meet. I smile back.

"I need to get back to the bar. I'll see you guys later. Have fun," Seb says, raising his hand in a wave before disappearing into the crowd.

"Why was he looking at you like that?" Paisley whispers from the side of me.

"Like what?" I ask.

"Like he wants to rip your clothes off."

I laugh. "How much have you had to drink?"

She narrows her eyes and holds my gaze. "You're sleeping together again, aren't you?"

"What are you two whispering about?" Ash asks, and I pick up the glass of wine Paisley has pushed in front of me, swallowing down a mouthful of the red liquid. I don't like lying to Paisley, but I know she won't understand what Seb and I have going on.

"Nothing. Paisley's just seeing things." I bump my shoulder with hers and she rolls her eyes. "What time is everyone getting to your parents' place tomorrow?" I ask Ash.

"About midday, I think."

"Do you need a ride? We can pick you up," Nash asks.

"Seb has offered to swing by and pick me up, but thanks."

He hasn't, but I'm hoping he'll want to stay at my place tonight and I can grab a ride with him tomorrow. I can feel Paisley's eyes on me, but I don't look at her. I can't lie to her twice.

I look out into the crowd of people, noticing a guy who keeps looking over this way. I watch him for a little longer, his eyes flicking to Ashlyn. He looks older than her, but he's hot, and I wonder if she knows him.

"Hey, Ash," I wait until she looks over. "I think you might have an admirer."

She frowns. "What? Who?"

"Yeah, who?" Nash asks.

I ignore Nash and gesture out onto the dance floor. "The guy in the blue shirt." She follows my gaze, her eyes widening and her cheeks flushing pink. "You know him?" I ask.

"Yeah. I know him."

I look back out into the crowd, seeing that he's staring at Ash. He smiles and starts making his way over.

"Who is he?"

"My boss."

"*That's* Principal Murphy," Paisley whispers.

Ash told Paisley and me about the guy at work that she'd become close to, but we haven't met him yet. It looks like that's about to change.

"Hey, Ashlyn. How's your Christmas vacation going?" he asks, his eyes fixed on her.

"Yeah, good. You?" He nods. "Guys, this is Ben Murphy, my principal. Ben, this is my family. My brothers, Wyatt, Nash, and Cade. And this is Cade's wife, Sophie, Nash's girlfriend, Paisley, and our friends, Ivy and Taylor."

He chuckles. "That's a lot of names to remember. Great to meet you all." After a round of hellos, his eyes go back to Ashlyn. "Can I buy you a drink, Ash?"

"Umm… sure." She stands and looks over her shoulder, grinning at me, Ivy, and Paisley. "See you in a bit."

Nash goes to say something, but Paisley beats him to it. "Have fun."

We watch as they disappear into the crowd.

"Is there something going on with them?" Cade asks. "He looks a lot older than her."

"It's her boss," Sophie says. "I'm sure he's just buying her a Christmas drink."

Wyatt snorts. "She looked very excited for a Christmas drink."

"You guys need to back off. She's a grown woman. Don't you want her to be happy with someone?" Paisley asks.

"Yeah, but not him," Nash says.

"Why?"

"He's too old for her."

"So? You're older than me."

"That's different."

"Why?"

"Because you aren't my sister."

Paisley rolls her eyes. "You're being ridiculous, Nash." She points at Wyatt and then Cade. "You two as well."

"We're always going to want to protect her from the assholes who want to hurt her," Nash says. "She's our baby sister."

"She's twenty-five, and not *every* guy is going to be an asshole. I know you mean well, but you all need to stop suffocating her."

"Yeah, maybe," Nash says, flicking his eyes to Cade and Wyatt. They both mutter something incoherent, and I know what Paisley's said has gone in one ear and out the other. They love her, but it's not hard to see how unhappy she is. They clearly haven't noticed, though, and as much as I care about Ash, it's not my place to say.

I finish the last of my drink and stand from the booth. "I'll be back," I say to Paisley, disappearing before she can say anything.

Knowing how busy Eden is, I want to help out for an hour so Seb can spend some time with his family. I worked in a bar for a year or so while I built up my editing business. I'm probably a little rusty, but I'm hoping it's like riding a bike and it will all come flooding back to me.

CHAPTER TWENTY-FOUR

Seb

Eden is packed. I can't remember the last time it was this busy. It doesn't look like I'm going to get any downtime tonight. I know Alex can't help being sick, but it couldn't have happened on a worse night.

I lift my head to serve the next customer, frowning when I see it's Ashlyn and some guy.

"Hey, Ash. What can I get you?" I ask her, my eyes flicking to the man standing next to her.

"Vodka lemonade and…" She turns to the guy.

He smiles at her. "A Heineken for me, please."

I look between them and see Ash roll her eyes. "Ben, this is my brother Seb. Seb, this is Ben, my principal at school."

"Nice to meet you, Seb," Ben says.

"You too," I tell him, relieved it's her boss and not some guy trying to pick her up. I make quick work of getting their drinks, sliding them across the bar. "They're on me. Merry Christmas."

"Thanks," Ben says, passing Ashlyn her drink. "Don't think this gets you out of me buying you a drink. We'll just have to make it another time," he says to her, and even in the darkness of the bar, Ash's cheeks flush pink.

Does she like this guy? He seems way older than her. He must know how old she is if he's her boss.

Before I can say anything, they disappear into the crowd, and I lose sight of them. Sighing, I focus on the next customer wanting a drink. I know Cade, Wyatt, and Nash will look out for her tonight. With how busy it is, I know I can't.

A few minutes later, I catch sight of Taylor waiting at the end of the bar. I wink at her, and she smiles. When I've finished serving, I wipe my hands on a cloth and make my way over to her.

"Hey. Are you having a good night?" I ask, just managing to stop myself from leaning down and brushing my lips with hers.

"I am, and I'm here to offer my services." I raise my eyebrows in surprise and smile. She slaps my chest. "Not *those* kinds of services! I mean my services behind the bar."

I pull my eyebrows together in confusion. "Behind the bar?"

She nods. "I worked in a bar in Pittsburgh for over a year. I know what I'm doing. I want you to go and spend some time with everyone while I cover for you."

"No! No way. It's Christmas Eve. I can't ask you to do that."

"You're not asking. I'm offering."

"It's still a no."

She crooks her finger and I lean in closer to her. "I'm doing this, Seb, so get used to it. I'm not taking no for an answer."

I grin at her. "Is this you being assertive again?" She nods. "You know I can't resist assertive Taylor."

She smiles and slips past me, opening one of the under-counter refrigerators and passing me a bottle of beer. "Go. I've got this." I start to say something, but she cuts me off. "Go." She pushes her purse into my hands and waves me away.

As much as I don't want it to, something shifts in my chest as I watch her lean over the bar to take a guy's order. She's beautiful inside and out, and I don't think she realizes what it means to me to have even one drink with my family tonight. She serves him like she's worked behind the bar forever, even managing to work the register before moving on to the next customer. Her eyes slide to mine, and she flicks her head to the back of Eden, where I know everyone is sitting. I smile at her and mouth a thank-you before heading through the crowd to the booth. I feel guilty that she's managed to talk me into letting her help. I'll just have this one drink and then I'll go back. She shouldn't miss out on Christmas Eve because I don't have enough staff.

"Hey, Seb," Nash says as I sit down in the booth next to him. "I thought you weren't going to be able to get away tonight."

"I had some unexpected help behind the bar," I tell him, taking a mouthful of beer.

"Did you see Taylor on your way over here?" Paisley asks. "She disappeared a few minutes ago."

I smile sheepishly. "Yeah. She's the unexpected help."

Paisley laughs. "She's behind the bar?" I nod.

"Does she know what she's doing?" Wyatt asks.

"She's a natural," I tell him. "I'm just having ten minutes and then I'll go back. She wouldn't take no for an answer."

"Sounds like Tay," Paisley says. "I'm going to go and see her in action." She stands from the booth. "I'll get some drinks on the way back."

"I'll come with you," Cade says. "It's my round."

I stand and let Paisley out of the booth, sitting back down when she and Cade disappear into the crowds.

"How've you been, Seb?" Sophie asks from across the table. I look over and smile. I don't have that crushing pain in my chest when I look at her anymore. She's not someone I'm desperately in love with. Instead, she's Sophie, one of my very best friends, although I haven't been much of a friend to her lately. I just needed time to heal, even though I know she won't understand why I've been so distant.

"I've been good, Soph. What about you? How are you feeling?"

"Come over here, quick!"

My eyes widen and I scramble out of the booth.

"What's wrong? Are you okay?"

She nods and reaches for my hand, tugging me to sit down next to her. "The baby's kicking." She takes my hand and places it on her swollen stomach. When nothing happens, I lift my eyes to hers and she smiles. "Wait." I hold her gaze, and a few seconds later, I feel a kick on my palm.

"Was that the baby?" I ask in awe, my eyes dropping to where my hand rests.

"Yep. I swear it's a boy and he's got the Brookeses' football gene."

There's another ripple of movement under my hand, and I grin. "That's incredible, Soph. I'm so happy for you and Cade."

"Can I ask you something?"

"Sure."

"Are we good? It feels like you've been avoiding me."

Fuck. I feel like the shittiest person, and I can't even explain why. I drag my hand through my hair. "I've just had some stuff going on. We're good, though. I'm sorry I've been a crappy friend."

She shakes her head. "You haven't been a crappy friend—"

"I have," I tell her, cutting her off.

"If you ever want to talk about anything…" She trails off. "I guess I just miss you."

I take her hand. "I miss you too."

"You should stop by the house and see the nursery."

"I will. I promise."

"Drinks!" Paisley shouts as she places a tray on the table, interrupting our conversation. "Taylor is killing it behind the bar."

I laugh. "I should go and take over from her. I don't want her working the bar all night."

"She told me to tell you that she's fine and to drink this first," Paisley says, sliding another bottle of Bud across the table to me. "She's loving it. I think you might have to drag her away."

"Hey! Do you know what I've just realized?" Wyatt shouts from across the table. We all turn to look at him. "Cade never had a bachelor party. We should do something."

Cade shakes his head. "I don't need a bachelor party."

"*Everyone* needs a bachelor party," Wyatt insists. "It doesn't have to be strippers and shit—"

"No strippers!" Sophie says, cutting him off.

"No strippers," Wyatt promises. "We could go fishing or something. What do you think?"

"I'm up for that. It's been forever since we've been fishing. Dad could come too," Nash says.

"Count me in," I tell Wyatt and Nash. "Cade, what do you say?"

He looks at Sophie, and she smiles at him. "Sure. I could get on board with a fishing trip."

"Yes," Wyatt says. "I'll see if I can set up a date in the new year."

"We could throw Sophie a bachelorette too," Paisley says, her voice etched with excitement.

"I'm not sure I'm up for a bachelorette," Sophie says with a chuckle. "I'll probably want to be in bed by eight!"

"We can make it a daytime pamper party," Paisley says. "Maybe *we* can have a stripper."

"There'll be no strippers, Paisley Prescott," Cade says, wrapping his arm around Sophie and pulling her against his side.

"I'm joking," Paisley assures him. "As if you guys would let us anyway." She turns and presses a kiss on Nash's lips.

"We wouldn't," Nash confirms, kissing her back.

She laughs as she pulls out of the kiss. "So, are we doing this? We could book a spa day. I'll arrange everything."

Paisley looks expectantly at Sophie, who smiles. "Sure. Why not? I could do with some pampering."

"Yes! We can do it the same day the guys go fishing." She turns to Wyatt. "Let me know when you've settled on a date, and I'll arrange everything for then."

"I'm sure Taylor and Ash will help," Wyatt says.

"Talking of Ash, I saw her at the bar with the school principal. Is something going on with them?" Paisley groans from the side of me. "What?" I ask, frowning at her.

"It's best you don't ask," Wyatt says with a chuckle. "We're all too over the top, apparently."

I look at Paisley, whose cheeks have flushed pink.

"Over the top in the best possible way," she says sheepishly. "Hell, I wish I'd had even one brother like you four to watch out for me. I think she really likes this guy, though, and things are going to be tough enough for them without you making it harder."

"What does that mean?" Nash asks, his eyebrows pulled together in a frown.

She closes her eyes and blows out a breath. "Fuck," she mutters. "Nothing. I've already said too much. Just back off a little. She's old enough to know what she's doing."

"Pais—"

"No, Nash," she says, interrupting him. "I love you, but I love Ash too, and I'm not about to break a confidence."

Nash nods and takes a pull of his beer. He doesn't look happy, and I hope whatever secret Paisley is hiding for Ash, it doesn't come between them. Out of all of us, it's Nash who's the most protective of Ashlyn. I guess it's the cop in him. What Paisley said has worried me too, though. As overprotective as we all are, it's only because we care.

CHAPTER TWENTY-FIVE

Taylor

I haven't worked behind a bar in over three years, but I can't believe how quickly I've fallen back into it. It's crazy busy, and I'm pretty sure I've spilled more drinks than Seb or Ryder would, but I can't deny that I'm loving it. I've had to ask Ryder how to make a few of the cocktails Eden offers. The bar I worked in back in Pittsburgh was more of a beer and wine place, but for everything else, it's like the three years have melted away. I'd forgotten what it was like to be a woman behind a bar, though, and I've been hit on by at least half of the guys I've served. I laugh off their advances and give them their drink. I'm not interested. I'm not looking for a hook-up.

When I look up to serve the next customer, it's Seb standing in front of me.

"Hey. What can I get you?" I ask him with a wink. He leans across the bar.

"You. In my office. Now." His voice is low and husky, and my stomach flips.

"There are people I need to serve," I tell him with a smile.

"Screw them. *I* need you." He flicks his head to the *staff only* area. "Come with me." He looks past me to Ryder. "We'll be five minutes," he shouts. I look at Ryder, who nods and grins knowingly. Despite keeping whatever's happening between the two of us quiet, Ryder is at Eden almost as much as Seb, and I know he must have seen Seb leaving my apartment this week. Not to mention him kissing me earlier.

When we're through the security door, Seb reaches for my hand and tangles his fingers with mine. We reach his office, and he opens the door, pulling me inside. He drops my hand and closes the door before engaging the lock. When he turns to me, I smile.

"Five minutes?" I ask, raising my eyebrows.

"What?"

"You told Ryder we'd be five minutes. I was hoping for a little longer than that."

His eyes flash with heat as they sweep over my body. He walks toward me, and I walk backward until my butt hits his desk. He gently pushes me to sit down and opens my legs, standing between them. His thick, inked arms rest on the wood on either side of me, and I tilt my head back to look up at him. He hasn't even touched me, but my heart is racing, and my breathing is labored already.

"You think I can't get you off in five minutes?" His eyes are fixed on my lips and my tongue darts out to wet them.

"Oh, I know you can. Maybe I wanted… more."

He grins. "What did you have in mind?"

I bite my bottom lip. Despite sleeping with him a handful of times, I'm still nervous to tell him what I want. I've never had someone who was bothered about what I wanted, and while I thought my sex life before him was good, I know for sure now that it wasn't. Taking a deep breath, I lower my eyes. "I want you to fuck me over your desk," I whisper.

He drags in a breath and tugs me to the edge of the desk, the growing bulge in his pants hitting me right where I need him. "Look at me, Taylor." I slowly raise my head, my eyes meeting his. "Do you have any idea how many times I've sat here and imagined doing exactly that?" I shake my head. "I've lost count."

"You have?" He nods. "I have a desk too," I tell him, wiggling my eyebrows.

He laughs. "I know. I had to assemble it with an image of me fucking you over it in my head. I hadn't seen you naked then, so the image was blurry. Now I know exactly what you look like, the picture in my head is clearer. The reality would be even better."

"You wanted to… you know… then?"

"Yes, Taylor. I wanted to fuck you then like I want to fuck you now."

He lowers his head and kisses me before I can respond. I wind my arms around his neck and moan into his mouth as he rolls his hips, his erection pressing against me. When he pulls away, he peppers kisses around my jaw and down my neck, his tongue licking over my pulse point. By the time his lips brush over my shoulder, I'm panting hard, and the ache between my legs is becoming unbearable. I wrap my legs around him and pull him closer toward me, rocking my hips against him. The seam of my jeans presses against my clit, and I gasp as it sends shots of pleasure through my body.

"God, I wish you had a dress on," he mutters as he pulls his lips off me and makes quick work of undoing my jeans and tugging them down my legs. I kick them off as he reaches for my cami and takes it off, leaving me in a strapless bra and panties.

"Holy fuck, Taylor," he says, pushing me gently to lie back on his desk. "Fucking perfection."

His fingers go around my neck before trailing between my breasts and over my stomach. When he reaches the edge of my panties, he runs his finger under the waistband, and I lift my hips.

"Please," I whisper, too far gone to care that I'm begging.

"I've got you, Tay." He removes my panties and tosses them on the floor with the rest of my clothes before swiping his fingers between my folds. I gasp and arch my back as his fingers brush against my clit. "So ready for me."

With his free hand, he reaches up and unhooks my bra, pulling the lacy material from my body. In seconds, he's taking one of my pebbled nipples into his mouth, and I cry out as he sucks hard on the sensitive bud. His fingers continue to strum my clit, and that familiar stirring in the pit of my stomach builds as his fingers and mouth work me over. My hands go into his hair as I hold his head to my chest. When he pushes two fingers inside me, I moan loudly, tugging gently on his hair.

"I'm going to come, Seb," I mumble, lost in my pleasure. I was already halfway there before he'd even touched me. It's always like that when I'm with him. It's like he knows exactly how to play my body as if we've been together more than the handful of times we have.

"You're so tight, baby. I can't wait to bury my cock deep inside you."

"Oh, God. That's so hot. I love it when you talk to me like that."

"Come for me, Taylor. Come on my fingers."

His words push me over the edge, and my entire body trembles as I come. Waves of pleasure crash over me, and I can't catch my breath as his fingers continue to play. When everything becomes too sensitive, I squirm underneath him and gently pull his head up to mine, kissing him like I might die if I don't.

He pulls away and rests his forehead against mine. "Every time

I look at this desk, I'm going to see you falling apart on it. I don't think I'm ever going to get any work done again." He chuckles when heat rushes to my cheeks.

"I need you," I tell him. "Do you have a condom?" He nods and kisses me again before reaching across the desk, opening one of the drawers and feeling inside. "You're wearing too many clothes," I tell him as he searches for a condom. I tug his shirt from the waistband of his jeans, and with trembling hands, my fingers fumble to undo the buttons. When he's found a condom, he places his hands over mine and holds my gaze.

"Hey, you're shaking. Are you okay?"

I nod. "I'm good." I can't tell him that he's the reason I'm trembling. I know I'm getting in way over my head with him, but I can't walk away. I love how I feel when we're together, even if he is ruining me for anyone who might come after whatever this is between us ends.

He frowns. "We don't have to do this, Tay—"

"No! I want to. I want you, Seb."

I sit up and kiss him, willing my hands to stop shaking as I undo his shirt, pushing it off his shoulders. My mouth waters as my eyes rake over his inked chest. Despite seeing him shirtless more than once, every time I do, he takes my breath away. My fingers go to his jeans, and I pop the button, sliding my hand inside.

"Mmm, no underwear," I whisper as my hand wraps around his hard erection. I pump his length, circling my thumb around the head of his cock, spreading the precum that's already leaking.

"Jesus, Taylor," he hisses. "I need to be inside you."

He takes a small step back, my hand falling away. I watch with wide eyes as he kicks off his jeans and rolls the condom down his length.

"Come here," he says softly, his hand reaching for mine. I let him guide me around the other side of the desk to his chair and climb on his lap as he sits down. His hands go to my waist and he squeezes gently as he lifts me up, and I sink down onto his length. I let out a long, breathy moan as he fills me, and I lower my head to kiss him.

"God, I can feel you so deep like this," I mutter against his mouth. He bites gently on my bottom lip, and I open up to him, my tongue colliding with his. He moans into my mouth as I roll my hips, and his fingers grip my waist tighter. My fingers dig into his shoulder as I ride him, and I drop my head back and close my eyes as pleasure races through me.

"Does this feel as good for you as it does for me?" I ask, his hips thrusting up beneath me.

"Fuck! Yes. You feel incredible, Taylor." His hands go from my waist to my chest, his fingers rolling and pinching my nipples. "I'm not going to last, Tay. You feel too good. Tell me you're close."

"I am," I assure him.

One of his hands snakes between our bodies, his fingers finding my clit. I drop my head into the crook of his neck as he massages the tiny bundle of nerves, pushing me headlong into an earth-shattering orgasm. My release must trigger his own, and he lets out a moan, his arms slipping around my waist as he holds me against him as we both come down from our orgasms. We're both breathing hard, and a fine layer of sweat covers our bodies. My head is nestled in his neck, and his arms hold me pressed against him long after our breathing has evened out. When I finally lift my head, his eyes search mine.

"You okay?" he asks quietly.

I nod. "Stay at my place tonight?"

He lowers his head and kisses me, which I take as a yes. I'm definitely in way over my head, and I'm beginning to feel things for him I promised I wouldn't. I assured him I was happy having a friends-with-benefits relationship, that it was just sex. I was kidding myself. I wanted more from the start, and now there are feelings involved, I know I should walk away before my heart gets broken when he inevitably walks away, but I can't. I know I should, but I can't.

CHAPTER TWENTY-SIX

Seb

"Merry Christmas, Taylor," I whisper against her hair as she stirs in my arms. She was asleep when I came up last night, and I didn't want to wake her. She'd left the door on the latch, and I let myself in, climbing into her bed and pulling her into my arms. I fell asleep with her nestled against me. I've never just slept when I've stayed over; there's always been sex. That's what our relationship is, after all. Sex. I can't help but wonder if it's becoming more than that, even though that scares the hell out of me.

"Merry Christmas," she mumbles, her voice thick with sleep. She sits up suddenly, leaning on my bare chest. "You didn't wake me last night. Unless I was more drunk than I thought."

I chuckle. "No. I didn't wake you."

She frowns. "Why not?"

"I figured you might need your sleep after your workout in my office." I wink at her and her cheeks flush pink.

She smacks my chest and pouts. "I would have been good for round two," she says, pressing her lips to my chest.

I flip her onto her back and bring my body over hers. "Is that right?" I whisper, dropping my lips to her neck. She tilts her head to give me better access, and I gently bite her skin before soothing it with my tongue. My lips find hers, and just as things get heated, my phone rings from the pocket of my jeans that I tossed on the floor when I undressed last night.

"Urgh. If that's Paisley…"

Taylor giggles. "She really has got a sixth sense if it is."

I reluctantly untangle myself from around her and reach for my jeans. My phone's still ringing, and I frown when Nash's name flashes up on the display. It's early for him to be calling. I hope everything's okay.

"Hey, Nash," I say, pressing the phone to my ear.

"Are you home? I've been buzzing your apartment but you're not answering."

"Umm…" I look at Taylor and cover the phone with my hand. "It's Nash," I whisper. "He's at my place."

"Is everything okay?" she whispers back. I shrug.

"I'm not there. Are you okay?" I ask, wondering what's going on.

He sighs down the phone. "I got into an argument with Paisley. I stormed out and didn't know where to go. I ended up at your place."

"Fuck. I'll be right there."

"Where are you?"

"It doesn't matter. I'll be five minutes." I end the call and turn to Taylor.

"I heard," she says before I can say anything. "Can you drop me at their place on the way?"

"Of course."

She climbs off the bed and heads to the bathroom. "Do you know what they were arguing about?" she shouts.

"No, but I can guess."

She pokes her head around the bathroom door, her toothbrush in her hand. "What do you mean?" she asks.

"Something to do with Ash and that guy she was with last night. Do you know what's going on with her?"

She sighs. "Yeah, I know." I hold her gaze when she doesn't elaborate.

"Should I be worried?"

"She's just trying to work some stuff out. If she needs to tell you all, then she will."

I frown, having no idea what she's talking about. "Is she in trouble?"

"No."

"This conversation isn't reassuring me."

"I'm sorry. I can't say anymore. I'm not going to break her confidence."

"That's what Paisley said to Nash, and I think that's what they've argued about."

"Talk to him, Seb. This is their first Christmas together. They shouldn't be arguing. Ash would hate that."

"I'll try."

We get dressed and head downstairs and out the back of Eden to where my bike is parked. It's only a two-minute ride to Nash's place, and I pull up on the driveway to let Taylor off.

"Do you think you'll be back before we need to be at your parents' place?" she asks as she climbs off.

"Yes. They need to talk."

"I hope they can work things out."

"They will."

I leave her on the driveway and, minutes later, pull into the underground parking garage at my apartment block. Nash's truck is parked in my space, and I park in front of him.

"Hey," I say as I turn off the engine and climb off the bike. "What's going on?" We walk in silence to the elevator, and when we're in the car and he still hasn't said anything, I try again. "Nash?"

He sighs and closes his eyes. "Fuck! I *hate* arguing with her."

The door opens and we walk out. "Then why are you? Is this about Ash?"

His eyes widen in surprise. "How did you know?"

"Because I saw how you reacted last night. You need to let it go."

He frowns. "Let it go? I need to know she's okay."

We've reached my apartment, and I open the door, stepping inside. Nash follows, and I toss my keys on the table in the entryway.

"She's okay."

He swings his body around to face me. "You know what's going on?"

"No."

"How do you know she's okay, then?"

"Because I asked Taylor, and she told me she was. That's all I need to know."

"But that guy is way older than her. You can't be happy about that."

"Fuck, Nash. I know better than anyone that you can't help who you fall in love with."

"She's in love with him?" he shouts, and I roll my eyes.

"God! I didn't say that. I have no idea if she's in love with him. If she does want to be with him, though, what are you going to do about it? Try and stop her?" I blow out a breath. "Maybe the girls are right, and we need to back off." He looks at me like I've asked him to run through the streets of

Hope Creek naked. I roll my eyes. "What happened with Paisley?"

"She got sick of me asking her to tell me what was going on."

"You can't let this come between you, Nash. Whatever she knows, it's not her secret to tell and you need to respect that. It's Christmas Day, man. You shouldn't be arguing. Ash would hate this has happened because Paisley was keeping a confidence."

He sits down heavily on the stool at the breakfast bar.

"I've been an idiot, haven't I?"

I raise my eyebrows. "Yeah, but you can fix it. Go home and talk to her."

"Thanks, Seb. I'm not sure when you became so good at relationship advice."

I laugh. "Trust me. I'm not."

He walks toward the entryway. "I'm an asshole for leaving her alone on Christmas Day."

"She's not alone," I tell him, walking up behind him.

He spins around and frowns. "Who's with her?"

I smile sheepishly. "Taylor."

"You called Taylor after I called you...?" He trails off before raising his eyebrows. "You were with Taylor last night."

It's not a question, more of a statement, but I answer anyway. "Yes."

"What's going on with you two?"

He walks out of the apartment, and I turn my back on him while I lock up.

"It's just sex."

"She doesn't want more?" he asks as we walk to the elevator.

"No. Neither of us does."

"You sure about that?"

"Yes."

We walk into the waiting elevator, and I push the button for the parking garage.

"I hope you've got a good present for Paisley," I tell him, hoping the conversation about me and Taylor is over.

He sighs. "Yeah, I did."

"What did you get her?" The elevator doors open, and Nash walks out without answering. "Nash?" I jog to catch up to him.

He stops by his truck and drags his hand through his hair. "A ring."

My eyes widen. "An engagement ring?"

"You think it's a bad idea?"

"No! I think it's great. Are *you* having second thoughts?"

"Fuck, no! Not about Paisley. She's the one, but I don't want to ask her to marry me on the back of an argument."

"Go and speak to her. I know for sure she's going to be as upset about arguing as you are. I'll follow you on the bike and bring Taylor back here."

He pulls me into a hug. "Thanks, man."

A few minutes later, I pull up on Nash's driveway and park behind his truck. I kill the engine but stay on the bike. He turns to look at me when he climbs out of the truck.

"I'll wait here for Taylor," I call to him. "Good luck."

He nods his head and walks up the driveway. It's only seconds later that the door opens and Taylor walks out.

"Hey," she says as she comes to stand next to the bike.

"Hey. How's Paisley?"

She blows out a breath. "Upset. What about Nash?"

"Same." I take her hand and pull her toward me. "They'll work it out. They belong together."

She smiles. "Yeah, they do."

"Come on. I'm ready for breakfast in bed."

I wriggle my eyebrows and she laughs.

"Sounds good to me."

CHAPTER TWENTY-SEVEN

Seb

A couple of hours later, I park the bike on my parents' driveway. Taylor's arms are wrapped around my waist, and I bring my hand over hers, tangling our fingers together. I kill the engine and we sit in silence on the driveway. After a couple of minutes, she squeezes my hand before releasing it and climbing off the bike. I watch as she removes her helmet and shakes out her long blonde hair. She's beautiful, and I don't know how I'm going to keep my hands off her today.

"You okay?" I ask.

She nods. "You brought my gifts over with yours yesterday, right?"

I borrowed Ryder's car yesterday and loaded my and Taylor's Christmas gifts into the trunk and drove them over to my parents' place. There's no way I would have been able to carry them all and ride the bike.

"Yep. They're already under the tree." She smiles, but it doesn't quite reach her eyes. I frown and climb off the bike. Reaching for her hand, I pull her against me. "Are you sure you're okay?"

She sighs. "I can't help but think about my mom. She loved Christmas. It was her favorite time of year." She smiles. "She used to decorate the house with a tree in every room, and lights all around the porch. She always made it magical, even though, as a single parent, I know she didn't always have the money."

I increase my hold on her, kissing her softly on the top of the head. "It sounds like your mom loved you a lot, Tay."

"Yeah, she did. I loved her too." She drops her head against my chest. "Last Christmas was so hard. She had no idea who I was. She kept lashing out and hitting me. The doctor sedated her in the end, and I had to go home. I spent Christmas Day on my own."

My heart slams in my chest knowing she was alone and hurting last year. "Fuck, Taylor. I'm sorry. I can't even imagine how hard that must have been."

"I miss her so much," she whispers, her voice choked with emotion.

"You're not alone now, Tay."

She takes a deep breath before leaning back and smiling sadly. "I'm sorry. I didn't mean to get upset."

"There's no need to apologize."

Before she can respond, Nash's truck pulls on the driveway, and she steps out of the embrace.

"I hope they sorted things out," she says, changing the subject and gesturing to the truck.

I watch as Nash helps Paisley from the truck, slides his arm around her waist, and kisses her head.

"It looks like they did."

"Merry Christmas," Nash calls out.

"Merry Christmas," Taylor and I reply in unison.

Paisley heads over, kissing me on the cheek and linking her arm with Taylor's. "Are you and Nash okay?" Taylor asks her quietly. I don't hear Paisley's answer as they walk arm in arm into the house.

When I look back at Nash, he's grabbing bag after bag out of the back of the truck, and I jog over to him.

"Let me help." I take a couple of bags out of his hands while he grabs the rest. "Are these all gifts?"

He laughs. "Yep, Paisley loves to shop."

"Did you two talk?"

"Yeah, we're good. Thanks for earlier. I appreciate it."

"There's no need to thank me, Nash. I'm glad you sorted things out." I grin. "So, should I be congratulating you both?"

His forehead furrows in confusion. "What?"

"Did she say yes?"

"Oh. No. I didn't ask her. I want it to be perfect and not like I was asking because we'd had an argument."

"I'm sure she wouldn't have thought that, but I get it."

"I'll be asking, and soon."

I chuckle. "I figured as much."

I follow him into the house and straight into the living room, dropping the bags by the large pile of gifts already under the tree. After a round of hellos, I sit down on the sofa next to Wyatt.

"I can't believe this time next year there's going to be a baby crawling around," Mom says, grinning widely.

Sophie laughs and pats her stomach. "Neither can I."

"Dinner smells great, Tessa," Taylor says from the loveseat across the room. "Thanks for inviting me."

"You're welcome, sweetheart." She smiles at her before her eyes flick to mine. "Seb, come and help me in the kitchen."

I stand and follow her out of the living room and into the

kitchen. I can't cook for shit, so I've no idea why she's asking for my help.

"Everything okay?" I ask when we get to the kitchen, but she makes no attempt to check on the food.

"Is Taylor okay?"

I frown. "Umm, yeah, I think so. Why?"

"She looked a little upset when she came in with Paisley."

I blow out a breath. "She's missing her mom."

"I saw you hugging on the driveway. Is something going on with you two?"

"No, Mom. We're friends and she needed a hug, that's all," I lie.

She narrows her eyes. "Okay," she says slowly, and I can tell by the way she's looking at me that she doesn't believe me. "It must be a hard time of year for her. I'm glad she decided to spend it with us."

I smile. "Me too." I look around the kitchen. "So, did you need any help with the food?"

She laughs. "No, Seb. I wanted to check on Taylor. You're useless in the kitchen."

I feign hurt and clutch at my chest. "Ouch! That hurts."

She rolls her eyes. "I think you'll live."

Taylor

Despite getting upset on the driveway when Seb and I arrived, I'm having the best time. Dinner was amazing, and I love the constant chatter and laughter that fills the room when everyone's together. It's easy to see how much this family loves each other, and I'm grateful I get to be a part of it, even for a little while.

"So, Ash. What happened last night with you and Ben? We want all the details," Sophie says when Tessa and Henry are in the kitchen, and the rest of us are in the living room, stuffed from the three-course meal we've all eaten.

Paisley stiffens next to me, and although she and Nash have sorted things out after their argument this morning, I can't imagine she wants it all brought up again. I lock eyes with Seb and subtly shake my head, hoping he knows not to give Ash a hard time about Ben.

"Nothing happened. We just had a drink," she says, her eyes on her lap.

"*Nothing* happened?" Sophie asks, her eyebrows raised in question.

She sighs. "I like him, but it's complicated." She looks at Nash, Seb, Wyatt, and Cade. "He's my boss—"

"And he's way too old for you," Wyatt says, cutting her off.

She rolls her eyes. "Yeah, he's older, but if I met a guy my own age, you wouldn't like that either."

"That's true," Wyatt concedes.

She shrugs. "I'm pretty sure he doesn't see me as anything other than a work colleague. A friend at best."

I take her hand in mine and squeeze gently. "I'm sorry, Ash."

While nothing might have happened between them last night, something definitely happened a couple of weeks ago, but Ben seemed to be struggling with their connection and was blowing hot and cold. I glance at Seb. I can't help but feel like I understand her frustration, despite our situation being different.

"Well, I'm not sorry this guy doesn't see you as more than a friend," Cade says. "Wyatt's right. He's too old. He's older than me."

"Okay, guys. It's Christmas. Maybe we should give Ash a break, if only for today," Seb says.

Ashlyn stands and goes to Seb, kissing his cheek. "Thanks, Seb."

"I hope I haven't upset you by mentioning him," Sophie says, her voice laced with concern.

Ashlyn waves off Sophie's comment. "Of course not. It's his loss, right?"

She sounds blasé, but it's not hard to see she's hurting.

"It's definitely his loss, Ash."

"Who wants a wine?" Ash asks, making for the door. It's clear she doesn't want to talk about Ben anymore and is keen to end the conversation.

"I'll have one," I tell her.

"Me too," Paisley says.

"I think I'm going to take a nap," Sophie says on a yawn.

"I'll come with you," Cade says.

She shakes her head. "No. Stay. I know where your old bedroom is. I'll only be an hour." She presses a kiss on his lips before leaving the room.

Paisley goes to Nash, who's sitting on the loveseat. He opens his arms, and she climbs onto his lap, dropping her head onto his shoulder. He kisses the top of her head, and I breathe a silent sigh of relief that the conversation about Ashlyn and Ben hasn't reignited their argument.

A few minutes later, Seb stands from where he's sitting on the sofa and leaves the room. Ash hasn't come back yet, and I wonder if he's gone to find her. Seconds later, my phone vibrates in my pocket. Sliding it out, my eyes widen when I see a message from him.

Seb: Meet me upstairs.

My stomach dips and I hold the phone to my chest, even though no one can see it. Glancing around the room, Wyatt and Cade are talking, and Nash and Paisley are too wrapped up in each other to notice anything. Biting my bottom lip, my fingers fly over the screen as I reply.

Me: What for?

Seb: Just come upstairs.

Nerves swirl in my stomach as I turn my phone over in my hand.

"I'm just going to the bathroom," I mutter as I stand and make for the door, bumping into Ash, who's coming back with the drinks. "I'll be right back," I tell her before she can say anything, slipping past her and into the entryway. I quickly climb the stairs, not wanting Tessa or Henry to catch me. When I reach the top, I'm met with an empty landing. Suddenly, a door to the left opens and I'm tugged into a room.

"Seb," I gasp as he closes the door and pulls me into his arms. "What are you doing?"

"Do you know how hard it's been not to touch you or kiss you today?"

I stare at him with wide eyes. "No," I whisper.

"It's been torture, Taylor."

"Oh."

He laughs and lowers his head, his lips finding mine. I wind my arms around his neck and slide my fingers into his hair. I moan as his tongue pushes into my mouth, and he lifts me up, his hands going under my ass. He places me on the vanity and opens my legs, standing in between them. Without taking his lips off mine, he tugs me to the edge of the counter, and I wrap my legs around him. His erection presses against me and I groan into his mouth. He pulls out of the kiss and rests his forehead on mine.

"I should stop before I end up fucking you in my parents' bathroom," he whispers, his voice breathless.

My stomach flips at the thought, and I close my eyes. "And that would be bad, right?"

He chuckles. "I think it would be hot, Tay, but it's not happening."

"Tease."

He kisses me softly before stepping back and rearranging his hard cock.

"We should go downstairs before we're missed." He helps me down off the vanity.

"Thanks for sticking up for Ash before."

He frowns. "I'm always going to stick up for her, Taylor." He drags his hand through his hair. "We're only the way we are because we care."

I cup his stubbled jaw. "I know."

He smiles and takes my hand, leading me to the bathroom door. "I'll check no one is out there."

I giggle and he looks over his shoulder. "What's funny?"

"All the sneaking around. It's like we're doing something we shouldn't."

He smiles. "Aren't we? Wait there." He opens the door and pokes his head around the doorjamb. "All clear." He guides me out of the bathroom and into the hallway. "You go down first, and I'll follow in a few minutes."

Even though we're not hidden away in the bathroom anymore, he pulls me into his arms again and brushes my lips with his. I step back and make my way downstairs, his words playing in a loop in my head. Are we doing something we shouldn't? We're both adults, and we're both single, so why *are* we sneaking around like teenagers?

CHAPTER TWENTY-EIGHT

Taylor

It's New Year's Eve and almost midnight. I'm sitting in a packed Eden, wondering what the hell I'm doing. Spending Christmas Day and every night since with Seb has me wanting things I know I can't have. We're always together, and it's feeling more and more like we're in a relationship. We're not, though, despite how much I want to be. I don't know how much longer I can keep pretending I'm okay with how things are between us. He made it clear at the beginning that he didn't want anything more than sex. I was the one who convinced him I could deal with that. I can't deal with it. Not at all.

"Should we go and find Seb before midnight? It doesn't look like he's going to be able to leave the bar with how busy it is," Ashlyn shouts over the noise of the crowd, pulling me from my thoughts.

"Yes! Let's go," Paisley says. "It sucks he can't get over here."

I blow out a breath and stand as everyone files out of the booth. I want to see Seb, and I want to ring in the new year with him, but I also want to kiss him at midnight, and I know that's not going to happen. While we might spend every spare minute together, it's always behind closed doors. He's not going to kiss me in front of everyone.

"Are you okay?" Ashlyn asks as she drops back from the others and links her arm with mine. "You're quiet."

"I'm good," I tell her, forcing a smile.

She bumps her shoulder with mine. "Maybe you and Seb can sneak off to his office for five minutes."

I stop walking and she stops with me. "What?"

She smiles. "I saw him kissing you in here on Christmas Eve, and I saw how he couldn't take his eyes off you on Christmas Day. What's going on with you two?"

I blow out a breath and tug her to the side of the room and out of sight of the others. I'm desperate to talk to someone about him, and it probably shouldn't be his sister, but right now, I don't care.

"I'm in over my head with him, Ash. It was just meant to be some fun, but I'm falling for him, and I don't know what to do."

Her forehead creases in a frown. "Have you told him how you feel?"

I shake my head. "He doesn't want a relationship. He was very clear about that before…" I trail off, unsure Ash is going to want to hear about her brother's sex life.

"Before what?" she prompts.

I sigh. "Before we slept together."

"But that was then. What if he wants something else now?"

"If he does, why hasn't he said anything?"

She smiles. "Maybe for the same reason you haven't. I've seen you two together. There's something between you. You should talk to him, Tay."

"I'm worried I'll ruin everything," I whisper. "I think I'm in love with him, Ash."

She pulls me into a hug. "Please talk to him. Promise me you will?"

I step out of her embrace and offer her a small smile. "Okay."

"We should find the others. It's nearly midnight."

I nod as she slips her hand into mine and leads me through the crowd to the bar. Despite promising to talk to Seb, I have no idea what to say. How do you tell someone you've caught feelings when you promised them you wouldn't? If he doesn't feel the same, I don't know how to go back to being just his friend.

"Where did you two go?" Paisley shouts as the bar comes into view. "You were behind me and then you were gone."

"I'll fill you in later," I tell her, and she tilts her head, her eyebrows pulled together in confusion.

"Are we getting shots to have at midnight?" Ashlyn asks, and I flash her a silent thank-you for distracting Paisley from asking any more questions in front of everyone. "As Ivy, Taylor, and I have no one to kiss at midnight, we're going to need something strong to drink when we ring in the new year."

"No shot for me," Sophie says, stroking her rounded stomach.

"Count me out too," Cade says.

"Well, I've got no one to kiss either, so I'll take that shot," Wyatt says, slapping both of his hands down on the wooden bar.

"Nash? Paisley?" Ashlyn asks.

"I think I'm good with a kiss," Nash says. Paisley grins as he pulls her into his arms and kisses her.

"It's not midnight yet," Ashlyn exclaims.

"I don't think they care," I tell her, jealous I can't just pull Seb into my arms like that.

"Just four shots, then?" Wyatt asks, waving to Seb, who's at the other end of the bar.

"Hey, what are you all doing here?" Seb asks as he stands in front of Wyatt.

"We figured you were too busy to come to us, so we came to you," Wyatt says.

He smiles and waves to everyone.

"What can I get you?" he asks Wyatt.

"Four shots of tequila."

Seb raises his eyebrows. "Who's on the tequila?"

"Ash, Ivy, and Taylor are complaining they have no one to kiss at midnight, so as we're the only single ones, we're seeing in the new year with a shot of tequila. You should get one too."

Seb looks past Wyatt, his eyes finding mine. He smiles, and a million butterflies take flight in my stomach.

"Sure. I'll get one."

He turns and reaches for a bottle of tequila, some wedges of lime, and a saltshaker. Placing them on the bar, he grabs five shot glasses.

"I think we should do a practice one," he says, filling each glass with the clear liquid and placing a wedge of lime next to each glass. "Who's going first?"

"Me," Ash says, moving closer to Wyatt and picking up a glass.

"Okay, so lick, shoot, suck," Seb instructs, and Ashlyn bursts out laughing.

"It's not my first time, Seb."

He rolls his eyes. "Why doesn't that surprise me?"

He pushes the saltshaker across the bar and she sprinkles some onto her hand. After licking the salt, she drinks down the tequila and snatches up the lime, sucking the juice into her mouth.

"Taylor! You're up," she cries, banging the glass down onto the bar.

I laugh. "Okay."

When I've done my shot, Wyatt, Ivy, and Seb drink down

theirs before Seb sets them up again. He's just finished when the music stops.

"Ten seconds," the DJ shouts over the noise of the crowd.

The entire bar begins to count down from ten, and Seb pushes a shot of tequila across the bar to me, Ash, Ivy, and Wyatt. We each shake some salt onto the back of our hands, and as the countdown gets to zero, we lick the salt and swallow the clear liquid. I squeeze my eyes closed and shake my head as the liquid burns my throat.

"Happy New Year!" Ash cries as she throws her arms around my neck and hugs me tightly.

"Happy New Year," I tell her, hugging her back.

She makes her way around everyone, hugging them as she wishes them a happy New Year. I follow her lead, and when I reach Seb at the end of the bar, he slides his arms around my waist and pulls me gently against him.

"Happy New Year, Taylor," he whispers in my ear, kissing me softly on my cheek.

"Happy New Year."

"Quick. Come with me."

He steps out of our embrace and laces his fingers with mine, pulling me away from the bar and toward the security door and his office. I glance over my shoulder, but everyone is celebrating, and they don't notice us slipping away. When we reach his office, he opens the door and guides me inside. Closing the door, he backs me up against it, his hands resting on the wood on either side of my head.

"What are you doing?" I ask, my voice breathless and my heart racing at being this close to him.

"Kissing you at midnight."

He lowers his head and brushes his lips with mine. Even though I know I shouldn't, I wind my arms around his neck and kiss him back. His tongue pushes into my mouth, and I open up to him, moaning as his hands go under my ass and he picks me up. I can feel his erection pushing against me, and I roll my hips, eliciting a groan from him. My fingers wind into his hair, and I leave them there as he pulls out of the kiss and rests his forehead on mine, both of us out of breath.

"Fuck. I wish I didn't have to go back to the bar and I could take you upstairs," he mutters. He kisses me again before lowering me to the ground. "I'll come up when we close."

I don't say anything, and he uses his finger to tilt my chin so I'm looking at him.

"Are you okay?" I nod, not wanting to ask him what's happening between us when he needs to get back to the bar. He frowns. "Are you sure?"

"I'm sure." I take his hand. "Come on. We're going to be missed."

He holds my gaze, and I wonder if he can tell I'm full of shit. After a few seconds, he reaches behind me and opens the door. When we get back into Eden, he squeezes my hand before dropping it and heading back to the bar. Spotting Ashlyn and Ivy waiting in line for a drink, I head over.

"Hey, where is everyone?"

Ashlyn smiles knowingly. "Where did you disappear to?" she asks, ignoring my question.

"Just the bathroom," I lie.

Her eyebrows rise, and she looks over to where Seb is. "Funny that both you *and* Seb needed to use the bathroom at the same time." I roll my eyes. "Did you talk to him?"

"No. He had to get back to the bar. He's coming over later."

"I hope you end up with the outcome you want, Tay."

She bumps her shoulder against mine and my stomach churns with nerves.

"Why is it so fucking hard to put yourself out there?"

"Tell me about it," she mutters.

I've been so consumed with my own mess of a love life, I haven't stopped to ask what's going on with Ash.

"What's going on with you and Ben?"

She sighs. "I've no idea. I haven't heard from him since Christmas Eve. I guess I'll see him when school starts."

"I'm sorry, Ash."

She shrugs. "Me too." She plasters a smile on her face and turns to me. "Let's get smashed!"

I laugh. "Yeah. Why not? I could do with some Dutch courage."

I have no idea how I'm going to form the words to tell Seb how I feel, but I know for sure I can't carry on sleeping with him. It's too hard. I pushed him into whatever this is between us, promising him sex was all I wanted. Now it's blown up in my face and I have no one to blame but myself.

CHAPTER TWENTY-NINE

Seb

When I finally lock the door behind the last of the customers, I breathe a sigh of relief that it's closing time. It's been one hell of a long night and I want nothing more than to climb into bed with Taylor and fall asleep with her in my arms. I hope she's still awake. She went up an hour or so ago and looked a little drunk. After Cade, Sophie, Nash, and Paisley left, she Ash and Ivy started on the shots. I served them at least three times, and I know Ryder served them too. If she's passed out, I have a spare key, but I don't feel comfortable letting myself in.

After tidying up and saying goodnight to Ryder and Alex, I take the stairs to Taylor's apartment two at a time before knocking softly on her door. I don't want to wake her if she's asleep, no matter how much I want to see her. "Taylor, it's me. Are you awake?" I say through the wood, hoping she's in the living room and can hear me. When there's no response after a couple of minutes, I turn to leave. As I do, the lock clicks and the door opens.

"Did I wake you?" I ask as she stands in the doorway with the comforter wrapped around her.

"I fell asleep on the sofa."

"I didn't mean to wake you."

"That's okay. Come in."

She stands to one side, and I walk past her into the living room. When she's closed the door, I pull her gently into my arms. She tenses, and I lean back, my eyes searching hers.

"What's wrong?"

She sighs and lowers her eyes. "What are we doing, Seb?" she whispers.

I frown and lift her chin with my fingers. "What do you mean?"

"This." She gestures between us.

"I thought you knew what we were doing."

"So did I, but I don't think I can do it anymore."

My heart pounds in my chest, and an uneasy feeling washes over me. She steps out of the embrace and my arms fall from around her.

"I thought I could do the whole *friends with benefits* thing…"

She trails off and moves away from me to sit on the edge of the sofa, her head in her hands. I pull my eyebrows together in confusion and go to her, kneeling on the floor in front of the sofa.

"What's happened? Whatever it is, we can work it out."

"I don't think we can."

"Look at me, Taylor." I wait until she lifts her head, my heart squeezing in my chest when I see tears pooling in her eyes. "Talk to me." She shakes her head. "Why not?"

"You won't want to hear what I have to say."

"Try me."

She sighs loudly but holds my gaze. "I'm falling in love with you, Seb."

All the air rushes from my lungs, and I sit back on my heels. "What?"

I hang my head and blow out a breath. She can't be in love with me. That's not how this was meant to go. My heart's pounding in my chest and noise rushes through my ears. This is what I was afraid of happening. I never wanted to be the reason for Taylor's hurt, and I never wanted to break her heart. I know all too well what that feels like. Regardless of that, it seems to be happening anyway. I know for sure I can't say the words back to her, even when there's a physical pain in my chest knowing I'm not going to be able to kiss her or hold her again. We got too close and spent too much time together. I should have seen what was coming, but I was selfish and didn't want to walk away.

"Say something," she whispers.

I can't bring myself to look at her, not when I can hear the hope in her voice. The hope that I'll say I feel the same, that I love her too. I can't let myself be that vulnerable again, no matter how much I might want it.

I sigh. "I don't know what you want me to say."

"That you feel the same or that one day you might." Her voice wobbles with emotion, and it takes everything in me not to pull her into my arms.

"Taylor." My voice is pained, and I know she hears it.

"It's okay. I get it."

It's not fucking okay, but I can't tell her what she wants to hear.

"I'm sorry," I whisper.

She gives me a small smile and pulls the comforter tighter around her body. "It's my fault. I was playing with fire from the second I saw you. It was only a matter of time before I got burned."

"Fuck," I mutter, standing up and dragging my hand through my hair. "I should go." I know I'm running away, but it seems easier than staying and facing up to what she's telling me.

"Okay," she whispers, and pain spikes in my chest. Despite that, I walk to the door, and she follows.

"Bye, Taylor."

"Bye, Seb."

I step outside and she closes the door behind me. I drop my head back onto the wood and close my eyes. I can't push down the feeling that I'm making a mistake. It feels like I'm losing my best friend. Maybe I haven't been as successful in guarding my heart as I'd thought.

CHAPTER THIRTY

Seb

The next couple of weeks drag by, and as much as I don't want to admit it, I miss Taylor. I miss holding her. I miss kissing her. Hell, I just miss being around her. I've seen her a handful of times in Eden and Ashlyn brought her to Thursday roast last week, but it's not enough. Things were a little awkward between us at my parents' place, and it's never been like that, not even when she was waving her pink vibrator in my face. I fucking hate how it is between us now. I'm a miserable fucker too, snapping at the staff and the customers. Ryder's had to ask me more than once to take a break.

It's my day off, and I sit on the sofa in my apartment, staring at my phone. I've typed out a handful of messages to Taylor but deleted them all. I have no idea what to say, but I miss her and desperately want to reach out. I jump when the phone suddenly rings in my hand. For a split second, nerves explode in my stomach at the thought that Taylor might be calling me, but when I look down, it's Cade's name flashing across the screen and I'm more than a little disappointed.

"Hey, man," I say as I answer.

"Hey, Seb. Are you busy?"

"Nope. What do you need?"

"Sophie's sick and I'm on call. I have to go out for an hour. Can you come and sit with her? I don't want to leave her on her own. I've tried Paisley and Ash but neither is picking up."

A couple of months ago, I would have freaked out if he'd asked me to spend some time alone with Sophie, and while I'm concerned she's sick, it's because she's a friend and nothing more.

"Sure. What's wrong with her?"

"It's the pregnancy sickness. She can go weeks and feel fine and then suddenly, out of the blue, it hits her. She'll probably sleep the whole time you're here."

"I'm leaving now. I'll be there in five."

"Thanks, Seb."

A little over five minutes later, I pull up outside Cade and Sophie's place. Cade is on the porch, and he jogs down the steps when he sees me.

"I've really got to go," he shouts from the driveway. "I won't be long. Make yourself at home."

I raise my hand in a wave and wait on the road while he reverses off the drive. Parking my bike where his car was, I climb off and head inside. The house is silent, and I guess Sophie's still asleep. Heading into the kitchen, I open the refrigerator and grab a can of soda before making my way into the living room and flopping down on their oversized sofa. I turn the television on with the remote and search for the sports channels. Finding a baseball game that's just started, I make myself comfortable, putting my feet up on the coffee table in front of me.

About twenty minutes into the game, there's movement on the stairs.

"Cade?" Sophie says, her voice thick with sleep.

"It's me, Seb. Cade had to go on a house call. He asked me to come over in case you got sick."

I stand from the sofa and go to the bottom of the stairs. She's only wearing one of Cade's t-shirts and some panties, the material stretched over her swollen stomach.

"He didn't need to get you to come over and babysit me. I'm sure you have better things to be doing." She stops on the stairs and pulls on the material of her t-shirt. "I should get changed."

I climb a couple of the steps and take her hand, guiding her down the stairs and into the living room. "Don't on my account, and I had no plans today. I don't mind. How are you feeling?"

She smiles. "I'm feeling a lot better after a nap. Cade worries about me. I would have been fine on my own while he went out, but thank you for coming." She sits on the sofa, curling her legs underneath her and covering herself with a throw that was over the arm.

"I think I was third choice," I say with a chuckle, sitting down next to her. "Paisley and Ash didn't answer his call."

"Well, I'm glad it's you that's here. I don't feel like we spend any time together anymore." She leans over and bumps my shoulder with hers. "No plans with Taylor today, then?" She raises her eyebrows in question, and I sigh.

I should be surprised she's asking me about Taylor, but it seems my entire family knows something was going on between us, despite us trying to be discreet. "No. I'm not even sure we're friends right now."

She frowns. "Why? What happened? You looked pretty friendly outside the upstairs bathroom on Christmas Day."

My eyes widen. "You saw us kissing?" She nods. "I didn't think anyone was upstairs."

"I'd gone up to try and take a nap. I couldn't fall asleep, though. I was just coming out of Cade's old room when I saw you. I went back inside until you went downstairs. I didn't want to embarrass you. It was clear if you were sneaking around upstairs, you didn't want anyone to know."

"We weren't sneaking around..." I trail off, knowing that's exactly what we were doing.

"Was that the start of something between you two?" she asks.

"More like the end, I think."

"What happened?"

I sigh. "We'd been messing around since just after she arrived in Hope Creek. Neither of us was looking for anything serious, at least not in the beginning."

"But it developed into more?"

"I guess it did for both of us, even if I couldn't admit it to myself. She told me a couple of weeks ago that she was falling in love with me."

"And you don't feel the same?"

"Yes. No. I don't know." I drop my head into my hands and groan. It should be weird to have this conversation with Sophie knowing how I felt about her a few months ago. I can't tell her the reasons I don't want to get into a relationship, or that starting something with Taylor scares the hell out of me, but regardless of all that, I need to talk to someone about it before I lose my mind. "It doesn't matter. I don't want to be in love. I don't want to get hurt aga—"

I stop mid-sentence, realizing I'm about to say too much. She heard me, though, and I groan internally as her eyes widen.

"Again? When did I miss that you'd fallen in love? With who? When? Did Cade know?"

"That's a lot of questions, Soph."

She smiles sheepishly. "Sorry. I'm just surprised, that's all. Why didn't you tell me?"

I shrug. "I didn't tell anyone." I'm not lying. I *didn't* tell anyone. Wyatt figured it out and Nash and Paisley overheard me.

"Who was she? Do I know her?"

I hold her gaze before shaking my head. "No. You don't know her."

"What happened?"

"She was someone I could never be with. She had no idea how I felt, but my feelings for her made me realize that love makes you vulnerable."

"Why didn't you tell her how you felt?"

I look away from her, uncomfortable that the conversation is going the way it is. "She loved someone else. It was never going to happen." I shake my head. "I don't want to hurt again like that, and the last thing I wanted was for Taylor to end up feeling like I did, but that's exactly what's happened, and I hate that I've hurt her."

"It sounds like what you had with this woman was completely different to what you could have with Taylor. From what you've said, it was always going to be one-sided. Loving someone who loves you back is completely different, Seb. No one can predict the future, but I think seeing what could happen with you two is a risk worth taking."

"I just don't know if I can open myself up."

"Love is scary, but the right person will make you want to take all of those risks, even if you don't realize it right away. You just have to ask yourself if Taylor is that person."

Before I can say anything, the front door opens and Cade walks in.

"Please don't say anything to him," I whisper. She nods and reaches for my hand, squeezing it gently.

"Hey, you're awake," Cade says as he drops his bag in the entryway and walks through the archway into the living room. He leans over the sofa and kisses Sophie. "How are you feeling?"

"Better. You didn't need to ask Seb to come over. I would have been okay."

"Humor me. It made me feel better leaving you when you were sick if there was someone here with you."

"You worry too much."

He leans down and kisses her again. "It's my job to worry."

She rolls her eyes and taps him gently on the chest.

"So, Seb, what do you have planned for the rest of your day off?" Sophie asks as Cade rounds the sofa and sits next to her, resting his hand on her stomach.

"Not much. You know I'm not good with time off from the bar. I'll probably end up stopping by Eden and checking everything's okay."

Cade laughs. "I'm sure everything is fine, Seb."

I smile. "I know. I should get going, though. Leave you guys to your day."

I've told Sophie I'm going to Eden, but I actually need to pick up her and Cade's gift for her surprise baby shower tomorrow. Cade knows about the arrangements, but we've managed to keep it a secret from Sophie. I can't wait to see her face when she shows up at Nash and Paisley's and we're all waiting for her. This pregnancy's been tough, and I know she hasn't been able to relax and look forward to the baby coming when she's been so sick. I hope this baby shower is the chance for her to do that.

I stand and Sophie starts to get up too. "Don't get up." I lean down and kiss her cheek. "Thank you," I whisper in her ear.

She smiles. "Thanks for coming and sitting with me. It was good to catch up. Don't be a stranger, okay?"

"I won't. I'm glad you're feeling better. I'll see you soon."

"I'll walk you out," Cade says, following me out of the living room and onto the porch.

"Thanks, man. I owe you," Cade says, pulling me into a hug.

"You don't owe me anything, Cade." I lower my voice. "I'll see you tomorrow. She still has no idea, right?"

He shakes his head. "She thinks we're going for a barbecue at Nash and Paisley's place."

"Good. If you need me to sit with her again, let me know."

"Thanks, Seb."

I raise my hand in a wave and jog down the porch steps to my bike. Climbing on, I pull on my helmet and start the engine. Despite needing to collect Cade and Sophie's gift, I find myself riding away from Hope Creek. Being on my bike clears my head and helps me think, and right now, all I can think about is Taylor. Sophie's words play on a loop in my mind, and I can't help but wonder if Taylor *is* the woman I want to take a risk for. If I'm honest, I didn't think anyone would ever make me want to put myself out there, but meeting Taylor changed everything, and I can't deny that anymore. I need to talk to her and tell her how I feel. I just hope she'll want to listen.

CHAPTER THIRTY-ONE

Taylor

It's the day of Sophie and Cade's baby shower, and I've spent the past week helping Ash to plan it all. I'm grateful she asked me to be involved. It's been a welcome distraction from thinking about Seb and what he's doing. I've seen him a handful of times. I guess it's hard to avoid him when I live above his bar. I didn't expect to see him when Ash invited me to Thursday roast, though. She assured me he wasn't going to be there. When he arrived five minutes after us, I'd seen her sheepish smile, and while I knew she meant well, trying to get us into the same room and talking, it just ended up being awkward and painful. It hurts to see him, and I know it will for a while.

"Do you think we need more balloons?" Ashlyn asks as she rushes into the living room, her arms full of bunting.

I look around the balloon-filled room with wide eyes. "Ash, if you put any more balloons in here, there won't be any room for *people*. No more balloons!"

"Okay. I just want it to be perfect."

I put my hand on her arm. "It looks incredible, Ash. Sophie is going to love it. Let's hang the bunting and then I think we're done until the food arrives."

"Shit! The food! It should be here by now."

"It'll be here," I assure her. I've barely finished my sentence when there's a knock on the door. "See. I bet that's the caterers now."

I chuckle as she tosses the bunting onto the sofa and rushes out of the living room to answer the door. I follow her, relieved when I see the catering company bringing in armfuls of food.

"The kitchen's through there," Ash says, holding the door open and directing them through the entryway. When they're all in the house, she closes the door and turns to me. "God, this is stressful. Remind me never to volunteer to organize anything again."

"Aren't you and Paisley organizing Sophie's belated bachelorette after this?"

She groans and drops her head back. "Paisley can do it!"

I laugh. "Let's get through one event before we worry about the next."

I take her hand and pull her into the living room where we spend the next fifteen minutes displaying the bunting. The room looks incredible when we're done, and I can't wait to see Sophie's face when she walks in here.

"We're back," a voice shouts from the entryway, and nerves erupt in my stomach. Paisley and Nash went to pick up Seb, and I can't help but feel apprehensive about seeing him today.

"I'll go and check on the caterers," I say to Ash. "See if they need anything."

She smiles sadly at me. "You can't avoid him all day, Tay."

"I can try," I whisper before turning and making my way into the kitchen through the door off the living room.

I breathe a sigh of relief when I've made my escape and spend the next ten minutes hiding in the kitchen. The caterers have everything under control, and if anything, I'm in their way. I can't force myself to leave, though, and I busy myself organizing and reorganizing the array of drinks that sit on the countertop.

"Taylor," a voice says from behind me. My stomach dips knowing it's Seb. Taking a deep breath, I slowly turn around. "Hey," he says quietly.

"Hey," I whisper, unable to stop my gaze from tracking all over him. He looks good. Too good. He's wearing black jeans that are pushed into lace-up boots and a dark green t-shirt stretches tight across his chest, his inked arms bulging from the sleeves. There's dark stubble on his jaw, and his hair is styled to look messy. My heart squeezes in my chest when my eyes finally find his, and I wish it didn't hurt so much to be this close to him.

"How've you been?"

I shrug slightly and lower my eyes. "I've been all right. You?"

"Yeah. Same." He sighs loudly, and I raise my eyes. He's dragging his hand through his hair and shifting nervously from foot to foot. "Do you think we could maybe talk later? After the shower, I mean."

A tiny flicker of hope ignites in my chest, and I nod. "Okay."

"I miss you, Tay," he says so quietly I almost miss it.

"I miss you too."

"Taylor. There you are," a voice shouts, interrupting our conversation. I look past Seb and see Tessa walking toward me. She pulls me into a hug. "Everything looks incredible, sweetheart. Thank you for all you've done to make this special for Sophie and Cade."

My eyes find Seb's over her shoulder, and he smiles.

"It was all Ashlyn. I just helped," I tell her as she steps out of the embrace.

"Nonsense," she says, waving off my comment. "Ashlyn said she couldn't have done it without you."

Suddenly, the kitchen door flies open, and Ashlyn appears. "Quick," she says, beckoning us with her arm. "Cade's just messaged. They're nearly here."

Ash's voice betrays her excitement, and I smile at Tessa.

"I'm not sure who's going to be more excited today," I say with a chuckle.

My eyes flick to Seb as I follow Ashlyn and Tessa out of the kitchen, and I can't help but wonder what he wants to talk about. A part of me hopes he's changed his mind and wants to give things a go, but I know that's unlikely. I've missed him so much these past couple of weeks. I've gone from falling asleep in his arms almost every night to barely seeing him at all. As much as I want to see him, it seems easier to keep my distance. It only hurts when I'm around him.

When Sophie arrives with Cade, she's overwhelmed by the surprise. Both she and Ash are crying within minutes, but they're undoubtably happy tears, and we spend the next hour playing baby-related games before Sophie and Cade open their mountain of gifts. As well as immediate family, Bree and Leo are here, and it's nice to catch up with Bree. I haven't spoken to Seb again, but I've caught him watching me a couple of times and my stomach erupts with butterflies every time his eyes lock with mine.

I'm in the kitchen grabbing a soda when pain explodes in my lower stomach. I grip tightly onto the refrigerator door and breathe deeply as I wait for the cramp to pass. I know what the pain means. My body has the worst timing. The pain instantly makes me feel sick, and as much as I'm enjoying the shower, the only place I want to be is at home.

When the pain has eased a little, I make my way into the living room where, thankfully, it's only the girls. The guys are out on the patio, toasting despite the baby not being born yet.

"Are you okay, Tay?" Paisley asks, her brow furrowed in concern.

Everyone turns to look at me and my face flushes with heat. "I need to go home, take some pain meds, and lie down." Paisley flashes me a sympathetic smile, knowing how bad my periods can be. I turn to Sophie. "I'm sorry I have to leave early, Soph. I hope you've had a great day."

She stands from where she's sitting, her face clouded with concern. "Do you want me to get Cade?"

I shake my head. "No. I'll be fine."

She frowns. "Are you sure? He won't mind."

I place my hand on her arm. "I'm sure. I just need to lie down."

She pulls me into a hug. "Okay. Thank you for helping Ash to arrange all of this, Taylor. I still can't believe it."

I chuckle and step out of her embrace. "You deserve it after everything you've been through. Enjoy the rest of your day."

I quickly say goodbye to everyone, and Paisley follows me into the entryway.

"I'll give you a ride," she says, picking up the keys to Nash's truck off the small table.

"No. Stay. I can walk."

"Taylor, I can see the pain on your face. There's no way I'm letting you walk. It'll take me five minutes to drive you home. No arguing."

"Thank you."

She waves off my thanks and links her arm with mine as we walk outside to Nash's truck. We're both quiet on the short drive to Eden, and when we pull up outside, she reaches across the cab and takes my hand.

"How are you doing? Aside from the cramps, I mean."

Paisley knows about what happened with Seb. She's been my sounding board as well as a shoulder to cry on over the past two weeks. She wanted to speak to him, but I begged her not to. If Seb wants to be with me, then it has to be his decision and not because anyone's talked him into it.

I shrug. "I'm okay. He said he missed me earlier and asked if we could talk after the baby shower."

"About giving things a go?"

"I don't know," I whisper. "I can't help but hope he might want to."

"I hope so too, Tay." She squeezes my hand. "Does he know you've come home?"

"No. I'll message him. Thanks for the ride."

"Feel better. I'll call you later."

I climb out of the truck and head into Eden. I'm grateful the bar's busy and I'm able to slip through the crowd and up to my apartment without being seen. Ten minutes later, I'm on the sofa with my sweats on and a heating pad pressed against my stomach. I've taken some Tylenol and I'm snuggled under a blanket. I'm just about to reach for my phone to let Seb know I had to leave when it chimes with an incoming message. Reaching for it, I find his name on the screen.

Seb: Are you okay? Paisley said you had to leave.

My fingers fly over the screen as I type out a reply.

Me: I'm okay. Taken some painkillers and doing better now.

Seb: Do you want me to come over?

I stare at the screen. Does he mean come over to see if I'm

okay or to talk? I don't want him to leave his brother's baby shower early to check on me.

Me: Later, if you still want to talk. Don't miss Cade and Sophie's shower.

Seb: I still want to talk, Tay. Do you need anything?

Nerves swirl in my stomach as I read his message.

Me: No, I'm okay, thanks. See you later.

Seb: See you soon.

I frown. I hope he doesn't decide to leave the shower early because of me.

CHAPTER THIRTY-TWO

Seb

When Paisley tells me Taylor's sick, the pull to go to her is like nothing I've ever felt before. I don't know how I ever thought we could just be friends. I'm in too deep. I should know after falling for Sophie that love isn't something you get a say in.

About half an hour after messaging Taylor, the baby shower is winding down and I'm helping Cade load his car with the mountain of gifts people have brought for the baby.

"Who knew you needed this much stuff for a baby," I say as I place the bassinet I bought them on the back seat of Cade's car.

He chuckles. "I know, right? We're going to need a bigger house and they're not even born yet."

When we get back inside, Sophie's in the entryway saying goodbye to everyone. She's teary again, and Cade goes to her, sliding his arm around her waist and tugging her gently into his side. After they leave, I briefly help to tidy up before making my excuses and leaving too. I'm just climbing onto my bike when Paisley comes running out of the house.

I frown. "Everything okay?"

She moves nervously from foot to foot and lowers her eyes to the ground. "I probably shouldn't say anything…" She trails off.

"But you're going to anyway?" I chuckle.

"Taylor told me what happened with you two." The laughter dies in my throat, and I sigh. "She's been a mess, Seb."

My heart twists in my chest, knowing she's hurting, and it's because of me.

"Fuck," I mutter.

"I know you've been the same as well. I don't think you were this miserable when you were getting over Sophie," she says. "You should think about what that means." She waves her arm. "I've probably said too much, but I care about you both and I want you to be happy."

I climb off the bike and pull her into a hug. She's right. As much as I thought I was in love with Sophie, how I feel about losing Taylor makes me question what I felt for Sophie. "I'm going to her place now. I finally got my head out of my ass like everyone said I should."

She steps out of my embrace and grins. "Go! Quickly!" I laugh as she pushes me gently toward the bike. "Tell Taylor I want to know *everything*."

I pull on my helmet and ride away, leaving an excited Paisley behind me. I stop at the grocery store, grabbing some chocolate for Taylor before parking at the back of Eden, bypassing the bar. I should check everything's okay, but I want to see Taylor. I take the stairs to her apartment two at a time but pause when I reach the door. Taking a couple of deep breaths, I lift my hand and knock on the wood. The door swings open and Taylor stands in front of me wrapped in a blanket.

"Hey. How are you feeling?" I ask, noticing how pale her face is.

"Hey, come in. I'm okay. The pain meds have kicked in."

"Good."

She turns and walks back into the apartment, and I follow her, closing the door behind me. She sits on the sofa, curling her legs underneath her.

"Help yourself to a drink. There's soda in the fridge."

I place the brown paper bag on the sofa next to her and walk across the apartment to the kitchen.

"Do you want anything?"

"I'll have a soda, please."

Reaching inside the refrigerator, I take out two cans and go back to her, sitting down.

"Thanks," she says as I pass her a drink. "What's in the bag?" she asks, sitting up and peeking inside.

I chuckle. "I got you some chocolate."

She looks across at me and smiles. "Thank you." She reaches inside and pulls out the large bar. Opening it, she breaks off a piece and holds it out to me.

I smile and take it from her.

"How did the rest of the shower go?" she asks when she's swallowed her mouthful of chocolate.

"It was good. I don't think I realized how much *stuff* a baby needs. We struggled to get it all in Cade's car."

She laughs. "There were a lot of gifts. I wish I could have stayed."

"I was worried when Paisley said you were sick."

She looks at me. "You were?"

I nod, taking the can of soda out of her hand and placing it on the side table with mine. Picking up her hand, I stroke my thumb gently over her skin.

"I'm sorry I was such an idiot when you told me how you felt.

I..." I trail off and drag my free hand through my hair. "I didn't know how to deal with it."

"You have nothing to apologize for. I knew the score when we started sleeping together. I should never have let things get as far as they did." She sighs. "I guess the more time we spent together, the more I hoped you'd start to feel things too."

"Taylor—"

"It's okay, Seb," she says, cutting me off and lowering her eyes to our joined hands. "Right now, I just want our friendship back. I miss you."

I continue to rub my thumb over the back of her hand and smile. "I don't think being friends is a good idea."

Her wide eyes meet mine. "You don't want to be friends anymore?"

"No. I don't think we can ever go back to being friends."

"What?"

She looks confused, and I guess after freaking out and avoiding her for two weeks, I can't expect anything else.

"I'm saying I want to give this thing between us a go, Tay. I'm not going to sit here and pretend to know what I'm doing, but I want to try. *You* make me want to try."

Nerves swirl in my stomach as I wait for her to respond. I guess I've been a jackass these past couple of weeks and there's a chance she doesn't think I'm worth risking her heart for. When she's silent for longer than I'd like, a wave of nausea washes over me and I realize I might be too late.

"I mean, if you've changed your mind—"

She smiles. "I haven't, Seb. I want to try too," she says, cutting me off.

Relief crashes over me and I reach for her, pulling her into my lap.

"You do?" She nods. "Thank God."

I cup her neck and bring my mouth to hers, kissing her softly.

Her lips brush against mine, and although it's only been a couple of weeks since I kissed her, it feels like forever. She pulls out of the kiss and rests her forehead on mine.

"I missed you so much, Seb."

"I missed you too." She lifts her head and worries her bottom lip. "What's wrong?"

"What made you change your mind? You seemed pretty set on not wanting a relationship."

I gently stroke her cheek, my hand still on her neck. "We were already in a relationship, even if it was one no one knew about. It took me a while to realize that. I wanted to spend all my time with you. That's more than sex."

"So, you're not afraid anymore?"

"Honestly?" She nods. "I'm terrified, Taylor. I don't ever want to hurt you and I don't want to get hurt either, but I want to take the risk with you. You're worth it."

"I promise to never intentionally hurt you, Seb, and I know you'd never intentionally hurt me."

"Haven't I already hurt you?" I ask quietly.

She sighs. "You were guarding your heart. I get it." She presses her lips to mine again in a soft kiss. "I hope one day soon you'll be able to tell me why you're so wary of love."

I hold her gaze. I don't know if I'll ever be able to tell her about Sophie. I hope I will, but I can't promise to. I don't want to start our relationship on a lie, though.

"I hope I will too. I'm so sorry I hurt you. That's the last thing I wanted."

"I know," she whispers, her head dropping onto my shoulder. I tighten my hold on her, loving how perfectly she fits in my arms.

When her body tenses, I know she's in pain. "Do you need more pain meds, sweetheart?"

She nods. "The Advil, please. I took some Tylenol earlier."

I brush a kiss on her forehead and stand up with her in my

arms. Lowering her onto the sofa, I go into the kitchen and grab the Advil, along with a glass of water. I hand both to her and she swallows them down, the heating pad covering her stomach.

"Lie down," I tell her, guiding her so her head is in my lap. I gently stroke my fingers through her hair, and it isn't long before her breathing's evened out and she's asleep.

I think if I'm honest with myself, I fell for her a while ago, I just wasn't ready to admit it. It took her walking away to realize what she means to me. After speaking to Sophie, I knew I didn't want to lose her. I wasn't lying when I said I was terrified. I've never done the whole relationship thing, and I have no idea what I'm doing. I do know I want to be with her, though. As scary as it is, maybe Nash was right when he said Taylor could be my big love. It's definitely starting to feel like that.

CHAPTER THIRTY-THREE

Taylor

"Hey, baby. You ready to go?" Seb calls out as he lets himself into my apartment.

"I'll be out in a minute," I shout back. "I'm just getting dressed." Seconds later, my bedroom door opens. Turning, I smile as he stands in the doorway. "I'm not ready yet."

My eyes sweep over him and heat pools in my stomach as I take him in. He's wearing dark dress pants and a white shirt. The top button is open, and his sleeves are rolled up, putting plenty of his ink on display. There's dark stubble on his jaw, and his hair is messy.

"You look sexy."

He chuckles. "So do you, sweetheart."

I giggle. "I'm not dressed."

"Exactly."

Before I can reply, he's crossed the room and I'm in his arms.

"We're going to be late," I mutter as his mouth drops to my neck. Despite that, I tilt my head to give him better access. "You're staying over tonight, right?" I moan as he bites gently on the skin under my ear before soothing it with his tongue.

"I stay over every night, Tay," he mumbles against my neck. "And now that I know what's going to be under your dress…" He trails off and runs his fingers around the elastic of my baby-pink panties. "I'm going to be hard all night."

My clit pulses at his words. We've done nothing more than make out since we officially got together, my period calling the shots. It's finished now, though, and I'm aching for him to touch me. I want to touch him too. How can I not when he looks like he does?

"Do we have to go tonight? We could stay here instead," he says against my skin.

"Your brother and my best friend just got engaged. I think they might be pissed if we don't show up," I tell him with a giggle.

"I've got another brother. I'll go to his engagement meal."

He kisses me again, leaving me breathless and unable to remember my name. When he pulls back, it takes me a few seconds to come back down to earth.

"We're going. Maybe we can sneak to the bathroom between courses?" I whisper in his ear.

With his arms still around me, he leans back, his eyes searching mine. "No way."

"Why not?"

"I'm not making love to you for the first time as my girlfriend in the bathroom of Franco's. It's not happening."

My eyes widen and a huge smile appears on my face. "Your girlfriend?"

He smiles back at me. "Yes, Taylor. My girlfriend. What did you think was happening between us?"

"You've never called me your girlfriend before."

"Do you like it?"

"I love it."

"I love it too. You'd better get dressed if you're insisting we go. Making love to you will have to wait until later."

He kisses me on the nose before releasing his hold on me and sitting down on the bed.

"What are you doing?" I ask as his eyes stay fixed on me.

"Watching you get dressed. The view's better in here."

I roll my eyes and open my closet, reaching inside for the electric-blue pencil dress I wore when we met up with Wyatt in Phoenix. I remember Seb loved it last time, and I'm hoping the same is true now. I hang the dress on the open door of my closet as I reach around and unclip my bra, sliding the straps down my arms. The dress is too low to wear one, and I look over my shoulder, Seb's eyes fixed on me. Laughing, I toss the bra at him before reaching for the dress and slipping it on.

"Can you zip me up?" I ask, standing with my back to him.

He blows out a breath as he stands and reaches for the zipper.

"You're killing me, baby," he mumbles, his fingers skating over my spine as he pulls the zipper up. I lift my curled hair over my shoulder as his fingers climb higher. When he's done, he brushes a kiss on my bare shoulder. "Turn around, Taylor." His voice is low and husky, and I love that I'm having this effect on him.

I slowly turn around and his eyes sweep over my body.

"You're so fucking beautiful. I'm not going to be able to keep my hands off you tonight."

"Then don't. I love it when you touch me, even if it's only holding my hand."

He smiles. "Let's go so we can get this over with and I can get you back here and naked."

I turn and slip my feet into my nude heels. "You don't mean that."

"I do!"

"Not the bit about getting the meal over and done with."

He sighs. "No. Maybe not that bit. I'm happy for them. I was wondering when he was going to pluck up the courage to ask her when he wimped out at Christmas."

"What? He was going to ask her at Christmas? Why didn't you tell me?"

"I didn't want to spoil the surprise."

"Why did he wimp out?" I reach out and place my hand on his arm. "He wasn't having second thoughts, was he?"

"Hell no! I think he'd have married her months ago if he thought she'd say yes. He was going to propose on Christmas Day and then they had that argument about Ash. He said he didn't want to ask her on the back of an argument."

I nod, remembering how upset Paisley had been when they'd argued. While they sorted things out pretty quickly, I think Nash was right to wait. Paisley had excitedly told me he'd taken her back to the lake where they'd had their first date and asked her to marry him. She had no idea he was going to propose, but there had been no doubt in her mind she wanted to spend the rest of her life with him. I couldn't wait to celebrate with them and the rest of the Brookes family. After everything she went through before she came to Hope Creek, she deserves more than anyone to be happy, and I've never seen her happier than when she's with Nash.

A few minutes later, we're ready to leave. The restaurant is just around the corner from the bar, so we're walking. It's a good thing we're walking. I'm not sure I'd be able to get on Seb's bike in this dress. I can't help but feel a little apprehensive as we head downstairs and into Eden. Despite meeting Seb's parents quite a few times since moving to Hope Creek, tonight will be the first time meeting them as his girlfriend. I already have a good relationship with everyone in his family, but it feels different now that we're together.

"You okay? You're quiet," Seb says as we reach the security door that takes us into Eden.

"Just a little nervous."

"Nervous? Why?"

"I'm going to be meeting your parents tonight."

He frowns. "You've met them tons of times."

"Not as your girlfriend. What if they like me as your friend but not your girlfriend?"

His eyebrows pull together in confusion. "You're serious, aren't you?" I nod and he wraps his arms around me, pulling me against his chest. "Baby, my parents love you. They're going to be happy. I promise."

I bite my lip. "Maybe you should have told them about us before tonight."

He shakes his head. "You have nothing to worry about, okay?" He holds my gaze and reaches his finger up to pull my lip from between my teeth. "Okay?" he asks again.

"Okay."

I'm still nervous, despite what he's said, but he slips his hand in mine and squeezes encouragingly.

"Come on. Let's get going."

We walk hand in hand into Eden, and Ryder smiles when he sees us.

"Have a great time. Tell Nash and Paisley I said congratulations," he shouts as we head past the bar.

"Will do," Seb shouts back, raising his hand in a wave.

When we get out onto the sidewalk, nerves bubble in my stomach. Seb's parents are just across the street from us, climbing out of their parked car. Although I'm nervous, I'm glad we're seeing them outside and not in front of everyone in the restaurant. As we get closer, Tessa's eyes drop to our joined hands, and she smiles.

"Well, it's about time," she says as she pulls Seb in for a hug. "I wondered how long it would take." She turns and hugs me too.

"What does that mean?" he asks, sliding his arm around my waist and pulling me against his side.

"It means it doesn't take a genius to see the connection between you two. Even your dad noticed."

"I can't decide if there's a compliment or an insult in that comment," Henry says as he shakes Seb's hand and smiles at me. His voice is full of humor.

"Oh, hush," Tessa says, waving her arm. She takes my hand in hers. "I'm happy for both of you."

"Thanks, Mom."

Seb squeezes my waist and I look up at him. He smiles and brushes a kiss on my lips.

"One son married, one engaged, and another in love. I thought the day would never come," Tessa says, taking Henry's arm and leaving us on the sidewalk as they head into the restaurant.

My eyes widen at her words. While I might have told Seb I love him, I know he's not there yet, and that's fine. I don't want to rush him into saying the words if he doesn't mean them. I know falling in love isn't something he thought would ever happen again after he got hurt before. I do love him, though, and I can't imagine walking away from him. I wish he'd open up to me. I've tried a couple of times to talk to him about his past, but he shuts me down every time. I have to admit, his reluctance to talk makes me a little nervous. I've been someone's second choice before, and I don't want to be second choice again.

"We should head inside," Seb says. "I think everyone else is already here."

We walk hand in hand into Franco's, and I smile when we're led into a private dining room where everyone's already seated. Chatter and laughter fill the air, and although I've only been in

Hope Creek for a short while, the people in this room are fast becoming the family I always longed for. While I wish every day that my mom was still here, it was only ever me and her growing up, and I can't deny that I was lonely sometimes. I don't think I could ever be lonely in Hope Creek, not with my best friend and the family she's going to marry into all around me.

CHAPTER THIRTY-FOUR

Seb

Nash and Paisley's engagement meal is the first time Taylor and I have been out together as a couple. Knowing I can hold her hand or kiss her whenever I want isn't something I thought I'd crave as much as I do. I don't think ten minutes have passed where I haven't been touching her, even if it's just a hand on her leg. I love that I'm able to be this way with her.

I saw her reaction when my mom mentioned me being in love. Despite Taylor telling me how she felt a few weeks ago, neither of us has mentioned the *L* word since. My mom's right. I'm pretty sure I'm falling in love with her. It feels too soon to voice it, though. I don't want to jinx anything. I'm happy as we are, and I think Taylor is too.

"Can I have everyone's attention," Nash says, standing and tapping a knife on his champagne glass. I look over, and he and

Paisley stand. "As well as thanking everyone for coming and celebrating with us tonight, we have an announcement to make."

"Another one," Wyatt shouts, humor lacing his voice. "You've only just announced the engagement."

"Shut up, Wyatt," Ashlyn says. I'm guessing from the way Wyatt yelps that she's kicked him under the table.

Nash chuckles. "So, as I was saying, me and my fiancée—"

A cheer erupts around the table when Nash refers to Paisley as his fiancée and Nash turns to her, pressing a kiss on her lips.

"Me and my *fiancée*," he exaggerates the word and grins at her. "Have set a date for the wedding. Neither of us wants a long engagement or a huge wedding, so we've set the date for February fourteenth."

"February fourteenth? That's in…" Ashlyn pauses and uses her fingers to count the days. "Three weeks!"

"Yep. Twenty-two days," Paisley says, smiling widely.

"I think we have some organizing to do," Mom says, standing from the table and walking to where Nash and Paisley are, hugging them both. "Have you thought about where you want the ceremony?"

"We were hoping we could get married at the house. Would that be okay?" Nash asks as he slips his arm around Paisley and pulls her into his side.

My mom looks across at my dad, tears pooling in her eyes. I flick my eyes to my dad, who smiles before standing and going to her.

"We would be honored, son," Dad says, pulling Nash into a hug and then hugging Paisley. "Your mom always hoped one of you would want to get married at the house."

"You did?" Nash asks. "You never said."

"I didn't want any of you to feel you had to but I always thought the backyard would look beautiful all dressed for a wedding."

"It's perfect. I hope you'll help us organize everything," Paisley says shyly.

From what Nash has told me, she doesn't have a relationship with her parents. Planning your wedding day must be hard without your family, but I know how much my mom and dad, along with the whole Brookes clan, adore her. She's got a new family now.

"Of course I will. You should both come over for dinner tomorrow and we'll get started. We don't have long." She gasps and reaches for Paisley's hand. "I'll call the bridal boutique in River Falls on Monday and schedule an appointment to go and try on some dresses. We might have to buy off the rack, but they'll still need some time for alterations, and then there's the flowers and the cake."

She finally pauses for breath, and I can't help but smile. Only twelve months ago, I can remember her saying that with how single we all were, she was never going to get the chance to help plan a wedding or become a grams. Now, Cade and Sophie are married with baby Brookes due soon, and Nash and Paisley are planning their wedding. It's incredible to think what can change in a relatively small space of time.

I glance across at Taylor, who's watching the exchange between Paisley and my mom. When a single tear slips down her cheek, I frown and reach for her hand.

"Are you okay, baby?"

She nods and wipes the tears away. "I'm so happy for them," she says quietly. "I never knew how desperately she needed to get away from Pittsburgh until she called me the day after Connor beat her up. I knew he was rough with her, but she never told me how bad it was. I should have done more."

I squeeze her hand. "It wasn't your fault, Taylor. You did all you could, and you helped her get away. She's happy now."

She nods. "Yeah, she is…" She trails off. "I never thought I'd see her again when I found out she was in Hope Creek. It's so far away from Pittsburgh."

I lean in and kiss her cheek. "I'm glad you decided to make the move here," I whisper in her ear. She turns her head so her lips are half an inch from mine.

"So am I," she says before pressing her lips to mine.

"Can I steal her away?" a voice says from behind me, and I reluctantly pull my lips from hers.

I smile, knowing it's Paisley. "I can share her for a few minutes," I say over my shoulder, and she smiles back.

"You two are so cute. I'm glad you managed to work things out. I won't keep her long. I just need to ask her something."

I stand and pull her into a hug. "Congratulations, Paisley. I'm so happy for you and Nash."

"Thanks, Seb."

She hugs me back and steps away, reaching for Taylor's hand. I wink at Taylor as she stands and lets Paisley pull her to the corner of the room. I can't hear what they're saying, but whatever it is has them both crying and hugging. I frown and lean across the table.

"Why are they crying?" I ask Nash, interrupting his conversation with Cade. I gesture with my head to Paisley and Taylor.

He looks over and smiles. "Because weddings make women cry."

When I look over again, Taylor's making her way back to me while Paisley goes to speak to Ash.

"Everything okay?" I ask as she sits next to me.

She nods. "Paisley asked me to be her bridesmaid."

"That's great, baby."

I lean in and gently swipe my thumbs over her cheeks, wiping away her tears. I know they're happy tears, but either way, I hate to see her cry.

"You'll be one of my best men, right?" Nash shouts across the table, interrupting our moment, and I chuckle.

"Try and stop me." I turn to Taylor and grin. "Looks like we're both in the wedding."

"Of course you are. You're his brother."

"I thought he might ask Cade as he's the oldest, but it looks like he's having us all."

She bites on her bottom lip and my eyes fall to her mouth. "I can't wait to see you in a suit."

I groan internally. I'm more of a jeans-and-boots kind of guy. I wore a suit for Cade and Sophie's wedding because Sophie asked me to. I didn't think I'd have to be wearing another one so soon, although the way Taylor's looking at me, I think being uncomfortable for a few hours will be more than worth it.

"Hey. We should share bachelorette parties," Sophie says. "Mine is next weekend anyway. What do you think, Paisley?"

"I'd love to. If you're sure."

"Of course I'm sure! You're already like a sister to me, and in a few weeks, you really will be my sister."

"We should do the same," Cade says. "A joint bachelor party."

"Sounds good to me. Aren't we doing our own thing in the day and then meeting up with the girls in Eden anyway?" Nash asks.

"Yeah, that was the plan. We have the spa booked while you boys go fishing," Ash confirms.

"This is going to get messy," Wyatt says, and a laugh erupts around the table.

I don't think for a second a fishing trip at the lake is going to get messy. I'm looking forward to it, though. We haven't all spent time together with Dad in a long time.

An hour later, everyone's leaving. After a round of goodbyes, I slip my hand in Taylor's and we walk back to Eden. The singer that was performing tonight has finished and some of the crowd from earlier has dispersed.

"Do you want a drink before we go up?" I ask as I guide her between the tables.

"Do you?"

I stop, turn, and hold her gaze. "No. I want to take you upstairs, peel your dress off, and kiss every inch of you."

She smiles. "Mmm, that sounds way better than a drink."

I lean down, my lips brushing her ear. "Good, because I don't think I can wait a second longer."

"Then don't," she says, tugging me through the bar and up to her apartment.

It seems she's as eager as me to be alone, and I love that.

CHAPTER THIRTY-FIVE

Taylor

We're barely through the apartment door and I'm in Seb's arms. He's kissing me like he hasn't seen me in weeks, and I love how urgent his kisses are. My fingers go to his shirt, and I pull the material free from his pants. Undoing the buttons, I slide my hands up his chest and over his shoulders, pushing the material off his body. When his shirt drops to the floor, I walk him backwards toward my bedroom, his lips still on mine. As we walk, his fingers go to the zipper on my dress, and he slowly lowers it. When his legs hit the bed, I pull out of the kiss and push him gently onto the comforter.

His gaze fixes on me as he sits up on his elbows and watches me with heated eyes as I slowly remove my dress, leaving me in just my lace panties.

"Holy fuck," he mutters, moving onto his knees and holding out his hand. "Come here, baby." I kick off my heeled pumps and climb onto the bed with him. He rolls me underneath him, bringing his body over mine. "You're so beautiful."

My cheeks flush at his compliment, and I wrap my arms around his neck and pull his head down to mine. "Kiss me," I mutter against his lips.

"With pleasure."

His lips find mine again in a searing kiss, and when he bites down on my bottom lip, I open up to him, our tongues dancing together. My fingers tug on the hair at the nape of his neck, eliciting a moan from him. His erection presses against the thin material of my panties and I lift my hips, trying to dull the ache that's growing there.

"God. You make me crazy, Tay," he mumbles, brushing kisses along my jaw and down my neck.

Despite it only being a few weeks since we slept together, it feels like longer, and my body aches for him.

"Please, Seb," I moan as his lips go lower, sucking one of my nipples into his mouth. I arch my back as his tongue circles my bud.

"Fuck! I need to be inside you," he says, climbing off the bed and kicking his pants to the side. My eyes drop to the erection that's tenting his underwear, and I watch as he palms himself through the material. My clit pulses, and I squirm on the bed. He quickly removes his boxers before coming back to me. He tugs my underwear down my legs and, taking himself in his hand, he starts to gently push inside me.

"Shit!" he says, pulling back. "I forgot the condom."

My eyes widen. I was so caught up in the moment, I don't think I'd have noticed if he hadn't.

He kisses me softly on the lips before leaning over the side of the bed and grabbing his wallet. In seconds, he's rolling a condom down his length before settling back between my legs.

"You okay?" he asks, his hand cupping my face.

I nod and tilt my head, pressing a kiss onto the palm of his hand.

He smiles before pushing gently inside me. I gasp and close my eyes as he fills me. My hands cling tightly to his shoulders and my nails dig into his skin as he begins to move.

"Open your eyes," he whispers.

I do as he says and our eyes lock. Our gazes stay fixed on each other as he continues to move against me. I've never had sex like this, and I've never felt as close to someone as I do right now. He lowers his head and kisses me before slipping his hand between our bodies and circling my clit with his fingers. I moan into his mouth as bursts of electricity shoot through my body at his touch.

"Jesus, Seb."

I wind my legs around his back and, using my feet, I drive him further inside me. As incredible as he feels, I want more.

"Can I go on top?" I ask, feeling a little shy.

He stills inside me and grins. "Baby, you never have to ask that. The answer will always be yes."

I squeal as he rolls us over, putting him underneath me. His hands go to my waist as I sit up, his cock still buried inside me. I roll my hips and he groans, his head dropping back onto the bed.

"Fuck, Tay. You feel so good."

"You feel good too."

I continue to roll my hips, and when his breathing begins to get ragged, he sits up and wraps his arms around me. When he moves, I gasp as my clit brushes against him with every thrust.

"I think I can come like this," I mutter, loving how he makes my body come alive.

"Is that a first like this?" he asks, his voice breathless.

I nod, and he smiles. He moves faster against me, and I hold onto his shoulders, my orgasm right there.

"Oh, God. I think I'm going to come."

His hand reaches up and pinches my nipple between his

LAURA FARR

fingers. That pushes me over the edge and my entire body shudders in his arms as my orgasm crashes over me. Wave after wave of pleasure rolls through me, and my release must trigger his own as he comes on a cry.

His arms hold me against him as our breathing evens out, and I can feel his heart pounding in his chest. I know mine mirrors his.

When he's caught his breath, he leans back, pressing his lips to mine.

"That was something else, Taylor." I smile and he smiles back. "I should clean up." He kisses me again before lifting me gently off him. "I'll be right back. Keep the bed warm."

He winks, and I watch him walk naked to the bathroom before flopping backward onto the bed. I can't remember being this happy in a long time, and after everything, I'm having to pinch myself to believe this is really happening.

When Seb finishes in the bathroom, he slides naked under the comforter and reaches for me.

"Come here, baby." He opens his arms and I scoot across the bed, pressing my body against his. "Are you okay?"

"I'm good." My fingers draw lazy circles over his chest. "Which was your first tattoo?" I ask, my eyes tracking over his ink.

He points to the top of the arm that's wrapped around me. "This one."

I sit up and drag my fingers over the tribal design that starts on his shoulder and descends down his arm.

"You were eighteen, right?" He nods. "What made you want to get one?"

"I wanted something that was just for me."

"What do you mean?"

"I love Wyatt. He's my best friend, but being an identical twin means you sometimes lose yourself. People tend to only see one person. When I got to eighteen, I wanted people to see *me*. The tattoos did that."

I frown. "I'm sorry you felt like that."

He sits up and reaches for me, pulling me into his lap. My legs straddle his, and he wraps his arms around me.

"Don't be sorry. I had the best childhood, and most of the time I loved being a twin." He laughs. "We had *a lot* of fun. I think getting the tattoo was just me telling people I was my own person."

"But you're covered in ink, Seb. How long did you feel that way?"

He smiles. "I didn't get the rest of my tattoos because of that."

"Why, then?"

"I got hooked. Plus, the girls in college loved them." He chuckles and tickles my side.

I giggle and push his hands away. "So, you got them because it made you look hot?"

He wriggles his eyebrows. "Did it work?"

I roll my eyes and wind my arms around his neck. "I'd say so, although you're the first guy I've dated with ink."

He grins. "Really?" I nod. "Was there anyone special back in Pittsburgh?"

"I thought there was, but it turns out he was hung up on his ex. Not that I knew until he left."

He presses his lips to mine, kissing me softly. "I'm sorry he hurt you, but I'm not sorry it led you to me. I know it took me a while to get my head out of my ass after you told me how you felt, but that guy must have been an idiot to walk away from you."

My cheeks heat at his words, and I drop my eyes.

"You never really said what made you change your mind about us."

He blows out a breath. "It was Sophie."

I pull my eyebrows together in a frown. "What do you mean?"

"Cade asked me to go and sit with her the day before the shower. She was sick and he needed to do a house call. He didn't want to leave her on her own." He pauses and his fingers trace up and down my spine. "She asked me what was going on with us." He laughs. "You know, we must have been terrible at keeping our feelings hidden when we were together. I think pretty much everyone saw something between us, although she saw us kissing at my parents' place at Christmas."

I smile. "Ash saw us kissing in Eden on Christmas Eve."

"She did?" I nod, and he laughs. "I guess we weren't exactly discreet either time, but I couldn't help myself and it's not like we were doing anything wrong."

"What did Sophie say?"

"That love is scary, but the right person will make you want to take risks." He strokes his fingers across my cheek. "She was right."

"It sounds like I owe her."

"I'd have come to the same conclusion. It might have taken me a little longer, that's all."

He kisses me again before maneuvering me off his lap and lying down, pulling me down to lie with him.

"Does Sophie know what happened before… when you got hurt? I know Paisley said you two are good friends."

"No, she doesn't," he whispers.

He doesn't say anything else, and it's clear he doesn't want to talk about it. I don't ask him after being shot down last time. I know we haven't been together long, but I hope he knows he can talk to me about anything.

CHAPTER THIRTY-SIX

Seb

"Taylor Jacobs, get your cute ass out here. I need a kiss before I go," I shout, grabbing my bag and slinging it over my shoulder.

"So bossy," she shouts from the bedroom. "Give me one sec." I chuckle and put my bag down, knowing her *one sec* is likely to be a couple of minutes at least.

It's Saturday and the day of the joint bachelor and bachelorette parties. The girls are booked into the spa in Hope Creek and the guys are heading to Lynx Lake for a day of fishing. The weather's good for the time of year and I'm looking forward to spending time with my family and relaxing. It's something I don't get to do very often.

"How do I look?" Taylor asks.

I look up and my mouth drops open. She's standing in the bedroom door in the smallest bikini I've ever seen. The pale pink material just covers her perfect tits, and as she spins around, I nearly swallow my tongue when the material of her panties disappears up her ass.

"Holy fuck," I exclaim, crossing the room and taking her in my arms. My hands go to her bare ass, and I squeeze gently, tugging her against me. "Have you any idea how sexy you look?" I whisper in her ear. "There are no guys at this spa, right?"

"I think the masseuse who's booked to do my full-body massage might be a guy."

Her voice is deadpan, and I lean my head back and stare at her. Her eyes dance with amusement and I narrow mine.

"Like hell it is," I growl.

She giggles. "I'm joking, babe."

"You'd better be."

Her arms circle my neck, and she pulls my mouth to hers. I kiss her urgently, my tongue pushing into her mouth. The moan that escapes her lips is like a direct line to my already hard cock, and I roll my hips against hers, showing her exactly the effect she's having on me. With her wrapped in my arms, a day fishing with my brothers and my dad suddenly doesn't seem all that appealing.

With my mouth still on hers, I walk her backward. Her legs hit the side of the bed and I pick her up, climbing onto the mattress with her in my arms.

"What are you doing?" she asks, her voice breathless against my lips.

"I need to be inside you."

"We don't have time. Paisley..." A knock on the door interrupts her, and she raises her eyebrows. "Is going to be here any second."

I groan. "It's like she knows."

She laughs. "She does not."

She extracts herself from my arms and heads into the living

room. I sigh and stand from the bed, adjusting my now aching cock.

"You're not ready?" Paisley asks Taylor as I walk out of the bedroom.

Taylor's cheeks flush pink and her eyes find mine. "I got a little distracted."

Her eyes go from Taylor to me before she grins. "Well, I can see why Seb might be distracted with you dressed like that. You look hot, Tay. I hope I didn't interrupt anything."

"You didn't," Taylor says.

"You did," I say at the same time, and Paisley laughs.

"Seb thinks you have some sort of radar and you know when we're about to get it on," Taylor explains.

"What?" she asks, looking between us.

Taylor waves her arm. "Never mind. I'll tell you later. We're going to be late. I'll just get dressed."

She walks toward me, and I pull her into my arms. "I should go. I was supposed to meet Cade ten minutes ago." I brush her lips with mine. "Have a great day." I lower my voice. "We'll finish what we started later."

"Promise?" she whispers back.

I smile. "I promise, baby."

Telling her I love her is on the tip of my tongue, but I hold back. I want to say the words, but not with Paisley watching. I do love her, though, and Sophie was right. Loving someone who loves you back is completely different to loving someone who never can.

Taylor

After Seb's said goodbye, I head into the bedroom and quickly get changed into a pair of yoga pants and a top, throwing my bikini and a towel into a bag. When I go back to Paisley in the living room, she smiles.

"It looks like things are going well with you and Seb."

"Yeah, they are." There's hesitation in my voice, and I know by the frown that clouds her face she hears it too.

"What's wrong?"

"Nothing."

"Tay."

I sigh. "I just wish he'd open up to me. Turns out he talked to Sophie about us, and she made him realize he wanted to give things a go."

"And that's bad?"

"No..." I trail off.

"But?" She pauses. "What aren't you saying, because you know you can say anything to me."

"I feel ridiculous even voicing this, but I'm a little jealous. I can't help but wonder if she knows more about his past relationships than I do. I know they're friends, and if he opened up to her, then that's great. I'm glad he had someone to talk about it with."

"I feel like there's another *but* coming."

"I love him, Pais. I want him to be able to tell me anything, but he shuts me down whenever I bring up this mystery woman."

She blows out a breath and sits on the arm of the sofa. "Maybe he just needs a little time."

"For what? If he's still hung up on her—"

"He's not," she says, cutting me off.

My eyes widen. "How do you know? Do you know more than you're telling me?"

"No, Tay." She reaches for my hand. "I know because I see

how he is with you. How he can't take his eyes or his hands off you. He's not hung up on anyone but you."

"I hope you're right," I whisper.

"This isn't like what happened with Eddie," she says, referring to my ex who went back to his previous girlfriend while my mom battled dementia.

I have no idea if this is the same or not. All I know is I was crushed when Eddie left, but I'd be completely devastated if Seb walked away.

I wave my hand and drag in a breath. "Enough about me. We have a bachelorette party to get to."

I take her hand and pull her toward the door. She pulls back and I stop, looking over my shoulder at her.

"Talk to him, Taylor. He'd hate that you're feeling like this."

I nod, knowing she's right. Despite me wanting him to be able to tell me anything, I'm just not sure how to even start this conversation with him when I know it's not something he wants to talk about. I don't want to push him away by demanding he tells me everything from his past. Maybe Paisley's right and he needs some time. I'll have to be patient and respect that.

An hour later, the seven of us are lying on heated loungers around the swimming pool at the Regency Spa in Hope Creek. As well as me, Paisley, Sophie, and Ash, Ivy, Tessa, and Bree are here, and other than the seven of us and an older couple, we pretty much have the place to ourselves.

"What time is the first treatment booked for, Ash?" Bree asks, turning sideways on her lounger.

"Eleven. You're booked in for a manicure."

"I can't wait. I haven't had my nails done since before Oliver was born."

"How's the little cutie doing?" Paisley asks.

"He's teething again, so he's grumpy. This spa day couldn't have come soon enough. I haven't slept well in weeks." She looks across at Sophie and grimaces. "Sorry, Sophie. I probably shouldn't be telling you how tired I am. You have all this to come."

Sophie smiles. "I can't wait." She rests her hand lovingly on her swollen stomach. "Even for the sleepless nights."

"It's totally worth it."

"Do you think you'll have any more babies, Bree?" Paisley asks.

"Yeah, maybe. Not for a couple of years, though. What about you?" She wiggles her eyebrows. "Is there a reason for the quick wedding? Something you're not telling us?"

Paisley laughs. "No. No reason other than I can't wait to be his wife."

"I can't believe you asked her that," Ivy says with a chuckle. "Her future mother-in-law is right there."

Tessa, who's lying next to Ash, has her head back and her eyes closed. She waves her hand in the air. "Don't worry about me. I remember what it was like to be young and in love."

"You're still in love," Ash says.

She opens her eyes and sits up. "Of course. I'm just old now." She laughs.

"You're all lying if you don't admit to thinking the same as I did," Bree says before turning to Paisley. "No offense."

"I'm not offended. I probably would have thought the same if it was someone else." Her cheeks flush pink and she smiles. "I hope it won't be long until I'm pregnant, though. We're trying," she says quietly.

"Oh my God," Ash exclaims. "I'm going to be an auntie again."

"It hasn't happened yet, Ash," Paisley says with a chuckle.

"But it will. I'm so excited for you guys."

"I'm going to pretend I haven't heard, otherwise I might cry," Tessa says, and Ash pulls her into a hug.

"Two grandbabies, Mom."

She smiles and reaches across Ash for Paisley's hand. "I'm so happy for you and Nash, Paisley. You deserve to be this happy." Paisley smiles at Tessa and I can see she's too choked up to speak.

"Me too, Pais," I tell her. "It's amazing news."

Ever since I've known her, she's always wanted a family. Miscarrying her asshole ex's baby after she arrived in Hope Creek can't have been easy, especially as she had no idea she was pregnant. She'd struggled for a while over feeling relieved to have miscarried, but no one would have wanted a child in her situation. This time will be so different. Nash adores her, and I know she feels the same way about him.

"Nobody tell Nash I've told you. I wasn't supposed to say anything yet," she says on a giggle.

"Your secret's safe with us," Sophie says. "It'll be great for this little one to have a cousin so close in age."

I'm so happy for my best friend. She deserves the world and more.

A couple of hours later after my full-body massage, I'm in the changing rooms when Sophie walks in, fresh from her *mother-to-be* pamper. She sits down on the bench next to me and smiles.

"That was amazing. I could do with one of those once a week," she jokes. "How was yours?"

"Really good. I think I fell asleep," I say with a chuckle.

"Are the others not out yet?"

I shake my head. "I don't think so, unless they're in the pool."

"I'm glad we've got a few minutes alone," she says. "I wanted to tell you how happy I am for you and Seb. He was a little lost before he met you."

"He was?" I ask, hoping she might tell me something I don't know.

She nods. "I'm sure he's told you what was going on with him now that you're together, but I've never seen him happier than he is now."

I don't want to tell her he hasn't opened up to me. Not when I don't know the reasons.

"I think I probably owe you a thank-you. He told me he spoke to you about us and that you gave him some great advice."

She smiles. "I didn't tell him anything he didn't already know, Taylor. He just needed pointing in the right direction. He'd have come to the same conclusion on his own."

"That's what he said, but either way, I'm glad he was able to talk things through with you. I know you two are good friends."

"Seb's the best."

"Yeah, he is."

She disappears to use the bathroom, and I sigh. As grateful as I am that he was able to open up to her, I want him to do the same with me. I know Paisley thinks I should talk to him about it, but I guess a part of me is nervous about what he'll say if I do. Clearly, something's holding him back. Maybe it's something he knows I won't want to hear.

The rest of the day is spent talking, laughing, and experiencing almost every treatment the spa has to offer. We've all been in the salon and had our hair and makeup done for tonight; everyone except Bree. She and Leo aren't coming to Eden. They need to pick the children up from Bree's parents, so she's going home. When we do get back to my place, all we need to do is get changed, but I'm so relaxed by the time we're ready to leave, going straight to sleep seems more appealing than drinks in Eden. I'm sure I'll wake up when I'm dressed for a night out and have a glass of wine in my hand.

CHAPTER THIRTY-SEVEN

Seb

After no one catches anything at the lake, we pack up and head to Eden earlier than planned. Despite the fishing being a bust, we've spent the day laughing and catching up, and it's been good to just relax and spend time with everyone. It's definitely something we need to do more often.

It's late afternoon when we walk into Eden, and it's starting to get busy already. I booked a band for tonight, so I'm expecting it to be packed later. I asked Ryder to reserve us two tables as I knew the girls wouldn't want to stand all night, and I notice he's saved us two by the stage where the band will be.

"Drinks?" Ryder shouts from behind the bar. I raise my hand in a wave and make my way over to him. "Beer?" he asks, and everyone nods. "How was the fishing?" he asks as he places five beers in front of us.

"None were biting today," Nash says as he grabs a bottle and swallows down a mouthful.

"What? None of you caught *anything?*"

"Nope. That's why we're here early. We gave up," Cade says, reaching past me and picking up a beer.

"Are the girls back yet?" I ask, knowing they were all planning to come back to Taylor's place after the spa to get changed for tonight.

"No. I haven't seen them." He grins. "Eager to see someone?"

"Fuck off, Ryder," I tell him, a smile pulling on my lips. I pick up my beer and move away from the bar, letting the others pick up their drinks.

"I don't want to say I told you so," he shouts after me. "But…"

I flick him the V over my shoulder, and I can hear him laughing as I walk away.

"Asshole," I mutter.

"How's it going with you and Taylor?" Wyatt asks as he catches up with me at one of the tables Ryder reserved.

"It's good, Wyatt. Really good," I tell him as we sit down.

He smiles. "Another Brookes brother in love." He bumps my shoulder. "I think you might want to hold off proposing or getting pregnant just yet. I don't think Mom could take the excitement."

Nash told us at the lake that he and Paisley are trying for a baby. We're sworn to secrecy, though. Apparently, they decided not to tell anyone they were trying in case things didn't happen as quickly as they hoped; although, knowing Paisley, I'm sure she will have told Taylor at least.

My eyes widen at Wyatt's comment. "I don't think we're quite ready for either of those things, Wyatt."

"You do love her, though, right?" Nash says, overhearing our conversation.

A cold sweat breaks out on the back of my neck as I glance

around the table and all eyes are on me. I drag my hand through my hair and blow out a breath.

"Yes, but—"

"I knew it," Nash exclaims, banging his hand down on the table.

I groan internally. "I haven't told her yet, so no telling Paisley."

"Why the hell haven't you told her?" Wyatt asks.

"I've never felt this way before. I don't want to fuck it up."

Wyatt's eyes widen, and I know he's asking about my feelings for Sophie. I subtly shake my head, answering his silent question with a silent answer. I thought I'd been in love with Sophie, and maybe I had, but what I feel for Taylor is so much more intense.

"You're not going to fuck it up," Nash says. "She loves you too. Anyone can see that."

I nod, knowing he's right. Although she told me she loved me a few weeks ago, I know without her saying the words. I can feel it every time we're together. I hope she knows how I feel by my actions. I hope that's enough until I have the balls to actually say the words.

About an hour later, my phone vibrates in my pocket. Reaching for it, I smile when it's a message from Taylor.

Taylor: Hey, we're heading back to my apartment now to get ready for tonight. Can't wait to see you.

"That's Taylor, right?" Nash asks.

I look up from the phone. "Yes. How did you know?"

"The dreamy-ass look on your face."

Everyone around the table erupts into laughter and I roll my eyes. "Like you don't have a *dreamy-ass* look on your face every time Paisley's around."

He waves off my comment and takes a pull of his beer. "What did she say?"

"That the girls are on their way here."

I lower my eyes to my phone and type out a reply to Taylor.

Me: We're already in Eden. Fishing was a bust. Stop and say hi before you go up. I can't wait to see you either.

Taylor: Okay. Be there in five.

Less than five minutes later, the girls arrive. I stand when I see Taylor, my eyes sweeping over her skin-tight yoga pants and tank. Her long blonde hair is curled in waves over her shoulders and there's something on her eyes that makes them pop. She looks beautiful. Reaching for her, I wrap my arms around her waist and pull her gently against my chest.

"You look hot," I mumble into her hair.

She laughs. "I'm wearing yoga pants."

I lean back and smile. "Baby, you'd look hot in a trash bag."

Her cheeks flush and she presses her lips to mine. "You're looking pretty hot yourself," she says when she pulls out of the kiss.

I sit down at the table and pull her onto my lap, my arms wrapped around her.

"Do you want a drink?" I ask in her ear.

"I think we're going to go and get changed in a minute."

"How was the spa?"

"Good. The male masseuse was excellent."

"Oi!" My hands tickle her waist, and she squirms in my lap.

"I'm joking. I'm joking." She giggles, pushing my hands away.

"No one gets to touch you apart from me," I say into her ear, my voice husky.

She stills on my lap and turns her head. Her eyes are wide and full of heat, and I'm sure they mirror my own.

"Do you think we could sneak to your office?" she whispers, her gaze dropping to my lips.

I chuckle. "I don't think so, baby. I think we might be missed." She pouts, and I laugh. "I'll make it up to you later."

"Hey, Taylor," Paisley shouts from across the table. "Let's head up to your place and get changed."

"Okay." She brushes her lips against mine again before standing up.

I grab her hand. "Don't be long."

She smiles. "I won't."

"I'll bring you some drinks up. Wine?"

"Please, except for Sophie. Oh, hang on." She says something in Paisley's ear, and I watch as they have a whispered conversation. "Yep, wine for everyone except Sophie. Thanks, babe."

I smile, knowing she was probably asking Paisley if she was drinking if they're trying for a baby. I knew Paisley wouldn't be able to not tell Taylor, just like Nash couldn't not tell us.

I head to the bar while they go up to Taylor's apartment. Mom stops at the table with Dad and the others. They're only staying for one drink before going home. The bar isn't really their scene.

When I've got a bottle of red and a bottle of white wine, along with a soda for Sophie, I make my way upstairs. Taylor left the door on the latch, and I walk into a scene of chaos. Despite there being no one in the living room, it's littered with clothes, shoes, and purses.

"Drinks delivery," I call out as I make my way through the living room into the kitchen.

"Be right out," Taylor shouts as I unload the contents of the tray onto the countertop.

I reach into one of the kitchen drawers, pulling out a corkscrew. "Red or white?" I shout, my back to the living room.

When arms suddenly circle my waist, I smile as Taylor presses her front to my back. Her hands come to rest on my chest, and after putting the corkscrew on the counter, I place my hands over hers.

"Hi," she mutters into my back.

I squeeze her hand. "Hi."

We stand in silence for a few seconds, her hands pressed over my heart. When she sighs, I turn around and hold her hands in mine.

"You okay?" I ask, my eyes searching hers. She nods and I frown. "Are you sure?"

Nerves bubble in my stomach as I wait for her answer. Something seems off, but I have no idea what. She was okay downstairs. I'm not sure what's changed in that time.

"I'm just tired." She smiles, but it doesn't quite reach her eyes. "I missed you today."

"I missed you too, baby."

I want to talk to her more, but Ashlyn and Sophie come out of the bedroom.

"Did I hear the word *wine*?" Ashlyn asks.

Taylor pulls her hands from mine and reaches around me for the corkscrew. "You did. Red or white?"

"Red, please."

I take the corkscrew from Taylor's hand and grab the bottle of red wine. "I'll open it."

It's only when she steps away from me that I notice what she's wearing. A pale pink strapless dress that hugs her body in all the right places and falls mid-thigh, putting her toned and tanned legs on display.

Putting the corkscrew and wine back on the countertop, I reach for her. "The wine will have to wait, Ash," I say as I circle my arms around Taylor's waist and pull her against my chest.

She smiles, and I breathe a silent sigh of relief that, this time, the smile does reach her eyes. Maybe she really is tired and it's nothing more.

"What are you doing?" She giggles as her arms wind around my neck.

"Telling you how incredible you look. You take my breath away, baby."

Her cheeks flush pink and she drops her forehead onto my chest.

"Put her down and open the wine," Ash groans. "You'll have her all to yourself later. Right now, we've got some drinking to do, and you boys are already ahead as you got here earlier than us."

I chuckle and brush my lips on Taylor's head before stepping out of the embrace. "I wasn't aware it was a competition," I tell Ash as I quickly open the wine and pour her a glass.

She doesn't answer and instead takes her drink back into the bedroom. Sophie laughs and picks up the can of soda I brought up for her.

"I hope that's okay," I tell her, gesturing to the soda.

"It's fine. Thanks, Seb." She looks from me to Taylor and smiles. "I'll leave you two alone."

She turns and disappears back into the bedroom where I can hear the chatter and laughter of the others.

"I should go and let you all finish getting ready."

"Okay. We won't be long. Ash is itching to get into the bar."

I laugh. "Sounds like Ash."

I lean down and kiss her. I'm going to tell her I love her tonight. I'm not afraid anymore. She's not going to hurt me, and I know for sure I'm not going to hurt her. She means everything to me and it's about time she knew it.

CHAPTER THIRTY-EIGHT

Taylor

I know Seb noticed I was quiet when he brought the drinks up earlier, and I know he's going to want to know why when we're alone later. Pushing down my apprehension at having to tell him, I follow the girls down the steps of my apartment and into Eden. I want to enjoy tonight and not worry about it. I'm sure I'm overthinking things anyway, and when I talk to him, he'll open up and everything will be fine.

Seb gets a round of drinks when we arrive, and after toasting Cade and Sophie and Nash and Paisley, Tessa and Henry decide to call it a night. After a round of goodbyes, they head out.

"Who wants to dance?" Ash shouts, standing up and drinking what's left of her drink before placing the empty glass on the table.

"Me!" Ivy says, standing with her.

"I'll come too," I say, pressing a kiss on Seb's cheek before standing and going to where Ash and Ivy are waiting. "Sophie?" I ask. "You coming?"

"I think I'll sit this one out," she says, her hand resting on her stomach.

"Okay. You coming, Pais?"

"Yep."

Seb stands to let Paisley out and makes his way to over to me. Slipping his arm around my waist, he tugs me against his side.

"Stay where I can see you," he whispers in my ear.

I wrap my arms around his neck. "Why? Don't you trust me?"

He smiles. "Of course I trust you, baby, but you look hot, and I don't want anyone hitting on you."

I roll my eyes. "No one is going to hit on me."

"You have no idea how beautiful you are, do you?"

Before I can answer him, Ash pulls on my arm.

"Put her down, Seb. It's girl time."

He chuckles and releases his hold on me. "Stay where I can see you," he says again.

"Yeah, yeah, we know," Ash says, pulling me away and toward the dance floor. I giggle and raise my hand in a wave to Seb, who's watching with a smile on his face.

"I guess as Seb's girlfriend, you get a taste of the Brookeses' over-protectiveness. Thankfully for you, it's only one of them. I get all four!" Ash says.

"I quite like it when he's like that," I admit.

"I'm the same with Nash," Paisley says. "I love it when he goes all caveman on me."

"Urgh, that's too much information, Paisley," Ash says, screwing up her nose. "When a guy who isn't your brother does it, it's hot. When it's all four of your brothers, it's just annoying."

"I guess." I take her arm. "Let's dance."

We spend the next half an hour dancing. There's a band playing tonight and they're good. They're playing songs we know

LAURA FARR

and I'm loving singing along badly to the lyrics. Paisley went back to Nash about ten minutes ago when her feet started to ache. As much as I want to stay and keep dancing, the balls of my feet are burning, and I need a drink. I gesture to Ash and Ivy that I'm going to sit down, and they nod, opting to stay dancing. When I get back to the table, Seb and Paisley aren't there.

"Where are Seb and Paisley?" I ask as I sit down and pick up my drink, swallowing a mouthful.

"Seb went to his office to check on something," Nash says. "Paisley's in the bathroom."

I nod. "I'll just go and see if he's okay."

"You do that," Nash says, laughing.

I leave him chuckling as I make my way through Eden. Reaching inside my purse, I pull out the fob that'll get me through the security door and close it behind me when I'm on the other side. The noise of the bar used to permeate through here, but since Seb installed the door, it's a lot quieter. When I reach Seb's office, the door is open slightly, and I'm about to walk in when I hear Paisley's voice.

"You have to tell her, Seb. You know what happened with her ex, right?"

I step closer, wondering what Paisley means.

He sighs. "Yeah, the jackass left her for his ex."

"She thinks because you keep shutting her down when she asks about your past, it's because you're still hung up on *your* ex."

"Fuck, Paisley. There is no ex."

"I know that, but she doesn't."

"I can't keep lying to her. She's my best friend. She loves you, Seb. I know you don't want anyone to know about Sophie, but Taylor isn't *anyone*, she's your girlfriend and she needs to know it was Sophie who broke your heart."

I stumble backward and all the air rushes from my lungs. I can't hear anything except the pounding of my heart. He was in love with Sophie? But Sophie's with Cade. Did something happen with them before Sophie and Cade got together? Does he still have feelings for her? Does Cade know? These and more questions race through my mind and I can't process them fast enough to even consider the answers. Was I the rebound? Am I still the rebound? I feel like an idiot. I'm second choice because he can't be with who he really wants to be with. I thought his heart had been broken after a failed relationship, not because he was in love with someone out of reach. Suddenly, I can't breathe, and I need to be anywhere but here.

I manage to make my legs work and pretty much run through the security door and out into Eden. My head is down as I make for the exit. I need some air. I should have gone out the back of Eden so I didn't have to see anyone, but I wasn't thinking clearly, and I can't go back now. I can't risk running into Seb or Paisley. I do run into someone, though, and I lift my head to apologize, my heart sinking when it's Ryder standing in front of me. Tears are running down my face, and he frowns.

"Hey, what's wrong? I'll get Seb," he says, his hand reaching for my arm.

"No," I shout. "I just need some air."

I shake off his hand and try to get past him, but he steps in front of me.

"Wait. What's happened?"

"Please, Ryder," I beg, looking over my shoulder. "Let me pass." When he still doesn't move, I lift my eyes to his. "Please." His eyebrows are pulled together in concern, but eventually, he steps aside. "Thank you," I whisper before rushing past him and out the door.

The cool night air hits my skin as I find myself on the sidewalk. I walk a little way along from Eden before stopping outside one of the storefronts and trying to catch my breath. My stomach churns with everything I've just heard. It somehow changes everything knowing it was Sophie who broke him. It wasn't a relationship that had run its course, but I still can't make sense of all of it. What does make sense is why Seb was so reluctant to open up to me. He wants to be with Sophie, but he can't, so he's settled for me. Hell, we even look alike, blonde hair and blue eyes. I've been such an idiot. Being second best isn't something anyone wants. I love him, but I know now he doesn't love me. I was just someone to fill the hole in his heart that Sophie knowingly or unknowingly left behind. My heart's breaking, though, and I've no idea what I'm going to do.

CHAPTER THIRTY-NINE

Seb

I follow Paisley out of my office and into Eden. She's right. I have to open up to Taylor. I don't want her to know how much of an idiot I was, falling for Sophie, but if what Paisley said is right, she has to know that she isn't my second choice. That isn't what's happening here. I should have told her. She's asked me often enough, but I was thinking of myself and not her. I was so intent on Sophie and Cade never finding out that I thought I could move forward without telling her. That it would be one less person in the world who knew. I know now that can't happen. Taylor's the most important person in my life and she has to come first, however awkward the conversation will be.

When we get back to the table, Taylor's not there. Ash and Ivy are sitting down, so she can't be dancing. Maybe she's in the bathroom.

"Where's Taylor?" Nash asks when Paisley sits down next to him.

"I was just about to ask you that," I say.

He frowns. "She went to look for you about five minutes ago. She came and asked where you were. I told her you were in your office. Didn't she find you?"

I shake my head, my eyes going to Paisley. "No. She didn't."

"She definitely went through the security door. I saw her," Nash says.

My stomach rolls and I feel like I'm going to throw up. "Do you think she overheard us talking?" I ask Paisley, whose eyes are wide, and her face is pale.

"I don't know," she whispers.

Nash looks between us. "What's going on? What were you talking about? I thought you went to the bathroom, Paisley." She leans in close to Nash and whispers in his ear. His eyes widen as he looks at me.

"Fuck! I need to find her," I say, turning from the table and walking away.

"I'll come with you," Paisley says.

I close my eyes as I hear Cade ask Nash what's going on. I don't really care who knows what right now. I just want to know where Taylor is.

I'm heading for her apartment with Paisley behind me when Ryder appears.

"I've been looking for you," he says, glancing past me to Paisley.

"Not now, Ryder. I need to find Taylor."

I start to walk past him when he grabs my arm. "Did you guys have a fight?"

I spin around. "What do you mean? Have you seen her?"

"She's outside. I tried to stop her, but she said she wanted some air. She was crying."

"Fuck!" I cry, looking at Paisley. "She overheard us, didn't she?"

I don't wait for her to answer before I'm jogging through Eden and out onto the sidewalk. When I don't see her outside, I begin to panic, and a cold sweat breaks out on the back of my neck.

"Taylor," I shout. "Taylor!"

"She's there," Paisley says, pointing up the sidewalk.

I look to where she's pointing. She's sitting on a bench a little way up the sidewalk that's half hidden by a large tree. I make my way to her and drop to my knees in front of her.

"Taylor. Look at me." She shakes her head. "Please, baby."

She slowly lifts her head, and when I see her tearstained face, my heart breaks. I reach my hand up to wipe away her tears, but she turns her head away from me and I pull my hand back.

"You love Sophie," she whispers, and I hate the dejection in her voice.

"No."

"But you did?"

"Yes, and I should have told you. I'm sorry you had to overhear my and Paisley's conversation."

Her eyes go past me to Paisley. "How could you not tell me?" she asks her. "You're my best friend and you lied to my face."

"Don't be mad at Paisley. I put her in an impossible situation," Seb says.

Taylor shrugs. "It doesn't matter now."

I frown. "What do you mean?"

"I can't be someone's second choice again, Seb. I *won't* be someone's second choice."

"Fuck, Taylor. You're not. You were never my second choice."

She lets out a sarcastic laugh. "I was! You couldn't have the woman you wanted, so you settled for me. We even look alike." She stands from the bench. "It's my own fault. I pushed you and

LAURA FARR

pushed you into being with me. If you really wanted me, I wouldn't have had to push that hard."

She starts to walk away from me, and I stand up and look at Paisley, not having a clue what to say to make this right.

"Taylor, wait," Paisley says.

"I don't want to talk to you, Paisley."

She stops and turns around. "Does Sophie know how you feel about her?"

"Felt. Past tense, and no, she doesn't. Cade either."

She sighs. "But everyone else does? God, they must think I'm an idiot."

"Paisley, Nash, and Wyatt know, that's all, and no one thinks you're an idiot."

"That's all? That's half your family, Seb."

"Taylor—"

"Were you thinking about her when we were together?" she asks quietly, her voice cracking with emotion.

"No! Never. Fuck, Taylor." I drag my hand through my hair.

"You went and spoke to her about our relationship," she says. "Why? Why would you get advice from someone you're in love with? This is so messed up."

"I'm not in love with her. I love *you*."

"I don't know if I believe you," she whispers.

My stomach rolls and I think I'm going to throw up. I have to make her believe me. I should have told her how I felt about her this morning. Hell, I should have told her days ago. "Let me explain, please." I drop to my knees on the sidewalk. "Please," I say again, not caring that I'm begging.

She stares at me kneeling on the floor and eventually nods her head. "Okay," she whispers.

Hope erupts in my chest, and I stand up and reach for her. She takes a step back and shakes her head. "Talk, Seb."

"I'll leave you two alone," Paisley says as she walks past us and into Eden. I barely see her go, my eyes fixed on Taylor.

I drag my hand through my hair and take a second to breathe. I know what I say to her in the next five minutes could make or break us. If it breaks us, I don't know how I'm going to live without her.

"I never wanted to have feelings for Sophie. They crept up on me. We're friends. That's all we've ever been, but somewhere along the way, for me at least, the lines got blurred." I pause and drag in a breath. "I thought I'd buried my feelings, but Wyatt figured it out, and Nash and Paisley found out by accident. Suddenly, it felt like everyone knew and I was so afraid Cade and Sophie would find out. I begged them to not say anything. Sophie and Cade had just gotten married and they were so happy. It would have ruined my relationship with Cade if he'd found out, and I didn't want that. So I dealt with it the only way I knew how. I threw myself even more into work and avoided my family at every opportunity. I thought it would be easier to stay away from everyone, but I hated it. I missed my family, and they were starting to wonder what was going on with me. Thanksgiving was the first time I'd seen anyone other than Paisley in weeks."

I step toward her and take her hands in mine before she can move away. She tries to pull her hands free, but I hold on tightly.

"I'm not going to stand here and lie and say that I wasn't still hung up on Sophie at Thanksgiving, because I was."

She lowers her eyes and I know this must be hard for her to hear but I've got to say it.

"But then there was you, and meeting you again that day changed everything for me."

She shakes her head.

"Yes, Taylor," I insist, releasing one of her hands and using my fingers to tilt her chin so she's looking at me. "I might not have known it right away, but everything felt a little easier when you were around, and the more time we spent together, the more I couldn't stop thinking about you."

Tears track down her cheeks and my heart physically aches knowing I caused them.

"You might have made the first move the night we slept together, but I wanted it as much as you. I didn't want to get hurt again, and I didn't want to be the guy who hurt you, which is what kept holding me back. I didn't think I could give you anything more than sex. I didn't think I could be enough for you."

I swipe my thumbs across her cheeks, wiping her tears away. I want to pull her into my arms and never let go, but I know I can't.

"I should have been open with you. I was so desperate for Cade and Sophie to never find out that I didn't think about what it would mean to keep it from you." I sigh. "You won't believe me, but how I feel about you, Taylor... it makes me question exactly what it was that I felt for Sophie."

"What do you mean?" she whispers.

"The thought of losing you. I can hardly breathe, Tay. I know I said I couldn't have the big love like Nash and Paisley, but I've found it. *You're* my big love and I don't think I'll survive if you walk away. You're not my second choice. You never were. You are the *only* choice. I don't want this with anyone but you."

She closes her eyes as more tears track down her cheeks. "I need some time to think."

My heart feels like it's breaking in my chest, and it's like no pain I've ever felt before. I can't lose her.

She's walking away from me, and I follow her along the sidewalk.

"Taylor..."

She stops on the edge of the curb and turns to face me. "I love you, Seb. I love you more than I ever thought possible, but I need some space."

She steps backward into the road, and the sound of screeching brakes pierces the silence. Her wide, scared eyes meet mine seconds before a car neither of us saw coming smashes into her, throwing her body into the air. It's like everything happens in slow motion and it seems like her body's in the air forever before she lands on the road with a sickening thud.

CHAPTER FORTY

Seb

Someone's screaming Taylor's name, and it takes me a second to realize it's me. My heart's pounding in my chest and nausea rolls through me as I run to her, dropping down onto the ground.

"Taylor, baby. Can you hear me?"

She's not moving, and her eyes are closed. There's blood on her face, and as my eyes sweep down her body, I see her leg is bent at a strange angle. I gently lift her hand, pressing my fingers over the base of her wrist. I breathe a sigh of relief when I feel her pulse under my fingers.

The car that hit her has stopped a little way up the road and the driver runs toward us.

"Fuck! She just stepped out in front of me. Is she okay?" he asks, his voice frantic.

"Call 911. Now!" I tell him. "It's okay, baby," I say to Taylor.

"You're going to be okay."

I look up when I see a guy coming out of Eden. His eyes widen when he sees Taylor in the road.

"Go to the bar," I shout. "Ask for Cade Brookes. Go!"

I keep her hand in mine, brushing my thumb over her skin while the driver of the car speaks to the 911 dispatcher.

"Is she breathing?" he asks, and I nod. "They said don't move her."

Suddenly, she moans. "I think she's waking up," I tell him. "It's okay, Taylor. Don't move, baby. Help is coming."

"Oh my God! Taylor!" Paisley shouts, and seconds later, Cade's by my side.

"What happened?" he asks, his fingers going to the pulse point on her neck.

"She stepped into the street and the car hit her."

"Fuck. Did she go over the hood?"

"I think so. It happened so quickly."

"Have you moved her?"

"No."

"Taylor, can you hear me?" he asks her.

"Seb," she moans.

"I'm here, baby."

Her eyes open and she starts to move, groaning in pain.

"Stay still, Taylor. Don't move," Cade says.

When she tries to get up, Cade stops her.

"No," she cries, trying to sit up.

"How long for the ambulance?" he shouts at the guy talking to 911.

"Two minutes," he replies.

"What's happening?" I ask Cade.

"I think she might have a head injury. We need to keep her as still as possible."

I'm relieved when I hear the sound of the ambulance in the

distance a minute later. I look over to the crowd that's gathered on the sidewalk. Sophie and Paisley are crying, while Nash and Wyatt try to comfort them.

When the EMTs arrive, I reluctantly move away from her so they can do what they need to. She's moaning and thrashing her arms around, and it's heartbreaking to watch. Paisley comes to me and pulls me into a hug.

"She's going to be okay, isn't she?" she asks, tears tracking down her cheeks.

"It's my fault," I whisper.

"What?"

"She was trying to get away from me, Paisley. She wasn't looking and stepped into the street."

"Seb, this is not your fault. It was an accident."

"She wouldn't have been out here if it wasn't for me."

"Hey. Stop it. This isn't your fault," she repeats, wiping her tears away. "She's going to need you, Seb. You have to be strong for her."

I shake my head. "I don't think she wants me anywhere near her."

"She loves you, Seb."

"God, I hope so. I love her so much, Paisley."

"She knows that. I promise you."

I don't answer her. I don't know what to say.

I'm numb as I watch them load Taylor onto a spinal board. There's an oxygen mask over her face and a line in the back of her hand. They load her into the back of the ambulance and Cade jogs over to us.

"They've given her something to keep her calm until they can get her to the emergency room. Her leg is broken, and they think she might have fractured her pelvis," Cade says.

I lean forward and rest my hands on my legs. I can't catch my breath, and I desperately drag in mouthfuls of air. Cade puts his hand on my shoulder and squeezes.

"You can go in the ambulance with her. We'll follow."

"Is she going to be okay?" I ask him. When he doesn't answer, I stand up. "Cade?"

"We'll know more when they get her to the hospital. I wish I could say yes, Seb."

Paisley bursts into tears and Nash pulls her into his arms.

"I'll see you at the hospital," I whisper before walking away from them and toward the ambulance.

I feel like I'm on autopilot as I climb into the back of the ambulance and sit on the pull-down seat the EMT points to. Seeing what happened to her and how violent the accident was, I know the human body isn't meant to be able to endure that. I'm praying for a miracle. I can't live in a world where she doesn't exist.

*

It's been hours since Taylor arrived at the emergency room. They wheeled her into trauma and I haven't seen her since. Everyone arrived minutes after we did, along with my parents, and we're all sitting in silence in the waiting room. The doctor came out not long after we arrived to tell us they were taking her into surgery. Imaging showed she hadn't broken her pelvis, but she had ruptured her spleen, causing internal bleeding. They needed to operate.

"How are you doing?" Sophie asks as she moves to sit next to me on the uncomfortable plastic chairs.

I close my eyes and drop my head into my hands. "What am I going to do if I lose her?" I whisper.

She takes my hand in hers. "Look at me." I reluctantly raise my eyes to hers. "You aren't going to lose her."

I shake my head. "You didn't see how she was thrown into the air." I bite back a sob and close my eyes. "I keep seeing it over and over again. It's all my fault. We were arguing. She was trying to get away from me."

She squeezes my hand. "What were you arguing about?"

I shrug. "It doesn't matter now. Nothing matters if she doesn't make it."

"She's going to make it, Seb."

"God, I hope so."

I pull my hand from hers and pace the waiting room. I feel useless sitting here doing nothing while she fights for her life in surgery.

"How much longer do you think, Cade?" I ask a few minutes later.

He stands and walks toward me. "I don't know, Seb. She's been down a while, so hopefully soon."

"I can't stand the waiting."

My mom walks over. "Come and sit down. Do you want a drink?"

She takes my arm and leads me to a chair. I sigh and sit down. "No, thanks."

Minutes later, the double doors leading to the trauma area open, and a doctor appears.

"Are you all here for Taylor?" he asks, nodding at Cade.

I stand. "I'm her boyfriend. Is she okay?"

"She's out of surgery and in recovery. We removed the spleen and stopped the bleeding. She's broken her leg in three places, so we've pinned it and she's in a cast."

"Is she going to be okay?"

"She's not out of danger yet." My mom slips her hand into mine and squeezes. "She suffered a head trauma in the accident. There's significant swelling and we've put her into a medically induced coma in the hope that the swelling reduces. When it does, we can wake her up."

"And if the swelling doesn't reduce?" I ask, fear creeping up my spine.

He smiles sympathetically. "Let's take one day at a time."

"Can I see her?"

"Not tonight, I'm afraid. She should be out of recovery in the morning."

I can't wait until then. I look helplessly at Cade, who steps forward. "Just five minutes, Bill."

He nods. "Okay. I'll send a nurse out."

Relief crashes over me as he turns and disappears through the double doors. I turn to Cade.

"Thank you," I tell him, pulling him into a hug. "She'll wake up, right? Once the swelling has gone down?"

"I hope so, Seb."

I pull out of the embrace when I hear soft sobbing. Looking past Cade, I see Paisley's crying in Nash's arms. Walking over to her, I place my hand on her back.

"Are you okay?"

She moves out of Nash's arms and turns around. "It should be me asking you that."

I frown. "You're her best friend, Paisley."

She shakes her head. "I think she hates me," she whispers.

"No. She doesn't. She loves you."

"I lied to her. She's got every right to be mad."

I pull her into my arms. "I should never have asked you to keep my secrets. I'm sorry, Paisley."

"I love you," she says, hugging me tightly.

"I love you too," I tell her. "I'm going to fix this. I promise."

"Taylor Jacobs' family," a voice says from behind me.

"Tell her I love her," Paisley whispers.

"I will."

I follow the nurse through the double doors and along the hallway. She stops outside a door with the word *RECOVERY* on it.

"There'll be lots of machines and wires, but don't let that overwhelm you. They're all there to help her," she says kindly.

I nod and take a deep breath as she pushes open the door. The sound of whirring machines fills the air, and she leads me past two curtained-off bays before she stops.

"If you need anything, let me know."

"Thanks."

Nerves erupt in my stomach as I step forward into the bay. My heart breaks when I see her lying in the bed. She looks so small and fragile. I frown when I see she's intubated. I wasn't expecting that. The machine connected to her breathing tube whirrs as it pushes air into her lungs, her chest rising and falling methodically. There's a bandage around her head, and the hair I can see poking out is matted with blood. A large graze covers the right side of her face, and her eye is swollen and bruised. Despite there being a blanket covering most of her, her right leg is uncovered, and a bright blue cast covers her foot up to her knee.

"Are you okay?" the same nurse from earlier asks as she comes up behind me.

"I don't know," I admit. "Why is she intubated? She was breathing after… after the accident."

"She just needs some help. We're letting the machines do all the work so her body can rest." She places her hand on my arm. "She's in good hands."

"Can she hear me?"

"We think so, yes. You should talk to her." She guides me toward a chair at the side of the bed. "You can hold her hand too." She smiles encouragingly, and I sit down. "I'll give you a minute."

Taking Taylor's hand in mine, I tangle our fingers together

before bringing her hand to my lips. Brushing a kiss on the back of her hand, I rest my forehead on our joined hands.

"I'm so sorry, baby."

I lift my head from her hand and stare at her face, willing her to wake up, even though I know she won't. I rub my thumb across the back of her hand.

"Everyone's waiting to see you. They love you so much, Tay." I blow out a breath. "I love you so much. Please come back to me."

I sit with her for another few minutes until the nurse appears again.

"I'm sorry, but I'm going to have to ask you to leave now. We don't normally let relatives into the recovery room. She'll be moved to her own room in the morning and you can come back then."

I sigh and nod. "Okay."

I reluctantly stand, her hand still encased in mine. Leaning over her, I brush a gentle kiss on her head.

"I love you, baby," I whisper in her ear. "I'm going to make this right, I swear to you. No more secrets."

I don't want to leave her, but I know I have to. As I walk away from her, I feel like I'm leaving my heart behind, and I know I'm going to be sleeping in the waiting room tonight. I can't go home and leave her here. She *is* my home.

CHAPTER FORTY-ONE

Seb

Taylor's been in an induced coma for two weeks. It's been the longest two weeks of my life. In the days after the accident, she seemed to be improving and a CT scan showed the swelling was beginning to reduce. Only days later, another scan showed a bleed on the brain. A subdural hematoma. The doctors had no choice but to operate again. She was in surgery for hours, and other than the night of the accident, I'd never been so scared. The doctors had hoped to try and wake her up after the surgery, but there'd been complications with a bigger bleed than expected and they'd decided to keep her asleep. She is breathing on her own now, though, thank God.

I look over my shoulder as the door to Taylor's room opens and my mom walks in.

"How's she doing?" she asks, kissing me on the cheek before going to Taylor and doing the same.

"No change."

"Have you been home yet?" I shake my head. I haven't left the hospital since she was brought in two weeks ago. "You need a break, Seb. Why don't you go home, take a shower and get something to eat? I'll stay with Taylor."

"No. I'm good," I tell her, lifting her hand to my lips.

She frowns. "I'm worried about you."

"I'm fine, Mom. I don't want to leave her."

She smiles sadly. "Okay." She sits on the chair opposite me and picks up Taylor's other hand. "Taylor's the one, isn't she?" she asks, her eyes meeting mine.

"Yeah, she's the one. I hope she feels the same way when she wakes up."

"What happened with you two?"

I sigh. "I should have been honest with her."

"About what?"

"My feelings for Sophie."

Her forehead creases in confusion before her eyes widen. "Feelings for Sophie…" She trails off. "That's why we didn't see you for weeks after the wedding."

It's not a question but I answer anyway. "It was easier to stay away, but meeting Taylor made me realize maybe my feelings for Sophie weren't as strong as I thought. They felt pretty real at the time, though."

"Oh, Seb. Why didn't you say anything?"

I shrug halfheartedly. "There was nothing to say."

"Do Cade or Sophie know?"

"No, but they will. I'm done with secrets. Secrets nearly destroyed everything." I look at Taylor, thinking they could still destroy everything if she doesn't pull through.

"Do you think that's a good idea? What are you going to gain from telling them now?"

"Taylor thinks I'm with her because I can't be with Sophie.

She thinks she's second best. *Nothing* could be further from the truth. I want her to know she's the most important person in my life and that I choose her over *everyone*."

"Even Cade?"

I nod. "Even Cade. I hope it won't come to that. I hope he'll see it for what it was."

"Which was?"

"An infatuation. I think I know now that I was in love with the idea of Sophie, that's all. If he doesn't, then I'll be devastated, but I have to show Taylor what she means to me."

"I'm not sure I totally understand, but you have to do what you feel is right."

"Thanks, Mom."

~

It's another three weeks before the doctors feel Taylor's well enough to be brought out of the coma. Everyone except Cade and Sophie is in the relatives' room while they wake her up. They're both at the hospital; they're in the maternity ward since Sophie gave birth a couple of days ago. I was so happy for them, but it feels bittersweet knowing Taylor's missing it all. I hope to God she wakes up today. I need to see her eyes and hear her voice more than I need my next breath.

I pace the room, wondering what's taking so long. It's been almost an hour since they asked us to leave her room, and I've no idea if that's how long it takes or whether something's gone wrong. I wish Cade was here to ask. At least he's talking to me now. Sitting him and Sophie down and telling them exactly what Taylor and I had been arguing about on the night of the accident had been one of the hardest conversations I'd ever had. Sophie had been embarrassed, but Cade had been pissed. It had taken him a while to come around. I'd been honest and explained that any feelings I had for Sophie were gone and I was in love with Taylor. I think we're okay now. I've only left the hospital a couple of times since Taylor was admitted, so I haven't seen him much, and while I want things with Cade to be okay, all I can focus on right now is Taylor.

The door to the relatives' room opens, and one of the nurses walks in. She smiles. "She's awake and she's asking for you, Seb."

Relief washes over me, and I let out a breath I didn't know I was holding. "She is?" She nods. "Maybe if you come in on your own first, so she's not overwhelmed."

"Okay."

I glance at Paisley, who's smiling as tears fall down her cheeks. Everyone looks relieved. It goes to show how much they all love her, even though she's only been in our lives for a short time.

"Tell her I love her," Paisley says, leaving Nash's side and pulling me into a hug.

"Me too," Ash says, her voice choked with emotion.

"You can tell her yourself. She's going to want to see you," I tell them both.

As desperate as I am to see her, I'm nervous as hell as I follow the nurse along the corridor to Taylor's room. She might have asked for me when she woke up, but that doesn't mean anything.

"The doctors explained what happened and the injuries she sustained. She was teary and scared and she's likely to be a little confused after being out of it for so long. She's going to need a lot of support."

"I'm not going anywhere."

She stops outside Taylor's room and smiles. "I know, Seb. You haven't spent a night away from her."

"I love her," I say simply.

"She's lucky to have you."

I shake my head. "I'm the lucky one." "I'll leave you two alone."

She walks away, and I take a deep breath before opening the door. Taylor's sitting up in bed, and she turns to look at me before bursting into tears.

"Seb," she whispers.

I cross the room in seconds and sit next to her, scooping up her hand.

"Please don't cry. Can I hold you?"

She nods, and I climb onto the bed next to her and wrap her in my arms. It feels so good to hold her. I don't ever want to let go.

"How are you feeling?" I ask a few minutes later.

"I've been better." She tilts her head and gives me a small smile.

"God, Tay. I was so worried about you." She lays her head back on my chest and I press a kiss on her hair.

"The doctor said I've been in a coma for five weeks." She reaches her hand up and cups my jaw. "You've grown a beard."

I chuckle. "I never got around to shaving."

"We were arguing, weren't we, when I got hit by the car?" she says quietly.

I sigh and nod. "You remember?"

"Yes."

"I'm sorry, baby. It was all my fault. If I'd just told you about Sophie from the beginning, then none of this would have happened."

"I stepped out into the road, Seb. It wasn't your fault."

"It feels like my fault. I was so scared I was going to lose you."

She sighs against my chest, and I wish I knew what she was thinking. I don't want to push her when she's just woken up, so for now, I'll settle for having her in my arms. There was a time after the accident when I thought I'd never see her again, let alone hold her. I'm not going to wait too long, though. She needs to know everything I said to her before the accident is true. I love her, and after nearly losing her, I'm going to fight with everything in me to make her mine again.

CHAPTER FORTY-TWO

Taylor

𝒜 hundred different emotions race through me as I lie in Seb's arms. When I woke up earlier, surrounded by faces I didn't know, the only person I'd wanted was him, especially when they'd told me how bad my injuries had been after the accident and how they weren't sure I was going to pull through. I guess we still have things we need to talk about, but I'm scared and overwhelmed, and no matter what, he feels like home.

"Knock, knock," a voice says from the doorway, and I lift my head off Seb's shoulder to see Paisley, Nash, and the whole Brookes clan waiting to come in. "Sorry, we couldn't wait any longer," Paisley says. "Are we okay to come in?"

"Of course you are," I say as Seb untangles his arms from around me, kisses me on the head, and climbs off the bed.

Paisley makes her way over and throws her arms around me. "I'm so sorry," she whispers. "I'm so glad you're okay."

"It's okay. I'm glad you're here." I fight back the tears as I hold her tightly. She's my best friend, and while I was upset she didn't tell me about Sophie, after everything that's happened, it doesn't matter anymore. I didn't tell her Seb and I were sleeping together at the beginning. I guess we both kept secrets.

"How are you feeling?" she asks, pulling out of the embrace.

"A little sore, and my throat hurts. The doctor said the cast can come off my leg next week."

She smiles and wipes away a tear. "That's great, Taylor."

My eyes widen as I remember why we were out for drinks the night of the accident. "Your wedding," I exclaim. "I missed it."

She takes my hand. "No, Tay. You didn't miss it. I couldn't get married when you were lying in a coma."

Guilt washes over me. "You cancelled your wedding because of me?"

She shakes her head. "Not cancelled, postponed."

"I'm so sorry," I whisper.

"I need my best friend next to me when I get married."

I reach up and pull her into a hug. "I love you."

"I love you too."

After a round of hugs from everyone, along with a lot more tears, I yawn and Seb ushers everyone out of my room, insisting I need to rest.

"You didn't have to make everyone leave," I tell him as I rest my head back against the pillow. "I'm okay."

"You're tired."

"I've been asleep for weeks, Seb."

"You yawned."

I chuckle. "I am hungry. Do you think you could find me something to eat?"

"Sure. Will you be okay on your own?" I nod. "What do you want?"

"Maybe a sandwich?"

"I'll see what the cafeteria has."

"Thank you."

He hesitates. "I know we have things to talk about, but can I kiss you? I've waited five weeks. I'm not sure I can wait any longer."

I smile. "Okay."

Relief washes over his face as he sits on the bed next to me. His hand comes up to cup my chin and his fingers stroke my cheek before he lowers his head and brushes his lips over mine. The kiss is soft at first, but it soon turns urgent as I push my tongue into his mouth. Despite it feeling like I only kissed him yesterday, I can't get close enough to him, and I wind my arms around his neck. We're both breathing hard when he pulls away and rests his forehead on mine.

"I missed you so much, baby. I can't even think about…" His voice breaks and he trails off.

I lean back and tilt his chin with my fingers so he's looking at me.

"You can't think about what?"

He sighs. "My life without you in it." He presses a kiss on my forehead. "We need to talk, but not right now. I'll grab you that sandwich."

He climbs off the bed and crosses the room, stopping when he gets to the door. "I won't be long."

"Okay," I whisper, watching him walk out and close the door behind him.

I bring my hand up over my eyes and burst into tears. I know for him it's been five weeks and I can't imagine what he's been through in that time, but for me, it's like I only found out about Sophie yesterday. I still haven't gotten my head around it, and with everything that's happened in between, I don't know when I will.

A few minutes later, there's a knock on the door. Knowing

everyone's left and that Seb probably wouldn't knock, I have no idea who it is. I wipe my eyes and sit up.

"Come in," I call out. I watch the door, my hand flying to my mouth when Sophie walks in with a baby in her arms. "You had the baby?" I ask, my eyes dropping to the bundle wrapped in blue. "A boy?" She nods. "When?"

She smiles. "A couple of days ago. He was a little early, so we're staying for a few days, but he's perfect."

"What's his name?"

"Hunter."

"I love it. I'm so happy for you and Cade." And I am. Regardless of Seb's feelings for her, she's my friend and I know what she went through to have Hunter.

"Thank you. How are you feeling? You gave us a scare." She sits in the chair next to my bed and reaches for my hand. "We were all so worried about you."

"I'm okay."

She frowns. "Are you sure? It looks like you've been crying."

I look down at my hands and fiddle with the edge of the blanket that covers me. "It's all a little overwhelming, that's all."

"I can't even imagine, Taylor. You've been through so much." She pauses. "I thought Seb might be here."

"He is. I asked him to get me a sandwich from the cafeteria."

She nods. "You know he slept at the hospital every night you were here?"

I look at her and raise my eyebrows in confusion. "He never said."

"Some of the nurses took pity on him and let him stay in here with you. Others didn't, and he slept in the waiting room. I think he went home twice in the whole five weeks and only then because Tessa made him."

"Why would he do that? He can't have slept well in weeks."

"I'd have thought that was obvious. He loves you." She squeezes my hand. "Taylor, whatever he felt for me, it's *nothing* compared to how he feels for you."

My eyes widen. "He told you?" I whisper, nerves swirling in my stomach.

She nods. "He told us both."

"Cade knows as well? Why?"

"You'll have to ask Seb that."

I bite my lip as I take in what she's telling me. I can't get my head around why he'd say anything. What does he have to gain from telling them now? Unless he thought I was going to tell them. I frown.

"I know what you're thinking, Taylor. He didn't tell us because he thought you might."

"Why, then? Why would he jeopardize his friendship with you and his relationship with his brother?"

"You need to talk to him, Tay."

"What did Cade say?"

"He was surprised. We both were."

"He wasn't annoyed?"

She sighs, and Hunter stirs in her arms. She releases my hand and gently strokes his face. When he's settled, she looks up. "He was pissed for a few days, but seeing how devastated Seb was as the weeks went by and you weren't waking up, it was easy for Cade to see how Seb felt about you. He's been torn up, Taylor."

My heart twists in my chest hearing he's been hurting these past few weeks.

"What about you?" I ask, knowing it must have been an awkward conversation for them all.

"I'm good, Taylor. I love Seb, but like a brother…" She trails off. "Are *we* good?" she asks quietly.

I take her hand again. "Yes, Sophie. It was never you I was

upset with. I knew you didn't know. I thought because he hadn't told me, he was settling with me because he couldn't be with you."

She shakes her head. "That was never how it was, Taylor."

"I'm beginning to see that," I say quietly.

"Promise me you'll talk to him."

I smile at her. "I promise."

She looks down at Hunter. "Do you feel up to a cuddle? He's been looking forward to meeting his auntie Taylor."

"I'd love to." She stands and places him in my arms. I gaze down at him as he yawns and stretches his tiny body out. "He's beautiful, Sophie."

"I think so, but I'm biased."

The door opens and Seb walks in with a handful of sandwiches. "I didn't know what you wanted, so I…" He looks up and trails off when he sees Sophie. His eyes flick to me holding Hunter and he smiles.

"Hey, how's my nephew doing?" he asks, crossing the room and coming around to the other side of the bed.

"He's perfect," I tell him, my eyes filling with tears as I stare at Seb. It's only now I see how tired and pale he looks. I'm not surprised knowing he spent every night here for five weeks. I guess that explains the beard too.

"I should take him back to the ward. He's going to need a feed soon," Sophie says.

"You'll come and see me again, right?"

"Of course we will." She takes Hunter from my arms and presses a kiss on his head. "I'll stop by tomorrow. I'm sure you'll be here then too, Seb." She chuckles.

"I'll be wherever Taylor is."

She smiles. "See you both tomorrow."

When she and Hunter have left, Seb sits down. "I didn't know what sandwich you wanted, so I got a selection."

"You told Sophie and Cade," I say, ignoring his comment about the sandwiches. His eyes meet mine and he nods. "Why?"

I hold my breath as I wait for him to answer. Despite what Sophie's told me, I still don't know why he'd tell his brother he once had feelings for his wife. He could have damaged his relationship with them both forever. Surely nothing is worth that?

CHAPTER FORTY-THREE

Seb

"You told Sophie and Cade," she says softly, and my eyes fly up to meet hers. I nod. "Why?"

I blow out a breath. I hadn't expected Sophie to say anything, and while we need to have this conversation, I thought I had a little more time to prepare. "Because I'm done with secrets, Tay—"

"But you could have jeopardized your relationship with Cade," she says, cutting me off.

I take her hand. "You're all I care about, Taylor. I nearly lost you because I was so set on no one finding out." She lowers her eyes. "Look at me, baby." I wait until she lifts her head. "I was thinking of myself when I should have been thinking about you." I release her hand and cup her face. "I messed up and I had to try and put it right."

She leans her head into my hand. "Seb," she whispers.

"I learned the hard way that secrets are toxic. They almost destroyed everything. You're the most important person in my life and it's about time you knew that."

"More important than your brother?"

"I love Cade, but if it came to it, I'd choose you, baby. Every time. Hearing you say you thought you were my second choice killed me. Nothing could be further from the truth. You're it for me, Taylor. I love you and I'll do whatever it takes to prove it to you. These past few weeks have been a living hell. If you hadn't pulled through…" I trail off, my voice choked with emotion.

"Hey," she whispers, "I'm okay." I nod and drag in a breath. She shakes her head. "I can't believe you did that for me."

"I'd do anything for you, Taylor. I didn't know that loving you was the best part of me until I almost lost you. Tell me I haven't lost you."

I can hear the uncertainty in my voice and I'm sure she hears it too. I hold my breath as I wait for her to answer. I've had five weeks to work through everything, but I know for her the argument feels like it happened yesterday. I'll wait as long as it takes, though, and if she needs time, I'll give it to her, but I have to know what she's thinking.

"Sophie said you spent every night with me." I nod. "You really mean everything you've just said, don't you?"

"Every word, baby. I'll keep telling you until you believe me."

"I do believe you," she whispers. "I love you so much, Seb. No one's ever fought for me like you have. I was an idiot to have ever doubted you."

Relief crashes over me and I climb on the bed next to her, taking her into my arms. "I'm the idiot, Taylor. I should never have given you any reason to doubt me. You're my whole world. I love you."

She rests her head on my chest and I can finally breathe again after five weeks. We lie holding each other, and after a few minutes, she tilts her head to look at me.

"Are you keeping the beard?"

I smile and reach my hand up to my chin. "I don't know. Do you like it?"

"I love it."

"Then I'll keep it." I lean down and brush my lips against hers.

When I pull back, she nestles against my chest. "When do you think I can go home?"

"I don't know. I'm guessing the doctor will be around soon and we can ask. Hopefully soon. I can't wait to fall asleep with you in my arms."

"I can't wait for that either." She pauses. "Have Nash and Paisley set another date for their wedding?"

"I don't think so. I think they wanted to wait until you were better."

She sighs. "I feel so bad they missed their wedding because of me."

I press a kiss on her head. "Paisley wouldn't have wanted to get married without you being there, Tay."

"I'm glad I haven't missed it, but I still feel guilty."

I hold her tightly and stroke my fingers up and down her arm. "Do you want to get married?"

She lifts her head and smiles. "Are you asking me?"

I smile back. "No. Not yet, but would you want to? Have you thought about it?"

"Have I thought about marrying you?" she asks, the smile still on her lips.

I hold her stare. "Just marriage in general. Do you see yourself married one day?"

"Yes. Do you?"

I nod. "What about kids?"

"Yeah, I want kids."

"I saw you with Hunter. It suited you."

She grins. "He's just the cutest. I can't wait for more cuddles. Do you want kids?" I nod. "How many?"

"Four at least."

Her eyes widen. "Four?"

I chuckle. "I want my kids to have what I have with my brothers and Ash. A house in Hope Creek with a wraparound porch, a white picket fence, and a pool in the backyard."

"I love what you have with your family. I want all of what you've just said, Seb. It sounds like you've given it some thought."

"It's all I've thought about these past few weeks. I knew if I got a second chance with you, I was going to grab onto it with both hands."

She tilts her head and kisses me. "I guess we'd better get a move on with the practice, then, especially if you want four." Her voice is deadpan, and I laugh.

"As soon as you're out of here and better, baby, try and stop me."

"I love you."

"I love you too."

I want it all with her. If you'd asked me even six months ago, I'd have said *not a chance*, but meeting Taylor changed everything for me. Now that I know she feels the same way, there's no doubt in my mind she's my future. There's no rush, though. We have the rest of our lives to be together, and I can't wait to see what that life looks like.

EPILOGUE

Taylor – A year later

"**D**o I really need to wear this?" I ask, my fingers coming over the blindfold Seb's insisting that I wear.

"Can you promise to keep your eyes closed?"

"Umm… no."

He chuckles. "Then you have to wear it."

"Where are we going?"

"I'm not telling you, Tay. Stop asking." I pout and he presses his lips to mine.

He takes my hand and leads me out the back of Eden.

"I borrowed Nash's truck," he says as I hear him open the door. He helps me into the passenger seat and closes the door. When I hear the driver's door close, I turn to him.

"Why did you need to borrow Nash's truck? Are we going far?" He ignores me, and music from the radio fills the cab. "Seb?"

"Just wait and see. We'll be there in a few minutes, okay?"

I grin. "Okay."

I feel his hand come to rest on my thigh and I tangle my fingers with his. I've no idea where he's taking me. He's giving nothing away, and up until half an hour ago, I didn't know we were going anywhere. It's been twelve months since my accident, and we haven't spent a night apart since I woke up in the hospital. Seb pretty much moved into my place above Eden. I didn't think it was possible to love him more than I did then, but I fall more in love with him every day. I've never been happier, and I know he feels the same.

When the truck comes to a stop and the engine cuts out, I bounce excitedly in my seat and Seb laughs.

"We're here. Wait there and I'll come and help you down."

"Okay."

Seconds later, my door opens, and he reaches around me to unclip my seat belt. Taking my hand, he helps me down from the truck.

"I'm going to take the blindfold off. Keep your eyes closed." I nod, and he chuckles.

He removes the blindfold and places his hands over my eyes. He knows me too well and knows that I'll peek.

"Can I look yet?" I ask excitedly.

"You can look."

He removes his hand and I open my eyes. It takes me a few seconds for my eyes to adjust, and when they do, I'm not sure what I'm looking at. We're standing in front of a beautiful house with a wraparound porch and a white picket fence surrounding the stunning front yard. When I turn to look at Seb, I notice a realtor board behind him, and my eyes widen.

"What's going on, Seb?" I ask, looking from him to the *For Sale* board.

"Do you like it? What you've seen so far, I mean?" He sounds nervous and I can't help but wonder what's going on.

"It's beautiful."

"Do you want to go inside?"

"Okay."

He takes my hand and guides me along the driveway, leading me up the porch steps to the front door. There's a porch swing off to the right which I couldn't see from the sidewalk, and I wait while he digs in his pocket for something. Pulling out a key, he opens the door and gestures for me to go on ahead.

If I thought the outside was beautiful, the inside is something else. The entryway opens onto an open-plan living room with a white wooden staircase leading to the second floor. Dark wooden floors flow throughout, and I walk through the living room, taking in the ornate marble fireplace and large sash windows on either side.

"Seb, this is beautiful," I tell him as he follows me through the living room and into the kitchen where there are white cabinets with dark marble countertops and the biggest island I've ever seen. Off to the right, double doors lead out into the backyard, and I press my nose on the glass, gasping when I see a swimming pool beyond the large, decked area just outside the doors.

The conversation Seb and I had in the hospital on the day I woke up after the accident flashes through my mind, and I spin around to find him standing right behind me.

"The porch and the white picket fence," I whisper. "The swimming pool in the backyard."

He nods. "If you don't like it, then we can look for somewhere else."

"No. I love it. It's perfect. It's exactly what we talked about."

"The realtor's holding it for us. It's ours if we want it."

"How long have you been looking at houses?" I ask, knowing that after talking about it at the hospital, we haven't mentioned it since.

He smiles sheepishly. "A couple of months. I wanted to find the perfect place. There are five bedrooms," he says with a wink.

I laugh. "For those four babies you want?"

He wraps his arms around me and pulls me into his chest. "I was thinking it was about time we made a start on the rest of our lives, beginning with this house. Then after we've moved in, maybe a baby or two? I am a twin, after all, and twins run in families, so… what do you say. Are you ready for the next chapter?"

His talking of twins should freak me out, but it doesn't. I can't wait to start the next chapter of our lives together, and doing it in this house is nothing short of perfect.

I smile widely. "It's a yes, Seb. A yes to the house, a yes to the babies, a yes to everything. I want it all and more with you."

He drops his forehead onto mine and drags in a breath. I wonder if he thought I'd say no. He's got nothing to worry about. Home to me is wherever he is, and I've never been happier than I am right now. I know there's so much more to come for us. I can't wait.

THE END

ALSO BY LAURA FARR

THE HEALING HEARTS SERIES

Taking Chances - Healing Hearts Book 1

Defying Gravity - Healing Hearts Book 2

Whatever it Takes - Healing Hearts Book 3

The Long Way Home - Healing Hearts Book 4

Christmas at the Cabin - A Healing Hearts Short story

STANDALONES

Pieces of Me

Crossing the Line

Sweet Montana Kisses

The Paris Pact

THE HOPE CREEK SERIES

Loving Paisley - Hope Creek Book 1

Echoes of Love - Hope Creek Book 2

SOCIAL MEDIA LINKS

Facebook Profile: https://www.facebook.com/laura.farr.547

Facebook Page: https://www.facebook.com/Laura-Farr-Author-191769224641474/

Facebook Reader Group: https://www.facebook.com/groups/1046607692516891

Instagram: https://www.instagram.com/laurafarr_author/

Twitter: @laurafarr4

Printed in Great Britain
by Amazon